DYNAMITE!

"There's only about three inches of fuse on these, so we'd better get rid of 'em damned quick." Windy pressed the glowing, oblong stick into Kincaid's hand. "Here, this one is yours."

Lobbing the dynamite out of the ditch, both men rolled onto their stomachs and covered their heads with their hands.

No more than ten seconds passed before twin explosions ripped the night sky. Screams and startled yells filled the air. Drawing his guns, Kincaid turned to fire. He could see several braves staggering to their feet to rush forward, and he fired four times and saw three of them fall. Windy's revolver was barking its deadly commands behind him.

"I think we've bought enough time to get back to the command, Windy," Kincaid said, rising to a crouched position. "Let's get the hell out of here!"

EASY COMPANY

EASY COMPANY
ON THE BITTER TRAIL

JOHN WESLEY HOWARD

A JOVE BOOK

First Jove edition published September 1981

First printing

Printed in the United States of America

Jove books are published by Jove Publications, Inc.,
200 Madison Avenue, New York, NY 10016

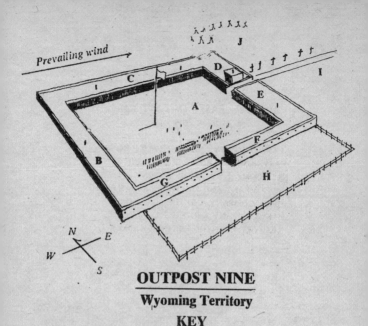

OUTPOST NINE

Wyoming Territory

KEY

A. Parade and flagstaff

B. Officers' quarters ("officers' country")

C. Enlisted men's quarters: barracks, day room, and mess

D. Kitchen, quartermaster supplies, ordnance shop, guardhouse

E. Suttler's store and other shops, tack room, and smithy

F. Stables

G. Quarters for dependents and guests; communal kitchen

H. Paddock

I. Road and telegraph line to regimental headquarters

J. Indian camp occupied by transient "friendlies"

INTERIOR   OUTSIDE

OUTPOST NUMBER NINE
(DETAIL)

Outpost Number Nine is a typical High Plains military outpost of the days following the Battle of the Little Big Horn, and is the home of Easy Company. It is not a "fort"; an official fort is the headquarters of a regiment. However, it resembles a fort in its construction.

The birdseye view shows the general layout and orientation of Outpost Number Nine; features are explained in the Key.

The detail shows a cross-section through the outpost's double walls, which ingeniously combine the functions of fortification and shelter.

The walls are constructed of sod, dug from the prairie on which Outpost Number Nine stands, and are sturdy enough to withstand an assault by anything less than artillery. The roof is of log beams covered by planking, tarpaper, and a top layer of sod. It also provides a parapet from which the outpost's defenders can fire down on an attacking force.

one

They moved slowly across the sloping stretch of broken ground, stooping low and occasionally kneeling to turn a rock over in search of insects or to snatch a handful of berries from the scattered brush. There were ten of them, six men and four women, and each of them carried a digging stick, approximately eighteen inches long, blunt on one end and sharp on the other, with the sharp end turned coal-black from fire hardening.

At certain selected bushes they would work their hands down to the base of the stem, test with their fingers, and then scrape the dirt away to expose tender white roots spreading beneath the soil in search of water. After the dirt was wiped away, some of the roots were eaten as they were drawn from the ground, while others were stacked in layered rows in wicker baskets by their sides. In the main, they were a pathetic-looking group, with their emaciated physical features covered by comical mixtures of clothing consisting of tanned leather contrasting with cast-off white men's garments.

But there was one young woman, in the lead and at the center of the group, who stood out from the others. She wore only traditional Indian clothing made from tanned antelope skin, which was fawn-colored and decorated at the neck and waist by rows of multicolored beads. Her dress was nearly ankle length, fringed from elbow to wrist, with the soft leather clinging to her shapely figure, especially against her well-rounded buttocks when she bent down to thrust her digging stick skillfully into the ground. Her long black hair, parted in the center and dangling past either shoulder in a twist of braids, took on a sheen in the lowering sun, and her lean, high-cheek-boned face was radiant with health and beauty. Her breasts, while not extravagant, were firm and full and their size was accented by the narrowness of her waist. She worked silently

1

with the others, apparently as oblivious to her natural attributes as she was to the eyes watching her from above.

There was a whiskey smell about him that reinforced the sullen ugliness of a face that might otherwise have been moderately attractive, were it not for the cruel, cold smile on his lips. Taking another drink from the bottle in his hand, he passed it back to his companions behind him and wiped his twisted lips with the backward swipe of a naked forearm. Mounted on a dun-colored horse, he was the picture of ferocity, his broad chest covered only by a leather vest, which touched the loincloth around his waist. The fringed leather leggings he wore clung tightly to the horse's ribs, and across his thighs lay a Remington repeater. The seven warriors behind him were similarly armed, each of them wearing a silver badge attached above the right breast. The shiny black hair of each man was adorned with a single feather.

A smaller Indian, perhaps three inches shorter than the lead warrior and boasting a ragged scar running from the bridge of his nose to the point of his chin, nudged his horse and moved up beside the warrior staring intently at the woman below.

"There she is, Wokana," he said with a leering grin and a gesture of the bottle toward the lowland. "Dark Star is waiting for you."

"I have waited long enough for her to come to me, Hunting Dog. I will wait no longer." Wokana took the bottle from Hunting Dog's hand and took a long drink before waving it with a drunken gesture toward the Indians below. "Look at them! Their men scratching the ground like birds looking for worms and working with women like they were women themselves, instead of hunting for meat like men. If they weren't so ugly, we would take them for our pleasure as we will take their women."

Hunting Dog laughed cruelly. "Remember, Wokana, they are nothing more than Paiutes, to be hunted and killed for sport instead of game. They do not fight to live, they *beg* to live. They deserve nothing but death at the hands of Bannock warriors, and their women's bellies should be filled with Bannock children to give some spirit to their blood."

Wokana continued to stare at Dark Star, whose entire concentration was given to the job at hand as she moved from bush to bush. There was a hunger in his eyes, which were slightly filmed with moisture from the effects of strong liquor. "The words you say are true, Hunting Dog," he said in a distant voice. "But Dark Star is mine. You can have the others."

A tight smile crossed Hunting Dog's lips, and when he spoke there was a taunting tone to his words. "She will not be able to refuse you this time, will she, Wokana? Like she has done so many times in the past?"

Wokana glanced sharply at his companion. "She has refused me only because she is blinded by that weakling Red Hand. After she has felt the power of a Bannock warrior, she will never again allow a Paiute to touch her."

"And Red Hand isn't here," Hunting Dog replied, his gaze drifting to search the lowland for the Paiute chieftain. "Black Bear will not be pleased. We were sent here to kill Red Hand, not the others."

"There is plenty of time to get him," Wokana said, raising the bottle and draining it before tossing it aside. "Right now I want only his woman." He turned on the blanket spread across his horse's back and looked at the warriors behind him. "Ride them down and kill them silently. Do what you want to their women, but leave Dark Star to me. When we have finished we will ride to the trading post and buy more whiskey. We have been paid for our work at the agency and I told Black Bear we would not return for one day. We deserve three. But first we will have our pleasure."

Wokana turned back, pressed his knees against the horse's sides, and sent the mount plunging down the slope at a gallop, with the others following close behind. Rocks clattered beneath their horses' churning hooves and dust rose in their wake.

The Paiutes looked up with fear-filled eyes as they recognized the agency police, Bannock warriors notorious for their brutality in enforcing their powers at the Sand Ridge Reservation. Leaving their baskets behind, they fled down the slope in a futile attempt to elude their pursuers, with women clutching skirts around their thighs and men ignoring fallen hats. The horses quickly closed on them and rifles were swung like clubs, sending the elderly Paiute men sprawling on the ground with crushed skulls or broken necks. There was a chorus of excited yips and yells as the Bannock turned their mounts on the fleeing women and the warriors slipped from their mounts to drag the women down into the sparse grass.

Clothing was quickly stripped away while the warriors, working in pairs, held the women spread-eagled on the ground.

Excited, muffled grunts rose in the still evening air as the Bannock took their turns mounting the women, and the occasional scream escaped from between hard fingers pressed over mouths.

Only one had not fled, and she watched the scene below her with a cold look of hatred and disgust before turning to stare contemptuously at Wokana, whose horse had stopped some five yards away. Dark Star's hate-filled eyes shone like obsidian in her tanned face, and she betrayed no fear as she suddenly raised her digging stick and threw it at Wokana's head.

The warrior ducked an instant before the sharpened point of the stick sailed past where his head had been and clattered harmlessly on the rocks behind him. He grinned and edged his horse closer.

"So?" he said, raising an eyebrow quizzically and glancing toward the warrior beside him. "The Paiute woman has more fight in her than her men do, Hunting Dog."

"And so does a crippled bird, Wokana," Hunting Dog replied with a scornful laugh.

"That's true, but this bird is not crippled. She is a beautiful woman who deserves to have a proud warrior lie beside her." Wokana looked closely at Dark Star. "Why did you not run with the others?"

Dark Star's eyes were riveted on Wokana's face and they never wavered. "Because I have no fear of you, Wokana. Just as I have no fear of other cowardly animals."

"Cowardly animals? You are talking to Wokana, the mightiest warrior of the Bannock tribe and chief of the agency police."

"I am talking to Wokana, coward, murderer and taker of women because he can get them no other way."

Wokana flinched involuntarily and his eyes became black slits. "You will pay for those words, Dark Star. I will show you what Wokana does with women and you will never forget it. You will never be satisfied with Red Hand again."

"*Kah!*" Dark Star replied, spitting at Wokana's horse. "After you touch me I will never sleep with Red Hand again because I will be filled with your filth and my shame. Red Hand is a proud man who does not need to *take* women. Women come willingly to him."

"Enough, woman!" Wokana snarled, leaping from his horse

4

and stepping forward to slap Dark Star with the back of his hand. "I will hear no more!"

Dark Star staggered backward under the force of the blow, but she did not fall, even though her cheek quickly turned crimson where Wokana's knuckles had landed. "You have not even enough power to knock a Paiute woman down, Wokana," she challenged. "How do you ever hope to satisfy one in bed?"

Wokana's face filled with rage and he lashed out again, striking the other cheek with an even more forceful blow. This time Dark Star went to her knees, and Wokana was on her instantly while her fingernails tore into his face and neck.

"Hunting Dog! Grab her hands and hold her down!"

The second warrior's powerful hands closed around Dark Star's wrists and he howled in pain as her teeth sank into his forearm. But he had control of her now and one hand went over her mouth while the other pinned her hands to the ground behind her head. Dark Star thrashed and kicked with her legs as Wokana ripped her dress up past her waist with one hand and worked his loincloth down with the other. Firm, well-proportioned thighs were exposed to him now, and when his hand touched the patch of soft black hair between them, a moaning grunt escaped his lips. He could smell the gentle hint of muskiness coming from her and could feel the smooth warmth of her skin as he lowered himself to take her. Their eyes were locked on each other, one set hating and defiant, the other set blurring and opaque with sexual excitement. And while he worked over her, his breathing came in sharp gasps and the pace of his thrusts became more rapid. Finally a shudder ran through his body and he lay still for several seconds before standing and rearranging his loincloth. There was a cruel smile of satisfaction on his lips as he looked down at Dark Star, motionless now and offering no resistance.

"You see how satisfied she is, Hunting Dog?" he said with a tone of triumph. "She lies there quietly and relives the pleasure."

The excitement on Hunting Dog's face caused the torn scar to take on a deep red hue and his hand trembled over Dark Star's mouth. His eyes remained fixed on her pubic region, and there was a quiver in his voice when he spoke. "She deserves two Bannock warriors, Wokana. I will be the second."

"No!" Wokana said sharply. "She is mine. Take one of the

5

others if you wish, but Dark Star is mine."

A hurt look filled Hunting Dog's eyes as he tore them from the damp hair and looked up. "She is nothing but a Paiute, Wokana. Why—"

"Because I said she is mine! Go now!" Wokana snapped, glancing toward the other warriors, now finishing with their victims. "The others have had their fill. Take what you want and then we leave."

After a moment's hesitation, Hunting Dog stood and trotted to the nearest woman, then dropped to his knees with a frantic tugging at his loincloth. Dark Star's eyes had followed him, but she looked away, rolling her head to stare up at Wokana once more.

"You and the others are filthy cowards, Wokana," she said, her voice surprisingly calm. "You are nothing more than dogs, not warriors. Red Hand will kill you for what you've done."

"Red Hand? Kill *me?*" he said with a cold laugh. "I would not be as kind to him as I was to you, Dark Star. I will kill him slowly and with great pain. You are my woman now. Tell him how much you enjoyed the feel of a Bannock warrior and he will cry great tears like the weakling he is. He is not a warrior, he's only a Paiute and no match for me." He paused and smiled down. "Once he is dead, you will have what a beautiful maiden deserves. A proud warrior to give you children."

"I would kill myself first."

"No, Dark Star, you wouldn't do that. If you did, I would kill every Paiute on the Sand Ridge. You would be taking their lives as well as your own." Wokana glanced again toward the lower ground and saw Hunting Dog stand and straighten his loincloth. "Hunting Dog! We go now! We have far to ride and much whiskey to drink!"

Wokana started toward his horse, then stopped and turned back. "I have never felt a woman like you, Dark Star. I will take you for my own." Then he stepped to his mount, swung onto its back and spun the horse around with a jerk of the hackamore.

Dark Star struggled to a sitting position and pulled the torn dress around her thighs before covering her face with her hands in shame.

The other warriors were mounted as well, and just as they started to leave, one of the elderly Paiute men who had been knocked unconscious attempted to struggle to his feet. The rearmost Bannock warrior raised his rifle and fired one shot, and the old man sprawled onto his back with a crimson hole torn in his chest. Then the Bannock rode away, and their exultant yells and cries drifted back to the silent patch of ground where the Paiute women were slowly crawling toward the three dead men.

Red Hand's head jerked up sharply at the distant crack of a rifle shot. The adobe jar in his hands was underwater behind the tiny dam he had made to capture the trickle of water seeping from the spring, and he cocked his head in the direction from which the sound had come. Two other jars filled with water lay beside his knees, and his keen eyes searched the distant hills. Seeing seven tiny specks galloping over the broken ground, he sprang to his feet, grabbed the jars and loped on foot toward where the others had been working.

He ran with well-paced, ground-eating strides, and his lean, lithe body showed not one ounce of fat. Bronzed skin was stretched tightly over sinewy muscle, and his shoulders spanned widely above a broad chest that tapered down to a narrow waist. He was nearly six feet in height, with raven-black hair tied in a single braid trailing down his back; his countenance was regal, and the snugly fitted leather leggings and breast cover made him appear even taller than he actually was. His high cheekbones and prominent nose gave an intensity to his dark eyes, and there was a wild handsomeness about him that few men could match.

At twenty-seven years old, Red Hand was the accepted leader of the Southern Paiute tribe assigned to the Sand Ridge Reservation, located on the western side of the southern tip of the Rocky Mountains. It had been a tremendous ordeal, being relocated into an unfamiliar region that was not suitable to the food-gathering lifestyle of his people, but Red Hand had obeyed the decision of the White Fathers and was trying to provide his tribe with the kind of leadership that would ensure their survival against overwhelming odds. Pinyon nuts, which were a staple of their diet and which grew in abundance in their home region of the Great Basin, were nowhere to be found. Sagebrush and juniper were also absent, along with the small game and insects that had sustained his people for so many generations. Oriented as they were to a water-scarce life on the fringes of the desert, the Southern Paiutes were a horseless tribe who lived a nomadic life in the constant quest of food.

But now, as Red Hand ran, he thought of only one thing: Dark Star and the safety of the tribespeople he had left behind to find water for their long journey back to the reservation. When he had heard the shot, he was more than a mile from the band. He crossed that distance in less than seven minutes. And when he slowed at the crest of ground above the swale and looked down, his breath rate was only slightly above that of a man who might have walked the same distance. He could hear the death chant rising on the shrill voices of women wailing over their dead husbands, and could see the four lifeless bodies stretched out on the ground. His eyes darted from woman to woman until he found Dark Star, clutching an elderly woman's shoulders and rocking back and forth in grief. Red Hand trotted toward her. There was a grim set to his tight lips, and the blank look on his face was that of a man who knew what he would find, but was desperately hoping he was wrong.

Placing the water containers carefully on the ground, he knelt beside Dark Star and gently touched her shoulder.

"What happened, little one?"

Dark Star's eyes had been closed and her cheek was pressed against the other woman's graying hair. When she opened them, there was a flood of tenderness and relief at the sight of Red Hand.

"I'm glad you're safe, Red Hand. Wokana and some of his warriors found us. They killed the men and . . . and . . ." She looked down, unable to speak anymore.

For the first time, Red Hand noticed the torn dress hanging loose across Dark Star's legs, and he could see a crimson spot of blood below her waist. He turned her face up to him tenderly and touched her cheek gently with his other hand.

"Don't tell me about it, little one. I think no differently about you now than I did before I left to find water." Then his voice turned as cold as the expression on his face. "But I want to know which one of them did this to you. Was it Wokana?"

Dark Star gazed deeply into his eyes before biting her lip and glancing away with a weak nod of her head.

"Was there anyone else?"

"No," Dark Star replied, her voice just above a whisper. "Wokana was the only one. He said I was his now."

"You will never be his, and he will never touch you again.

8

Believe that, little one." Red Hand picked up one of the containers and held it to Dark Star's lips. "I have fresh water. Drink now, you and the others, then wash yourselves clean. I will turn away while you do so and then I must cover the dead. When I am finished, I will take you back to the reservation."

Dark Star accepted a drink and then took the container from his hands while searching his face with darting eyes. "Do you think the agent will punish them for what they have done, Red Hand? Will he make them leave us alone and let us live in peace as the White Father promised?"

Red Hand gazed at her for long seconds before shaking his head with sad resignation. "No, he will not. They are his police and the white men cannot be trusted any more than the Bannock can. We can never live in peace here as they promised. Peace is only a dream, just like the food and clothing we were supposed to have. I have never wanted war, but now I have no choice. I must lead our people away from here, to a new land and a new hope, and when I do they will come after us. But we will fight them now, both the whites and the Bannock, and if we must die, we will die with our heads held high in pride."

Red Hand squeezed her shoulders tenderly and stood. "Clean yourself and help the others," he said, moving away. "I will be waiting on the ridge until you have finished."

Red Hand climbed slowly up to the crest and stood there, a lone figure silhouetted against the darkening sky. The golden rays of the setting sun washed across his body and he stared at the gigantic mountain range to the northeast, glowing red in the distance. He could see the indentation known as South Pass, where the Iron Horse crossed the narrow divide, and instinctively he knew what he must do. And he knew as he stood there that many of his people would not survive, especially the elderly and injured, but he also knew he had no other choice. Escape into an unknown land dominated by whites was the only choice they had, and even if it meant certain death, he had no other alternative. In that moment of solitude he longed for his desert home while the harsh chill of the coming night closed about him. But he felt certain that he would never see his native land again. Many minutes had passed before he heard Dark Star call to him, and he turned wearily to retrace his steps and begin covering the bodies of the slain with rocks.

two

Even if he had been smiling, there would have been a mean, ominous look about the dark face of Dennis Michael Harbert. He was a man of unusually large proportions, standing six foot three with thick, muscular shoulders sloping down as though pulled earthward by his brawny arms. Hammerlike fists worked in impatient clenching motions by his sides, and there was an absence of waist to his broad torso, although he was flat of stomach and devoid of fat. Beneath the brow of his broad-brimmed hat, steel-gray eyes stared impatiently through the window by which he now stood, and those eyes were hooded by heavy black eyebrows that matched the full crop of hair on his head. Wearing a white shirt and dark vest, with matching pants tucked into high leather boots, he held a coiled blacksnake whip in one hand while the other hovered over the big revolver sagging from his right hip.

But Dennis Michael Harbert was not smiling. Known as Big Mike to friends and enemies alike—the former being far smaller in number than the latter—he had held the post of agent at the Sand Ridge Reservation for nearly a year and he had ruled with an iron hand. Now, though, with the recent change of administration in Washington, he knew his days were numbered. The "Indian Ring," as the appointments made under Grant had been called, was being cleaned up and eliminated, and men more sympathetic to the Indian cause were finding favor with the political thinkers back East. As a consequence, Harbert knew that if he was to turn his tenure at Sand Ridge into the profits he had envisioned at the outset, he would have to move quickly.

If there was any one thing about Big Mike that made him unique, other than his size, it was his fiery Irish temper and will to win at any cost. And that temper was at a full boil now as he watched Wokana slip from his horse's back and walk unsteadily toward the agency office through the deepening shadows of twilight. Harbert turned at the sound of knuckles rapping on his door, and his face turned even darker with the flush of anger rising within him. The bushy mustache above his lip quivered slightly and his baritone voice was a booming rumble when he responded to the knocking.

"Come in!"

Just as Wokana opened the door, the blacksnake whip lashed out, and the leather "popper" at its tip snapped the air barely inches from the Indian's face. Wokana jumped back, nearly fell, then righted himself. Even though he attempted to mask it, there was fright in his eyes and he stared cautiously into the gloom.

"I said come in, dammit!" Harbert snarled.

"The snake in your hand says otherwise, Black Bear," Wokana said hesitantly while taking a second pensive step into the office. Harbert accepted the appellation of Black Bear from his agency police, since they couldn't pronounce his last name.

"If I'd wanted to hurt you I would have," Harbert replied, coiling the whip with angry motions. "Take your eyes out one at a time I will, if you ever disobey me again. Now get your butt in here and close the door."

Wokana did as instructed and stood silently before the glowering agent, who studied him for a moment, then spat, "You're drunk!"

The Indian could feel the whiskey fire raging in his stomach, and he glanced down once before looking up at the agent. "It was our day off. We drank some whiskey."

"Exactly my point. I gave you a day off, not three! Where the hell have you been?"

"The trading post. After we did what you told us to do, we wanted to have a drink and celebrate."

Harbert slammed the coiled whip down on his desk and turned away from Wokana. "That would be acceptable, if you had done what I told you to do."

"You told us to teach the Paiute a lesson about wandering from the reservation," Wokana said with a questioning look in his eyes and a plea for understanding in his voice. "We did that, and they will never wander again."

"They won't, huh?" Harbert demanded, spinning on his heel with remarkable agility for a man so huge. "Did you see any Paiute in their huts when you came back?"

11

"No. I wasn't looking for them."

"Just as well, 'cause they ain't there. What about Red Hand?"

"Red Hand?" Wokana asked with the first hint of concern in his voice. "He wasn't with the others. I'll get him tomorrow. He will come to me now."

"Like hell he will! I don't know what you think you've done, and I don't give a damn, but Red Hand was supposed to have been killed. He's the only one around here with enough guts to lead his tribe off the reservation."

"Like I said, Black Bear, I'll get him tomorrow, or tonight if you want."

Crossing his massive arms across his chest, Harbert smiled coldly and leaned against his desk. "You will, huh? How you gonna kill him if he ain't here to be killed?"

"I . . . I don't understand."

"Sure you don't understand. The reason I made you and your Bannock warriors agency police was to keep the Paiute in line and *on* the reservation. You've had it damned good—all the women you wanted, special quarters and extra rations. Now that's all gonna have to change."

"Why?"

"Because of your three-day drunk, that's why!" Harbert closed on Wokana and put his face not six inches from the Indian's.

"Why do I need you to ride herd on the Paiute when there ain't a goddamned Paiute on the whole damned reservation?"

Wokana's first instinct was to back away, but he knew better and held his ground. "The Paiute have gone?" he asked in a lowered voice.

"Every damned one of 'em. And I'm sure it's Red Hand that's behind it all. After I sent you out to do that little chore three days ago, I had to go into town to take care of some business. I thought you'd be back here to take care of things, so I stayed overnight and came back the next day. When I got here, the storage room had been broken into and two cases of rifles were missing, along with Red Hand and his people. Before I left, there were one hundred Bannock and half again that many Paiute here. Now there's only Bannock, and all the little shitty chores that the Paiute used to do are going to have to be done by your tribe."

Straightening, Harbert turned away and a different tone

came into his voice. "That is, of course, unless you can catch those Paiute and bring them back. They've got at least a two-day lead on you right now."

Wokana stepped forward and said earnestly, "We'll catch them, Black Bear. They have no horses, so we can find them within a day. When we do, we'll kill Red Hand and bring the others back."

"All right, I'll give you another chance. See that you don't waste it. Deputize as many of your Bannock as you'll need to do the job, but I don't want any more Paiute killed than necessary. I need them. They probably headed south toward the desert, so you head that way first light in the morning."

Now Wokana's mind was working in the manner for which it had been trained, that of a cunning hunter calculating the moves of his prey. He thought silently for several seconds before responding. "They might run for the desert, where we can't follow them with our horses, like you say, but I think Red Hand is too smart for that. It would take him at least eight days to get beyond the water holes. He knows we can catch him in three. I think he might head for the great pass and hope to hide in the open land beyond."

"You think he'd do that?" Harbert asked in a tone of grudging respect. "Even though it's summer, they could damned well freeze to death up that high. He would be taking a real risk with the lives of his people."

Wokana smiled, pleased that the agent was having to depend on his judgment. "The Paiute are like all other cowardly animals, Black Bear. They will fight only when cornered and they will do anything to avoid a fight. I believe Red Hand will hope we think he went toward the desert. If we can be tricked, it will give him time to escape. Just to be sure, we will hunt toward the lowland tomorrow, and if we find no sign, we will turn and head for the mountains."

"Fine. I don't give a damn what you do as long as you get them back here." Harbert studied his thoughts while his hand played absently with the whip. "Just to be sure, I'm going to send a telegram. There's an army outpost about a day's ride east of the divide. I'll send a telegram to the Bureau of Indian Affairs saying that an armed band of Paiute have jumped the reservation, and that they must be captured and held until we can return them to the agency. I'll make it damned good and they'll notify the outpost mighty quick. I'll be gone all day

13

cause I've got some other business to take care of, so when I get back I'll check the bucket out by the well. If it's upside down, I'll know you didn't find them to the south and went toward the mountains. If it's right side up, I'll know you are still tracking them toward the desert. Whichever way, I'll take off and catch up with you and personally supervise their return."

"Whatever you want, Black Bear," Wokana said with a hint of disappointment. "But your Bannock police will have no trouble with the Paiute."

Even the slightest indication of independent thought from Wokana enraged Harbert, and his eyes narrowed to tiny slits. "Just like you had no trouble killing Red Hand? Your job is to find them, hold them and bring them back, and that's all. My job is to make damned sure that you do. Now get the hell out of here, I've got some thinkin' to do!"

Wokana didn't respond, backing instead toward the door, stepping out and pulling the latch closed behind him. But the hatred he felt in his heart for the big agent was nearly uncontrollable, and that hatred was now mentally directed toward the Paiutes. They are the ones who have put me in the position of having to crawl before the Bear, he thought. They are the ones who have made me lose face, and they will pay for it. There will be plenty of time to torture them before he catches up with us. And Red Hand will be the first to be tied between our horses and torn in half.

The thought of what he would do to his rival chieftain mellowed Wokana's black mood considerably, and he was almost smiling as he moved through the darkness toward his quarters.

The heat of midday pressed down upon Outpost Number Nine, and with the dinner hour at hand, there was little activity on the parade, which comprised the center portion of the fortress. Designed in a square configuration, with high lumber-and-sod walls, it was located in the vast nothingness of the Northern Plains and situated to protect the vital communication link known as the South Pass over the Rocky Mountains, about a day's ride to the west. In the absence of wind, the flag hung limply from its pine pole, and the occasional soldier of Easy Company, United States Mounted Infantry, could be seen strolling casually from the mess hall to his barracks to relax

14

for a few moments before work began again. Sentries prowled their guard posts atop the walls and stared into the rolling "sea of grass" that surrounded them, in seemingly endless undulations, to the horizon.

One place inside the outpost, however, did not share this apparent tranquility. It was the telegraph shack, located between the ordnance stores and the guardhouse, on the eastern side of the parade. Inside the small office stood a single desk that supported the wood-and-brass telegraph sending and receiving equipment. Along one wall were the shelves that supported banks of acid-filled glass jars, which were the wet-cell batteries that powered the telegraph equipment, sending the streams of coded dots and dashes flowing along the uninsulated copper wire stretching from one pine pole to the next, parallel to the road that extended eastward from the post's main gate. This road and the adjacent telegraph wire were the outpost's main lines of communication with regimental HQ, many miles to the east. Now the telegraph key sounded its frantic rattle in response to an incoming message, and since all communication received from the key sounded urgent, Corporal Williams took up pad and pencil and began to translate the clicking of the key into readable words. The more he wrote, the more intense the look on his face became, and he cocked his head toward the device to prevent misreading a single letter of the code. And when the machine finally ceased its clatter, he hastily reread the words on the pad, then jumped from his chair and raced for the door. He read the message again as he crossed the parade to the orderly room, directly opposite, and when he threw the door of the orderly room open, Sergeant Ben Cohen looked up in surprise.

"What the hell's the meaning of this, Williams?" asked the big, rawboned first sergeant. "That door was designed to open so there is no need to tear it down."

"Sorry, Sarge," Williams replied, shoving the sheet of yellow paper across the desktop, "but this just came in over the wire. Sounds mighty damned urgent to me, and I thought the captain should see it as quick as possible."

Taking up the message, Cohen leaned back in his chair while his eyes skipped over the words. When he finished, he looked up at Williams again. "You're right, Corporal. The captain should be back from lunch any minute, and—"

A tall, distinguished-looking man in his mid-forties, with

15

hair slightly graying at the temples, stepped into the orderly room. There were silver captain's bars on the shoulders of his blue uniform and his body was still trim in spite of long years and numerous military campaigns. There was a look of confidence about him, the look of a man born to command, yet self-assured enough to understand the meaning of compassion. Captain Warner Conway, born a Virginian, had served as a lieutenant colonel under General Grant during the Civil War, and even though, along with hundreds of other officers, he had been reduced in rank at the end of the conflict and was overdue for promotion now, there was not the slightest indication of bitterness about him.

"Good afternoon, Corporal Williams, Sergeant Cohen," he said to the two men who stood at attention before him. "As you were, gentlemen," he said, then noticed the paper in Cohen's hand. "Do you have something that I should see?"

"Definitely, Captain," Cohen said, handing the message across. "Williams thought it was pretty important and I agree. Here, sir, have a look for yourself."

Conway's eyes skipped over the words and a puzzled, calculating look filled his eyes as he lowered the message. "I find this a little strange, Sergeant, but we'd better move on it. Find Windy and Matt and send them to my office as quickly as you can, and after that have two full platoons battle-ready and prepared to move out." The captain turned to Williams. "Thank you for your prompt action on this, Corporal."

Williams came to attention again and snapped a smart salute. "You're welcome, sir. I'll be waiting to send any response you might have."

"Very good," Conway replied, returning the salute and moving toward his office. "Carry on."

Ten minutes later, two tall men stepped into the office. Their height was their only point of similarity. The first man through the door was First Lieutenant Matt Kincaid, a graduate of West Point, currently serving his second tour of duty on the frontier. In his mid-thirties, he was broad-shouldered, narrow at the hips and exceptionally handsome in a rugged, athletic sort of way. With his lean build, he was the sort of man whom the designers of uniforms must have had in mind, and his tanned face was set off nicely by the blue collar around his neck.

An entirely different manner of man came in behind Kin-

16

caid. Wearing fringed buckskins, with a revolver sagging from one hip and a bowie knife from the other, Windy Mandalian was the embodiment of frontier strength and spirit. His rugged face was dominated by a hawklike nose, and his dark features and taciturn ways might have labeled him as much of an Indian as those he had fought against for so many years as an army scout. In fact he was the native son of an Armenian furrier and a French Canadian lady, with perhaps a touch of Cree in his bloodline. He was known by all in the High Plains country as a fearless, formidable force on the field of combat, while he was also admired for his fairness of mind and desire to resolve issues without a fight. But when fighting was the only possibility, there were few, either Indian or white, who wished to cast their lot against him.

Conway had been reading the message one final time when the two men walked into his office, and he looked up from the document with a pleasant smile. "Hello, Matt, Windy. Thanks for coming. I've received a rather unsettling communique from the Bureau of Indian Affairs this afternoon, and I'd like a professional opinion from you two as to its content."

The captain looked down at the paper again and held it up to the light. "This came over the wire just after lunch." He handed the message to Kincaid, and Windy peered over the lieutenant's shoulder as he read it.

Att: Captain Warner Conway
From: Bureau of Indian Affairs
Subject: Sand Ridge Reservation

Captain Conway:
Approximately three days prior to this missive, a band of Paiute, numbering in the vicinity of one hundred fifty, jumped the reservation at Sand Ridge and are presumed to be heading in your direction via the South Pass. Having stolen weapons from the storage room at the reservation, they are to be considered armed and extremely dangerous. While there are no exact figures on the casualties and/or deaths they have inflicted, it has been determined by the agent in charge, one Dennis Michael Harbert, that they are prepared to kill to maintain this insurrection. Their leader, one Chief Red Hand, has vowed never to be taken alive and he has previously been known to

17

instigate attacks against the peaceful Bannock tribe living adjacent to the Paiute on the reservation. If they are seen, you are instructed to capture and hold this renegade element from Sand Ridge until such time as Mr. Harbert arrives to take them back to their assigned area. Again, consider them to be hostiles and take whatever means necessary to rectify this breach of the legal treaty between the United States of America and the Paiute nation.

Please advise as to action taken.

Yours truly,
Bradly Warington
Director, Bureau of Indian Affairs
Washington, D.C.

Conway laid the message on his desk and looked up. "Well, what do you think, Matt?" he asked his second-in-command.

"Sounds pretty strange to me, Captain," Kincaid said, shaking his head. "Why would the Paiute head up this way if they were going to jump their reservation? Their native land is desert country and they neither own nor ride horses, which we all know are essential to survival on the Great Plains. It seems to me that if they were going to quit their reservation, they would head south instead of northeast."

Conway nodded and looked at Windy. "What Matt's just said kind of rattled my brain a little bit too, when I first read that telegram. Got any thoughts or opinions, Windy?"

Windy pulled the knife from his left hip and cleaned a fingernail in thoughtful silence before glancing at the captain. "According to that message, they're armed and considered dangerous, right, Cap'n?"

"Right."

"And they're quartered at Sand Ridge Reservation?"

"Yes, although I'm not exactly familiar with where that's located."

"I am. It's a day, maybe a day and a half's ride west of the South Pass. Worst place in the world for a tribe of Paiute."

"Why do you say that, Windy?"

"First off, Cap'n, I know more'n a hatful about the Paiute, and I ain't never seen one that was dangerous unless his back was to the wall. They're very primitive, peaceable people, and they live where they live 'cause there ain't nobody else that

18

can survive there, so they think they'll be left alone. Their main interest is finding food, not a fight. They don't even hunt worth mention, just dig up roots and such. Second, like Matt said, they wouldn't head north unless there wasn't any place else for them to go. Puttin' 'em on a reservation this far north is like tryin' to grow horns on a bullfrog. If they jumped their reservation, I'd say it's more for survival than because they got a war feather up their ass."

"There has to be some reason for this message, Windy," Conway said, more as a question than a statement.

"I'm not denying that, Cap'n, and there may well be. But like I said, the Paiute are normally a peaceful nation with home grounds around the fringes of the Great Basin in Utah Territory, not under the armpit of the Rocky Mountains. Only somebody named . . . what was that, Tadbry Barrington?"

"Bradly Warington," Conway corrected.

"Just as bad. Only somebody with that kind of name would assign the Paiute a reservation on a place where they couldn't hope to survive. Not to mention putting them next to Bannock."

Kincaid had been watching the scout and now he said, "You mentioned the Bannock, Windy. I'm familiar with them, but not to the extent that you are. According to what I've read, they're a pretty nasty lot."

"They're so rotten, Matt, they shouldn't even be on a reservation by themselves. We all know how tough and mean the Sioux, Cheyenne and Arapaho are, but even they don't want any part of the Bannock. Not out of fear, mind you, but out of disgust. The Bannock kill for sport, mutilate the dead for the hell of it, and haven't an honorable bone in their bodies. Their favorite target, when they get their blood up, are the Paiute. To them, the Paiute ain't no more'n varmints, to be killed like rabbits or coyotes, and they do a damn good job of it. Putting them on a reservation with Paiute is like askin' a naked virgin to walk through the enlisted men's barracks over there and come out the other end with her maidenhood intact."

"That's pretty much what I've heard, Windy," Matt said with an agreeing nod while turning toward Conway. "While I'm by no means an expert on the subject, Captain, I did study Indian cultures quite a bit when I was at the Point. The Paiute, Bannock, Shoshone and Utes all share the same language, known as Uto-Aztec, and possibly that's why the BIA, in its infinite ignorance, lumped the Bannock and Paiute together.

19

Apparently the Bannock retained more of their cultural heritage from the Aztecs, who were the sophisticated executioners in Mexico, than did the others. At any rate, the Bannock are known as Horse Utes, obviously due to their adaptation to mounted travel, and they are a nasty, arrogant offshoot of the Shoshone. Their culture is similar to that of the Comanche, but they've adapted to life on the fringes of the Great Basin, where sagebrush substitutes for grass, and antelope provide what the buffalo do here. The Bannock are considered to be bastard cousins even by other Indian tribes sharing the same heritage. They are highly skilled horsemen and they have used that skill in the worst possible ways. Like Windy said, they raid, steal and kill for no apparent reason other than that they think it's fun. Putting them side by side with the Paiute is like filling a rainbarrel with fish and handing some sadistic bastard a rifle."

"Sounds to me like you did your homework pretty well, Matt," Conway said. "Too damned bad some of those high mucky-mucks back in Washington didn't take the same course. Apparently, to their way of thinking, since all Indians have red skin, there are no differences between them. That's like saying two white men, one a Catholic and the other a Protestant, haven't got a damned thing in the world to argue about."

"Yup," Windy added. "A sparrow and an eagle both fly, so that makes 'em birds. Be wastin' your time tryin' to point out the difference to some intelligent son of a bitch in the BIA."

"Well, even as much as they screw up, I suppose we can't be too hard on them," Conway said. "It has to be more than a little difficult to legislate from two thousand miles away and make decisions about people you've never met in a land you've never seen."

Windy returned the knife to its sheath and leaned against the wall. "There's plenty of people to ask, Cap'n. People who do know what the hell's goin' on out here."

"Sure there are, Windy," the captain replied with a wry smile. "But that's not the government's way of doing business. The BIA is a political plum to be handed out not on merit but in payment for favors. The War Department falls into the same category, unfortunately for us."

"Speaking of war, Captain," Kincaid said, turning the message on Conway's desk and glancing at the words. "What are we going to do about these Paiute? Says here that they're armed and dangerous, and if they're running scared, it's damned hard to tell just what they might do."

"I know, Matt. I've got two platoons ready right now, and we'll have to approach this thing from the standpoint of an armed rebellion. If you leave now, you and Windy should be somewhere near the South Pass by noon tomorrow. You'll have to bivouac tonight, but the sooner we get there, the better it will be for all concerned. When you do make contact with them, give the Indians a chance to surrender and maybe we can end this thing without any bloodshed. If you're fired on, however, you'll have to use whatever means necessary to hold and detain them until their agent arrives. Use your own best judgment, but if they have sick or wounded, maybe you'd better march them back here for detainment and medical treatment."

"All right, sir. We'll ride out as soon as we can saddle up. Which platoons are we taking? The first and the third are due up for combat patrol, according to the rotation chart."

"Yes, I'm sure they're the ones Ben has alerted. Besides, I'd like to see how Lieutenant Dalby performs in the field. He seems to think that high marks and being made brigade captain at West Point automatically makes a second lieutenant one step below the rank of general and a seasoned combat veteran."

"He's still pissin' civilian water, Cap'n," Windy said laconically as he hunched away from the wall. "The biggest difference between a green second lieutenant and an idiot is the fact that the idiot knows how dumb he is."

Conway laughed. "We're all the same, Windy, when we first start out. That gold bar on our shoulders invariably separates the brain from the rest of the body. Unfortunately, Dalby seems to have suffered a more complete division than most. Put him through his paces out there, and when you get back, let me know how he performs. Good luck and happy hunting."

Sergeant Cohen had just stepped into the orderly room when Matt and Windy left the captain's office. "The first and third are mounted and prepared to move out, sir," he said, stepping to one side to allow the two men to pass. "Lieutenant Dalby has them lined up like they were going to stand a regimental inspection instead of going on combat patrol."

Kincaid sighed wearily and nodded. "I suppose he has, Ben. I wonder if there's anything in that rulebook of his that tells how men are supposed to die?"

The old veteran of many battles smiled and took a seat behind his desk. "Of course there is, sir. Standing at attention with creases straight, with a gig mark for any fresh blood on the uniform."

"Sounds about right," Kincaid allowed with a chuckle. "Thanks for getting things lined out, Ben."

"No thanks needed for a man doing his job, Lieutenant. Oh, by the way, there's one more thing. He's got Private Holzer holding the company guidon."

"Oh shit! What the hell's he want with that damned thing?"

The first sergeant grinned again. "I guess he wants you people to be able to tell who you are."

"I'll put a note in my pocket," Kincaid said dryly as he stepped out of the building. "See you in a couple of days."

He looked across the parade and saw the two platoons lined up like twin rows of blue corn, with all men mounted and sitting at attention, their eyes locked straight ahead. He couldn't help but allow an inner smile to spread through him when he saw Sergeant Gus Olsen, a seasoned veteran with more battles under his belt than the lieutenant had teeth, sitting there with a pained expression on his face. And when his eyes found Private Wolfgang Holzer, with the guidon staff held stiffly in his hand, Kincaid shook his head and walked toward the mounted units. Dalby sat his horse proudly before the two platoons.

As he moved across the parade, Kincaid thought about Private Wolfgang Holzer. He was as near to being an automaton as any man the lieutenant had ever seen, and he would carry out to the letter any order given him—any order he could understand, that is, because the private could speak hardly any English. He had been signed into the army by a recruiting sergeant on the New York docks when he stepped off the boat from Germany, and he had been more than a little confused throughout his basic training and trip out West. Until he arrived at Outpost Number Nine and his assignment with Easy Company, he had been entirely convinced that the paper he had signed was an application for a homestead.

The guidon propped against Holzer's right stirrup, and held stiffly in his right hand, was a large square of cloth with a triangular portion having been cut out of the trailing edge. It was divided into two equal halves, the top half being a field of blue with the letters US standing out in bold white, while the lower half was white with a blue E. There was a spear-tipped emblem at the top of the staff, decorated in gilt, and the staff itself was nearly six feet in length.

When Kincaid drew near, Dalby snapped a smart salute. "First and third platoons prepared to move out, sir!"

Kincaid returned the salute. "Thank you, Lieutenant. Put the men at ease."

"At ease, sir?"

"Yes, Lieutenant. We are going on a combat patrol on the High Plains, not a parade down Fifth Avenue."

Dalby's neck reddened slightly. "Yes sir. Sergeant Olsen! Put the men at ease!"

"Yes sir. At ease!"

The soldiers relaxed in their saddles. Kincaid watched them momentarily before looking at the lieutenant again. "Thank you, Lieutenant. Now have Private Holzer return the guidon to the orderly room."

"The guidon, sir? According to the book, it is to be displayed by any unit in the field as a demonstration of military might, strength and solidarity."

"That's fine, but experience has shown without a shadow of doubt that all the guidon provides when on military maneuvers is an early grave for the poor bastard holding it—in this case, Private Holzer there. He wants a homestead, true, but I think he wants something a little more commodious than a three-by-six hole in the ground. Invariably the bearer of the colors is the first man shot, and while there always has to be a first casualty, I see no point in painting a target across someone's chest. Get rid of it, Lieutenant. I'm as proud of our company as the next man, but there is a time and place for all things. On a combat patrol there is neither time nor place for military pomp and ceremony."

"Yessir." Without changing expression, Dalby snapped over his shoulder, "Sergeant Olsen! Have the guidon returned to the orderly room!"

"Yessir," Olsen replied, turning to the German. "Holzer, I know you're not going to understand this, but I'm going to give it a rip anyway. I'll speak real slow and easy, and you listen exactly the same way. Take-the-guidon-back-to-the-or-derly-room."

"*Vas?*" Holzer replied, his desire to please displayed openly on his amiable face.

"I said take-the-guidon-back-to-the-orderly-room."

"*Vas?*" Holzer repeated.

"I said . . . ah, to hell with it. Private Marlow!"

"Yes, Sarge?" a young soldier behind the sergeant replied.

"Take the goddamned thing back to the orderly room on the double."

"Sure, Sarge," Marlow said, swinging down and taking the guidon staff from Holzer's hesitant grasp. "Sorry, Wolf, old boy, but you'll have to dry your laundry another time."

"*Vas?*"

"And that too," Marlow said with a grin as he furled the flag and trotted across the parade.

Private Wolfgang Holzer made an empty gesture with his hand and shrugged his shoulders while watching Kincaid with bewildered eyes.

"Let's just say you've been given another day to live, Private," Matt said as he swung onto his saddle while watching the bulky soldier. "You're a big enough target as it is."

"*Vas,* sir?"

Windy edged his horse up beside Kincaid's "'Vas,' whatever in hell that means, doesn't seem to be doing him a whole hell of a lot of good, Matt. This is the American army, ain't it?"

"Yeah, supposed to be. But to some recruiters, a body's a body. Wienerschnitzel, strudle and sauerkraut not withstanding. What the hell, he still squeezes a trigger in English."

"The universal language, Matt. And understood only by the unfortunate few. I'll ride point if you want."

"Do that, Windy. We'll use our standard signals."

The scout reined his mount away while turning in the saddle with an easy grin. "*Vas?*"

"Get the hell out of here, you old bastard. One Wolfgang is more than I need."

Continuing to grin, Windy walked his horse toward the gates and adjusted the Sharps rifle cradled in the crook of his left arm. Private Holzer looked at Kincaid in continued puzzlement and said, "*Vas,* sir?"

Matt picked up his reins and moved his horse to the head of the column. "Forget it, Private. Inside joke, and one you couldn't possibly understand."

Smiling now, Kincaid shook his head and indicated to Sergeant Olsen to move the patrol out. Saddles creaking softly, Easy Company rode through the main gates and onto the plains.

three _____

It came suddenly, with little warning, a summer storm raging across the high peaks of the Rocky Mountains. Flashes of blue lightning hissed and sizzled in the black night, and even the driving rain could not muffle the cracking boom of rolling thunder. They were illuminated briefly, struggling upward with the wind ripping at their tattered clothing, and then plunged into darkness again, but the band of Paiute, strung out in long, formless ranks, continued their blind flight toward the crest.

It was bitterly cold, and occasional waves of sleet stung their faces. At an altitude of over seven thousand feet, their breathing came in ragged gasps as their totally inadequate clothing flapped around their bodies in the ceaseless wind. No one knew how many had been lost in the darkness, lying down beside a boulder or outcropping of rock to shield themselves from the biting cold, only to perish there alone in the inky blackness. But a singular, solitary figure could be seen at the head of the column, walking straight and proud and occasionally turning back to help the lame and elderly over a particularly rough stretch of terrain. One would have thought he felt no ill effects from the freezing temperature or thin oxygen at that altitude, and he seemed mindless of sparse clothing as he placed an arm around those less strong to comfort them and offer words of encouragement to continue the journey. His face, when illuminated by the occasional flashes of blue, revealed a desire and desperation and commitment to purpose, written there as though etched in stone. We must go on, was Red Hand's continuous entreaty; we have nowhere else to go.

The storm, for all the misery it created, did provide one solitary blessing. Knowing his people were suffering greatly from the cold, Red Hand had taken ten of his strongest braves and set out in search of clothing and blankets when they neared the Union Pacific switching yard at South Pass City, now several miles behind them. He was completely aware of the railroad men's contempt for Indians and realized he could expect no help merely for the asking. Under cover of darkness they had approached what appeared to be a storage building of some sort, had broken out a window, and were rummaging around inside for any article of warmth when they were discovered by a guard. Several shots had been exchanged before Red Hand and his braves could escape, and one young Paiute had been shot through the shoulder. He was being helped now by the others up the long grade, but Red Hand knew that when the storm broke, the railroad men would come after them and the wounded man would be taken captive.

There was little doubt in Red Hand's mind that Wokana and his Bannock police would be searching for them as well, and he wondered for a moment which group would be the more inclined to show mercy. His automatic conclusion was that they would receive no mercy from any quarter, and that they were in a fight to the death with all who opposed them. Realizing there was little or no chance of victory for his people, Red Hand's chest tightened with inner resolve. They were armed with forty rifles and as much ammunition as they could carry. If fight they must, they would not go down without a struggle.

Dark Star was walking several paces behind him, and Red Hand stopped to help her over a rain-slick boulder while lightning cracked across the sky again. Even though she offered a tired smile of thanks as his strong grip closed about her arm, Red Hand could see the strain on her face and an aching filled his heart.

"How are you feeling, little one?"

"I'm very tired, Red Hand. Very tired. But I'll make it. Save your strength to help the others. How much farther do we have to go?"

"We're nearly to the top now, and we'll rest there for a few minutes. It will be much easier going down the other side. But we have to keep going, we have no other choice. The men of the Iron Horse will be coming after us at dawn, and Wokana can't be far behind. If we can get to the lowland, maybe I and the healthy ones can hold them off while you and the others escape."

Dark Star stopped abruptly and reached up to touch Red Hand's face gently with her fingertips. "I will not go without you, Red Hand."

Red Hand smiled tenderly and pressed his hand against hers. "Yes you will, little one. You must lead our people away as I would. If we are victorious, we will catch up with you. If we aren't, you are the only one strong enough to do what must be done."

"I don't want you to die, Red Hand. I love you and I don't want you to die."

"I love you, little one, and I don't want to die. But the choice is no longer mine." Another driving sheet of rain swept over them and Red Hand put his arm around her trembling shoulders and pulled her to him in an attempt to shield her from the cold. "My life is as nothing compared to the lives of the others. Let's talk no more of death and think only of how warm the sun will be when we are on the lowland tomorrow."

The others were straggling past them now, and the two braves supporting the wounded man paused by Red Hand's side.

"How do you feel, Standing Crane? Can you make it a little farther?" he asked, turning the young brave's dangling head up to him.

Standing Crane opened his eyes slowly and they were blurred in feverish delirium. "I can make it, Red Hand. It is very hot, but I can make it."

"I know you will, Standing Crane, you are brave and have strong medicine. When we get to the greasy grass, the Dream Singer will sing you a cure and you will again stand as straight as those from whom you took your name."

Standing Crane nodded before his eyes closed and his head sank again. A sudden flash of light swept over them and Red Hand glanced toward the sky. The clouds were breaking up, and brilliant moonlight pierced the blackness as scudding clouds filtered past. Red Hand moved forward again with renewed determination.

"We must go now. The storm is passing and it will freeze when the clouds have gone. We must get down to the greasy grass or we all will die."

The ragged column straggled toward the crest, which was now occasionally visible, and the rain lessened to occasional showers while the gusting wind became a steady howl across the summit. Two ribbons of steel glistened in the moonlight, and when they reached the crest, Red Hand could see powerful lights far below and could hear the straining chug of three locomotives pulling their load up the long grade. He turned and led his people down the side of the mountain away from the railroad tracks, and the flat blackness of the prairie beckoned them from far below.

Michael Harbert stepped down before the rough-cut lumber building and tied his horse to the hitching rail. It was early evening, and from the direction and smell of the breeze he knew a storm would come that night. Off to the left, the black hole of a mine shaft yawned its dark welcome into the side of the mountain. The cleared land around the cabin was littered with crates filled with mining equipment. The four horses in a corral across the way lifted their heads from the drinking trough and watched Harbert with pricked-up ears in expectation of more grain, but the agent stamped his boots on the steps instead and crossed the porch to knock on the door.

A chair scraped on the floor from within, followed by heavy steps and less-than-welcome words. "Who is it?"

"It's me, Bill. Mike Harbert."

An iron bar clanked back and the door opened cautiously before swinging wide. A big man, equal in height and size to Harbert, stood in the doorway with his hands on his hips. He wore a red woolen shirt, high boots, and baggy pants held up by wide suspenders flanking his modest paunch. His curly hair was reddish in color and joined at the point of his chin by a flourishing beard, while his cheeks and upper lip were shaven, but now bristling with a single day's growth. His blue eyes were set rather close together in his head, and that placement gave them a hard, staring quality. When he spoke, there was a profound lack of humor in his voice.

"What the hell are you doing here?" Bill McCauley asked.

"I had to talk to you, Bill. We've got a slight problem."

McCauley's bushy eyebrows arched suspiciously. "A problem? What kind of problem?"

"Nothing we can't handle. Mind if I come in? I'd rather talk inside."

Shrugging, McCauley stood to one side and waited for Harbert to enter before closing and bolting the door again. The room was barren with the exception of bedrolls spread out on the floor and a single table in the center of the room, at which three other men sat. They nodded to Harbert without expressing greeting and the agent pulled up another chair, reversed it, and lowered himself onto the seat with his arms crossed on the backrest. The table was nearly covered with maps and diagrams, which McCauley shoved to the floor with a sweeping motion of his arm before taking a seat and reaching for the whiskey bottle. He splashed a generous ration into a dirty tin cup and pushed the drink toward Harbert, then filled cups all around.

"Here's to ya," Harbert offered, raising his cup in salute.

Again, the three nodded without response and McCauley drank silently without acknowledging the toast. He wiped a filthy sleeve across his lips and continued to stare at Harbert.

"You mentioned a problem. I'd be listenin' now to hear what it is."

Harbert matched the stare for a few seconds before smiling weakly and glancing away. "Like I said, it's nothin' we can't handle, Bill. My Paiute jumped the reservation two days ago. Not a damned one left on the place when I got back from that meeting with you."

"What! And you say that's not a big problem?" McCauley snapped. 'You couldn't have a bigger problem, Mike. Now explain."

"Well, like I said, I'm going to be a day or two late in filling my contract with you, that's all. It's nothing to get excited about, and—"

"Nothing to get excited about! This entire operation hinges on that contract. I've got a goddamned bundle of money invested in this thing, and in you as well, and any delay is too goddamned long! According to our original agreement, you would have one hundred Paiute here the day after tomorrow to work in that fucking mine out there, with another fifty as backup to fill in for those killed and injured. You were also going to supply some of your police to keep things in line and encourage them featherheads to a little better production."

McCauley's eyes narrowed and his right hand moved toward the revolver lying on the table. "And for that you would be paid a hundred dollars a head, plus ten percent of whatever the mine produces. You've already been given a twenty-five-percent advance, which was a good-faith gesture. Now, I'd say that $8,250 is one hell of a lot of good faith, and I don't aim to see one nickel less come my way."

"Just calm down, Bill," Harbert said, holding his hands up defensively. "Everything will be taken care of and our agreement will be met as stipulated in the contract. It's just going to take me a day or two longer than I had originally planned, that's all."

"Too goddamned long! We're set to go day after tomorrow, and you know as well as I do that I ain't got till next Christmas to get this job done and get out. I've got exactly two and a half months, no more. That rich old bastard Huntington doesn't know what we're up to here. He thinks I am only a mining engineer who is going to assess his claim and determine if it's worth a dig. He doesn't know there's a vein of ore back in there as wide as your goddamned hand, which won't be there when he gets back from his trip to Europe. That jolly little voyage and vacation is going to take him exactly two and a half months, and he's coming straight here when he gets back. I don't plan to be around when he shows up."

"Neither do I, Bill, and we won't be. My police are tracking the Paiute now and should have them back within a couple of days. I'll supervise their return personally and bring them straight here. We'll be in operation as soon as I get back, and we'll just make them work a little harder to make up for lost time."

McCauley stared into his cup and thought a moment. "Where the hell do you think they went?"

"Most likely up over the South Pass, but my boys are checking the lowland first to make sure they didn't cut a trail for the desert. If they did head up over the mountain, we've got them bottled up. I sent a telegram this morning to the Bureau of Indian Affairs, and they notified an army outfit stationed north of the pass to cut them off and hold them for me."

Harbert took another drink of whiskey and was satisfied with the look on McCauley's face as he lowered the cup. "Actually, Bill, this could work to our advantage. If we come up missing a few Paiute at the end of this thing, we can pass them off as having been killed trying to escape the reservation again. The army doesn't give a damn what happens to a bunch of Indians, and the BIA will believe whatever I tell them."

"Yeah, maybe so," McCauley allowed. "All I want to see

31

is them ore carts filled with gold-bearing rock and heading for the crusher. There's no doubt that some of your Paiute are going to die, either from exhaustion or accidents, and we might need a cover until we've sapped that vein."

"And we've got one. Now, what say we have another drink in friendship before I head back to the reservation?"

"Sure, Mike. But there ain't no need in you goin' back tonight. We've got more whiskey than the five of us can drink, and you might as well go over these plans with us so you'll know what your Paiute are supposed to do."

"Sounds fine to me," Harbert replied with a grin, reaching for the bottle. "Let's get started on the whiskey now and the plans a little later?"

McCauley nodded his bearlike head and squinted at Harbert. "You're not a bad sort, Mike. But don't ever cross me. Understand?"

"Wouldn't think of it," Harbert said, the grin widening while he rocked back in his chair and propped a boot on the corner of the table. "I'm a firm believer in honor among thieves. Now, we *are* thieves, wouldn't you agree, Mr. McCauley?"

McCauley grunted and sloshed more whiskey into his cup. "We only take advantage of the situation at hand, Mr. Harbert. If that be thievery, then so let it be. There are the advantaged and the disadvantaged. I'm an advocate of membership in the former."

"As you should be," Harbert responded, raising his cup again. "To the success of our venture?"

It was obvious that McCauley was not given to toasts, but he grudgingly raised his cup. "Yeah. Let's just get on with it."

At eight o'clock the following morning, Michael Harbert reined in beside the well in the front yard of the agency. When he saw the bucket inverted on the ledge of the well, a sly smile crossed his lips and he turned his horse north in the direction of the mountain range that loomed in splendor above the horizon.

The deep grass glistened in the brilliant morning sun, and Matt Kincaid could feel the warming heat spread across his shoulders. There was not a cloud in the high blue sky and the air smelled clean and fresh, washed by the drenching storm of the night before. Prairie dogs perched on the mounds above their dens to bask in the welcome heat. There was an aura of peace and serenity about the vast, rolling plains, belied only by a big roan horse quartering toward the two platoons at a dead run.

Kincaid held up his right hand to halt the column, and watched the buckskinned rider steer his horse clear of the "dog town." When the scout reined his horse to a plunging stop beside Kincaid, the animal's mouth was flecked with foam; its legs and chest were wet, and yellow seeds from the damp grass clung to its dark hide.

"Nice day for a massacre, Matt," Windy said, turning his mount beside Kincaid's to face the mountains, approximately five miles away.

"What do you mean by that, Windy?"

"Not exactly sure. I found some of those Paiute, but the strange thing is, there aren't any young braves with them. Just women, children and a few old men. The only young feller with 'em looks like he's been shot. If I remember right, they were supposed to be armed and dangerous, weren't they?"

"Yeah, that's what the message said," Kincaid replied, his eyes sweeping over the stretch of grass between them and the foothills. "Is that what you meant by 'nice day for a massacre'? That those with weapons are lying in wait for us to try and take the defenseless ones?"

Windy broke off a chew of cut-plug and nestled it comfortably in his cheek. "Could be. The main band is down in a deep draw, and they look like they've been rode hard and put away wet. Must've crossed the divide in that storm last night, and it don't look like the whole tribe of 'em working together could pull a sick whore off a pisspot."

"Could their warriors be hiding in the next draw, waiting to climb up to the top of the rise and fire down on us when we ride into the low ground?"

"That's the way the Sioux or Cheyenne would do it," Windy replied, spitting and chewing the tobacco to work up flavor. "Can't tell about the Paiute, but if they are, they'd have to be on the west side, 'cause I had me a good close look at the one between us and them. Nothin' but bumblebees and butterflies."

"All right. Are they due west of us?"

"Due west."

"Lieutenant Dalby!" Kincaid called, turning around in his saddle. "Come up here!"

Dalby pressed his horse forward with more than a hint of eagerness and reined in beside Kincaid. "Yessir?"

"Windy's made contact with the Paiute. They're due west of us about . . . how far would you say it is, Windy?"

"Two and a half, maybe three miles."

"Good," Matt said, turning again to Dalby. "We'll work a pincers maneuver. You take the third platoon and angle off northwest and I'll take the first and head southwest. They're in a deep draw and it's mostly women and children, with a few oldtimers thrown in. The ground is clear between us and them on this side, but we don't know about the opposite side. When you're in position, you wait as a reserve unit and I'll take my platoon in. If you hear our bugle call for assistance, be prepared to close from the north."

"Fine, sir," Dalby said, tight-lipped now. "But if you'll pardon my asking, sir, why don't we take them with a frontal assault? We have them outmanned and outgunned, so—"

"We don't know that, Lieutenant."

"But you just said they are mostly old men and women and children, sir. It would be good for morale to take them in a classic manner."

"It would be better for morale if everyone survived this operation, including the Paiute. Have you ever seen what a nightingale does when you get close to her chicks, Lieutenant?"

A confused look crossed Dalby's face. "No, sir, I can't say that I have. What does that have to do with anything?"

"Everything, and especially when you're fighting the noble savage. She'll act like she has a broken wing, calling out in pain and flopping around like she's helpless, while leading whatever is threatening her brood away from the nest. That little trick hasn't gone unnoticed by the Indians."

"You mean they're using their women and children as decoys, sir? That's less than noble in my book," Dalby said with a hint of superiority.

"Your concept of honor and the Indians' concept of honor are two entirely different things, Lieutenant. Victory is their primary purpose, and they're damned adept at achieving that goal. I want you to fully understand one thing: we don't consider the band in the draw to be a threat. They are not to be fired upon and neither is anyone else who doesn't make a show of hostile intent. Is that clear?"

"Yessir," Dalby responded almost contritely.

"Good. Now move out. Take our bugler, Corporal McBride,

with you, and if you get jumped, sound the call for help."

"Very good, sir. But we won't get jumped."

Kincaid and Windy watched the young officer ride away at the head of his platoon and Windy made no attempt to disguise the contempt in his voice.

"They're all the same, Matt. They'd charge hell with a bucket of warm water if they thought it'd get 'em a medal or a promotion."

"Yeah, I suppose so, and I imagine I was the same way. But unfortunately, too many second lieutenants wind up in hell empty-handed. Let's go, Windy. We'd better get there before Dalby does."

Nearly an hour had passed before the first platoon skirted the southern lip of the deep draw, and they could see the Paiute below them, huddled in a mournful group, with the stronger ones ministering to the needs of the weaker. They passed by the depression, seemingly unnoticed by the Indians, and Kincaid halted the unit and called his platoon sergeant forward

"Yessir?"

"Sergeant Olsen, we'll dismount here and move forward on foot in echelon formation. Keep one squad back in reserve and we'll communicate through hand signals as we advance. Pass the word along not to fire unless fired upon and—"

The staccato rattle of rifle fire erupted from just over the next rise, and Kincaid's head snapped in that direction in conjunction with Windy's. They could distinguish the opposing sound of return fire, but no combatants were visible to the eye.

"What do you think, Windy?" Kincaid asked without looking at the scout. "Did they jump Dalby?"

The scout's eyes were locked on the horizon as well. "Can't say for sure, Matt. If they did, he was sure as hell out of position. He should be north, and that firing is coming from the west. I'd make it three, maybe four hundred yards."

A shrill bugle call split the air, but it was not the sound Kincaid had expected. Instead of the call for help, it was the call to charge.

"Now what the hell's that for, Matt?" Windy asked with a sharp glance at Kincaid. "Surely he wouldn't charge into an ambush."

"I don't know, Windy, hard to tell what he'd do, but we'd better find out."

The rifle fire coming from beyond the next ridge continued unabated, and Kincaid wheeled his horse. "Sergeant! Take two squads and—"

"Matt! Look over there!" Windy shouted, pointing toward the north.

Matt's head swiveled in the direction indicated, and he saw the third platoon break the crest of the rise in the spread-out formation of the classic cavalry charge, with Dalby in the lead and heading down toward the startled Paiute.

"That damned idiot!" Kincaid snarled. "Windy! Cut across and head him off! Stay low, 'cause we don't know what the hell's waiting behind the lip! Sergeant Olsen! You stay here with the third squad and give Windy covering fire if needed. I'll take the rest of the platoon and see what the hell's going on over that next rise!"

"Yessir!" Olsen said and yelled over his shoulder, "Third squad, dismount and assume prone firing positions! First and second! Move out with Lieutenant Kincaid!"

By the time Olsen had finished giving the command, Windy's horse was streaking down the slope with the scout crouched low to his mount's neck and his body pressed forward to provide the smallest possible target.

While the third squad spread out in a firing line along the crest, Kincaid heeled his horse to a dead run and led the other two squads toward the continuing rifle fire just over the next rise. Approaching the crest, he slowed his mount and gave the signal for the two squads to dismount and spread out in a diamond formation. With handlers holding their horses, the mounted infantrymen moved cautiously forward with rifles held at the ready and bodies crouched low to the ground. Below them they saw roughly forty Paiute, sprawled on their bellies in the grass and firing at mounted Indians racing in zigzag patterns while firing back at the prone Indians. Kincaid saw two warriors go down before his eyes darted to the right in response to a third field of fire. He could make out bowler hats, black against the surrounding green, and checkered flannel shirts hugging the earth behind blazing weapons.

"First squad! Fire above the heads of the mounted Indians below. Second squad! Fire above the heads of those people off to the right, whoever they are!"

Instantly the army weapons exploded and the soldiers expertly jacked spent rounds from their single-shot Springfields and fed fresh rounds into the smoking chambers.

Confused now, the mounted warriors retreated, but the men in the bowler hats turned their rifles on the crest. Slugs ripped into sweet grass and thudded into the gray earth, but the men of Easy Company still did not aim to kill while continuing to rain down their steady salvo of pinning fire. The Paiute lay in their positions while craning their necks rearward, before half of them twisted around to fire at the targets above. The firefight went on for nearly five minutes before Kincaid saw Windy lead the first platoon into position behind the group off to the right and heard Windy's uncompromising words.

"Lay down those guns, boys, or lay beside 'em! Your choice!"

Rifle fire from that position came to a sporadic halt and Kincaid raised his head slightly. "You down there!" he shouted in the direction of the Paiute. "Lay down your weapons! If we have to fire again we will be aiming to kill!"

After a moment's hesitation the Indian weapons were silent as well, and Kincaid rose slowly to his feet. "Corporal Wilson! Corporal Miller! Keep them covered while I go down and find out what in hell's going on here! If so much as one shot is fired, you're instructed to kill every last one of them. Windy!"

"Yeah, Matt," the scout called back in a relaxed voice.

"Have Dalby get whoever is in charge over there and bring him down! You mount up two squads and go out and get whoever is the leader of those mounted Indians and bring him down as well!"

"Right, Matt!"

Kincaid worked his way down, and he could feel a familiar chill tingling along his spine as he moved forward, entirely exposed to enemy fire. Before him, one tall Indian stood and walked silently toward him, while off to his right a barrel chested man walked ahead of Lieutenant Dalby. When they met at the bottom of the draw, Kincaid looked first at the white man and then at the Indian.

"My name is Lieutenant Kincaid, E Company, United States Mounted Infantry. Now who the hell are you?"

The Indian stared at Kincaid and there was defiance in his

eyes. "My name is Red Hand. I am chief of the Paiute."

"All right," Matt replied, looking at the white man. "And who are you?"

"I'm Fritz Dugan, section chief for the Union Pacific over at South Pass City."

"You're a little ways away from your railroad aren't you, Mr. Dugan?" Matt asked. "How do you explain your actions against these Paiute?"

"Don't need to explain," Dugan replied sullenly. "A thievin' Injun is a thievin' Injun and he deserves what he gets."

"Could you be a little more specific, Mr. Dugan?"

"Damned right I can. Yesterday evenin', this feller and some of his kind broke into my storehouse. Took a couple of shots at my guard and tried to steal everthin' we had. I don't take kindly to thievin' Injuns."

"Apparently not," Kincaid replied, looking now at the Paiute. "And you, Red Hand? Did you attempt to steal from Mr. Dugan here?"

Red Hand's face went tight and his lips barely moved. "I speak to no white man."

"You just did, Red Hand. Are you from the Sand Ridge Reservation?"

Red Hand only stared impassively at Kincaid until the sound of two horses walking toward them caused him to turn his head. There was instant hatred in his eyes when he saw Wokana, but when he looked at Windy, his expression changed slightly.

"Matt, this fellow here says his name is Wokana. Claims to be chief of the agency police on the Sand Ridge, and says he came to take the Paiute back. He and his warriors are Bannock, and I think you remember our little conversation yesterday with the Cap'n regarding their opinion of the Paiute."

"Yes I do, Windy," Matt replied, glancing at the fierce-looking warrior. "Who sent you after the Paiute?"

Wokana's head turned toward Red Hand and a twisting sneer curled his lips. "Black Bear. The agent who was sent to us by the Great White Father. Red Hand has broken our treaty with the white man. We will take them back now."

"Not quite so fast, Wokana. Where is this agent of yours?" Kincaid asked, noting the obvious blood hatred between the two Indians.

38

"We will meet him on the way back to our land. The Paiute will go with us."

"I don't think so, Wokana. They have sick and injured who must be treated. I'll take them back to Outpost Nine and your agent can come for them there."

"No! They go with me! I am chief of the agency police and they have broken our laws. We will see that it never happens again."

"I'll bet you would," Kincaid said, noting the expression on Wokana's face and the hatred in Red Hand's eyes, "but I am the military law here and I'll decide what's best for all parties involved. Mr. Dugan?" he asked, looking at the railroad man. "Exactly what was taken from your storeroom?"

Dugan hesitated before looking down to nudge a clump of grass with the toe of his boot. "Nothin'. We jumped 'em before they could get their hands on anything."

"And that's cause to attempt to kill them?"

"We gotta fend for ourselves out here, mister," Dugan snapped, his head jerking up and a hot flush crossing his face. "The army sure as hell ain't been much help."

"Thank you for the vote of confidence, Mr. Dugan," Matt said dryly. "You railroad people haven't been exactly princes to work with, yourselves. Now I want you to go back to your place of business, and if you have any complaints to file against these Paiute, you place them through proper channels." His eyes shifted to the Bannock warrior. "And you, Wokana, go back to your reservation and inform your agent that these people will be released to him only on proper authority."

"They go back with me," Wokana grunted.

"Like hell they do. If you're not out of my sight within two minutes, I'll arrest you on the spot. Is that understood?"

Wokana glowered at Kincaid for several long seconds before turning his horse away with a final glance at Red Hand. "You do not deserve to be called a man, snake belly. I can wait until Black Bear comes for you."

"Kah!" Red Hand hissed, slamming his rifle across the neck of Wokana's horse and causing the mount to rear on its hind legs. Wokana only grinned and galloped across the plains with a wicked laugh trailing behind.

"He's everything you'd expect from a Bannock," Windy said, watching the warrior disappear over the rolling swell.

39

"Yeah, a real nice fellow," Matt replied, turning to Dugan. "You're free to go, Mr. Dugan. I suggest that you do."

"I'm gone, Lieutenant, but you haven't heard the last of this incident. The Union Pacific carries a lot of weight with the government."

"I'm sure it does, and feel free to do whatever you think necessary. But don't expect any sympathy from the military."

Dugan glared at Kincaid before jabbing a blunt finger toward Red Hand as he turned away. "You, redskin! If I ever see you on our land again, you'll be pushin' up daisies with your toenails!"

Red Hand smiled easily and spoke for the first time. "Your land? You own nothing. This land belongs to all."

"You show me your deed and I'll show you mine!" Dugan snapped, spinning on his heel and walking toward his men, standing on the high ground.

"Seem to be a matched set, him and Wokana," Windy said, resting his Sharps across the pommel of his saddle.

"Proves there's bad on both sides, Windy," Matt replied, turning again toward the lone Paiute. "Red Hand here says he won't talk to me, but he just might fill you in on what's happened to him and his people. Why don't you try to get the story out of him while I go off to one side and have a little chat with Lieutenant Dalby?"

"Sure, Matt. Come on, Red Hand, let's take a little walk."

Red Hand nodded and followed Windy away, while Kincaid turned on the second lieutenant, who swallowed with some difficulty and looked away from his commanding officer.

"Now, Lieutenant," Matt began, "I want to know exactly what you thought you were doing over there. You were given orders to provide a flanking element to come to our aid if attacked. Why in Christ's name did you attack?"

"I . . . I . . . heard the rifle fire and—"

"Look me in the eye when you talk to me, Lieutenant!"

"Yes, sir," Dalby said, allowing his head to turn reluctantly toward Kincaid's. "I thought you were under attack and I felt it my duty to come to your rescue."

"My rescue? You're just damned lucky you weren't the one to be rescued, if that had been possible, which I doubt. If there had been an ambush laid out as we thought there might be, you and the rest of the third platoon would have been cut down like new-mown hay. What you have to utilize out here, Lieutenant, is common sense, not textbook tactics. You will never fight against any armed force more cunning and wily than the Indians you will face during your tour here on the frontier. Most have only one chance to learn that and still survive. You've had your first and last chance, and if you are to be depended upon to protect anyone's flank in the future, you damned well better not forget it."

"I . . . understand . . . sir. I apologize for my overreaction."

"Your apology is fine, Lieutenant, and accepted. But how do you apologize to a man with a bullet through his chest?"

"You don't, sir," Dalby managed before glancing away.

Kincaid watched him and a different tone came into his voice when he spoke again. "My first instinct would be to say, 'Don't be too hard on yourself, Lieutenant,' but I don't believe in that. Your men are trained to follow wherever you lead, and it's your responsibility to make damned sure you know what the hell you are leading them into. Enough said. Now assemble both platoons and be prepared to escort these Paiute back to the post. Disarm the young braves and provide whatever help you can to the sick and injured. They are people to us, Lieutenant, not Indians. Never forget that."

Kincaid returned the sad-faced lieutenant's salute, watched him walk toward the third platoon, waiting on the hill, and noted Dalby's erect military posture despite the embarrassment of an upbraiding. He'll make it, Matt thought, and then his mind went to the task at hand and he wondered about the agent whom Wokana had called Black Bear. He knew they would meet soon and he was equally certain that it wouldn't be a pleasant experience. For some reason and without ever having met the man, he disliked him somehow and a nagging anger touched his mind. He looked around at the pristine land and an unsettling revelation came to him.

"We were sent here to protect the white men from the Indians," he said softly. "And now the situation appears to be reversed, with us protecting everybody from everybody. Who the hell knows what's going to happen next."

four _____

'What's your name, son?" Kincaid asked as he knelt over the young Indian who lay stretched out before him on an army blanket.

Standing Crane remained silent and watched with fevered, untrusting eyes while the white man opened the medical satchel beside his right leg. The other Paiute watched as well, from a short distance away, and the Dream Singer ceased shaking the rattle in his hand and the wailing chant died on his lips.

Matt smiled his understanding as his fingers drew disinfectant and a roll of white bandages from the bag. "I don't blame you for not wanting to talk to me," he said while gently unbuttoning the young man's tattered shirt, "and I know you think your friend there with the rattle could do you more good than I can, but you're wrong in this case. If I don't get you patched up and to some proper medical treatment damned quick, he'll be singing your death chant instead of trying to heal you."

Again the Paiute did not respond, and made a feeble attempt with weak hands to push Kincaid away. "Just hold on there," Matt soothed, pulling the blood-encrusted shirt away to examine the torn wound just above the left breast. "You've been shot up pretty good, but I've seen worse." He dampened a cloth with water from a canteen and began dabbing the swollen, discolored flesh around the hole. "If you're going to die, it will only be after I've made every attempt to save your life."

From the corner of his eye he saw Windy and Red Hand stop on the crest of the swell, then his full attention went again to the task at hand. An instant before he heard Windy's voice, he thought he had caught the sound of running feet.

"Matt! Watch out!"

Kincaid glanced up just as Red Hand's shoulder slammed into his side and he sprawled onto his back in the grass. The Paiute scrambled to his feet, prepared to lunge again, and Matt drew his knees up to protect his stomach and chest. Red Hand dove through the air with arms extended, and a second before he landed, Kincaid's boots shot out and caught the Indian squarely in the chest. A grunt escaped Red Hand's mouth and a startled look filled his eyes as he flew backward and slammed to the ground with the breath knocked from his lungs. Matt was standing over him before he could recover, with one boot pressed against the Indian's Adam's apple and the other braced to provide pressure.

"I don't know what the hell you're up to, Red Hand," Kincaid said through gritted teeth, "but I do know I could kill you right now if I wanted to."

Hatred welled in Red Hand's dark eyes, but the pressure on his throat denied him speech and the two men stared at each other in silence while Windy trotted to Kincaid's side.

"I believe he thinks you're trying to hurt his friend, Matt," the scout said. "He hates white men as much as he distrusts them, and from what he told me, he has damned good reason."

"Yeah?" Matt replied, neither increasing nor lessening the pressure. "I'm not too fond of Indians right now myself. What's his story?"

"They've been given a pretty shitty deal by the white agent on their reservation. They are bullied by the agent's Bannock police, their women are raped at will, and their people are killed more for the hell of it than anything else. According to Red Hand, they weren't trying to start a rebellion, only escape. They knew the Bannock would be after them and had no choice but to head in this direction. Lost quite a few people for their efforts, most of them old men and women who died from the cold, crossing the pass."

"How many?"

"He doesn't know for sure. Maybe as many as fifteen."

A different look came into Kincaid's eyes and he lifted his foot from Red Hand's throat before squatting on his haunches beside the prone Indian. "Just because some whites are bad, that doesn't mean we all are. We are here to help your people, not hurt them. Your friend over there will die if he isn't treated damned quick, just like you and the rest of your people would have if we hadn't shown up."

Turning toward Lieutenant Dalby, Kincaid said, "Lieutenant, have the men take the blankets from behind their saddles and distribute them to the most seriously injured. Do the same with our field rations and make them as comfortable as you can before we start back. Provide them with water and arrange for one of our horses to be made available to the wounded man over there."

"Yessir," Dalby responded, turning to issue the orders while Kincaid looked down at Red Hand again.

"You and your people will be taken back to our outpost, where a decision will be made regarding what should be done with you. You will be talking personally with Captain Conway, and I can assure you there is no man, either white or red, who commands more respect on the High Plains than he does. He is fair, firm and honest. Now, are there any questions before I go back to try and save your friend's life?"

Red Hand watched silently while Kincaid's orders to the lieutenant were carried out, and a look of grudging respect crossed his face when he looked up again. He had seen the soldiers moving among his people, covering them with warm blankets and comforting the sick and elderly.

"Yes. I have one question," he said finally, his eyes locked on Kincaid's. "Why?"

"Why, what?"

"Why are you doing this for us?"

Matt smiled, and reaching down with his hand, he offered the Indian assistance to his feet. "Because we wish only to live in peace with you. To help you if we can, to protect you if necessary, and above all to make certain that all agreements signed by our two peoples are met to the fullest."

There was a sadness about the young chief's face as he declined Matt's offer of help and sprang unassisted to his feet. "We have nowhere to go. We wish only to live in peace with you, but there are certain white people who say no. If we could return to our homeland, we could live without your help, but we cannot. We must live where we are told to live, and for that we all will die."

Red Hand's gaze drifted again to his people, and then to the open plains. He stared stoically into the distance, his head turning in a one-hundred-eighty-degree arc, before his eyes centered on Kincaid again. "We cannot survive here. We cannot trust the white man and we cannot fight the Bannock with any hope of winning. We would be better off put to death now than to be made to go back where we came from."

"Don't get too hasty, Red Hand," Kincaid replied, touching

the Indian's arm lightly with his fingertips. "As I said, Captain Conway is a fair man. Whatever decision he makes will be in the best interest of all concerned. Now, may I go and give your friend medical attention?"

Red Hand looked first at the young Indian and then back to Kincaid. "Yes. If he lives, I will have you to thank." The dark eyes shone with determination and his lips were drawn tightly across his teeth. "If he dies, you will be my enemy forever."

"Forever is a long time, Red Hand. I'm no doctor and don't pretend to be one. But I will help your friend to the best of my ability. What's his name?"

"His name is Standing Crane. He is my younger brother."

Matt whistled under his breath and heard Windy say beside him, "Matt, I know you ain't a doctor, but you'd better learn mighty damned quick how to be one."

"I know, Windy. The problem is, if the boy had been treated before he lost all that blood, he could easily have been saved. As it is now, he's fevered and weak. To tell you the truth, I don't think he has a chance in hell of making it, but we've got to try."

"Have at 'er, Matt. Give it your best shot and nobody can ask any more of you than that. Not even Red Hand, even though he won't understand it. Maybe you ought to let the Dream Singer have the responsibility."

"No, I can't do that. He has two chances with our type of medicine—slim and none. With that fellow shaking a gourd full of beads over his head, his chances are down to one—none."

"All right. You never backed off in a tight spot before," Windy said, pulling a square of cut-plug from his pocket and carving off a corner with his knife. "I'll be right close to Red Hand here, so don't worry about your backside."

"Thanks," Matt replied, stepping toward the wounded man and kneeling down to resume his treatment. "This isn't going to be easy, son, but then nobody said it would be."

It was a strange-looking procession that worked its way across the prairie that afternoon. The Paiutes, walking as a disheveled band, with dull gray army blankets draped around the shoulders of the elderly, were flanked on either side by a platoon of mounted infantry. The uniformity of the army forage blues and

45

bay-colored mounts contrasted with the ragged, ill-matched clothing of the Paiute. They walked their horses in stride with the Indians, making no effort to hurry them or intimidate them in any way. It was a silent procession, with Red Hand and Dark Star walking at the head of the column, the soft jangle of bit chains and equipment being the only violations of the silence. Standing Crane slouched awkwardly in the saddle, his eyes closed and head bobbing in time to the movements of the horse, while two soldiers were doubled up on a horse to the rear.

In the distance behind them and occasionally visible over the rolling swells, the Bannock police kept their distance, much like coyotes shadowing a herd of cattle, making no effort to advance but never losing contact with their slow-moving prey.

Late in the afternoon, Standing Crane died. He slumped forward in the saddle, his head resting on the horse's mane, before sliding off to one side and toppling to the grass on his back, to stare upward with sightless eyes and mouth slightly agape. He made no sound in death, and even the impact of his falling body was muffled by the thick grass.

"Lieutenant!" the soldier nearest Standing Crane shouted toward where Kincaid rode at the head of the platoon. "We've got a problem back here, sir!"

Kincaid and Windy both turned in their saddles and looked back toward the stalled rear portion of the column before wheeling their mounts and racing toward the silent figure lying beside a motionless horse. Matt leaped down and knelt quickly beside the fallen Indian, pressing an ear against his chest and testing the pulse in his throat at the same time. Remaining mounted, Windy glanced toward the band of Paiute and saw Red Hand sprinting toward them.

"His brother's comin', Matt," the scout said softly.

Kincaid didn't reply, listening instead for the faintest heartbeat, probing for the weakest indication of pulse. He found neither.

Red Hand slowed when he neared, and after a brief pause, Kincaid looked up at him. "I'm sorry, Red Hand. He's dead."

There was not the slightest flicker of emotion in Red Hand's eyes. It was as though he might have been looking at a stone that he had never seen before and that held no meaning for him. He might have been alone on the prairie, so isolated did he seem as he watched his dead brother. Then, slowly, his eyes moved to Kincaid's face as if he were a man in a trance.

"You killed him."

"No, Red Hand," Matt said, "you've got it wrong. I tried to save his life."

"No, you killed him."

"How did I kill him?" Kincaid asked softly.

"You are white."

"What does that have to do with his death?"

"If it weren't for your people, we would not have been put on the reservation. We would have lived far away from our enemies and this would not have happened to Standing Crane. He was nothing more than a boy, but he would have been a great man. Now he has died with your white medicine in him, and his spirit will never go to the Distant Place."

Matt stood and squared his broad shoulders before the Paiute. "Our medicine has nothing to do with his death. If I hadn't treated his wounds he would not have lived this long. I don't know anything about that Distant Place you mentioned, but if having white medicine in him has anything to do with his not being able to get there, then you've got a pretty lousy selection process."

Windy had been watching the Indian closely, his hands folded across the saddle horn and shoulders hunched slightly forward. "Red Hand, you and me had a pretty good little chat this mornin', like we trusted each other. I'd like to think we still do. Now, I'm gonna ask you to listen to me one more time. The lieutenant had nothing to do with your brother's death, just like he says. True, you've gotten a mighty rotten deal from Indians and whites alike, but your hatred ain't gonna put ducks back on the pond."

The Indian's head swung up toward the scout. "Standing Crane was killed by white men. The men of the Iron Horse."

"For a fact he was," Windy allowed. "And those same white men would have killed me or Matt here if they caught us in their warehouse. They weren't shooting at Indians, they were shooting at what they thought were thieves. Granted, that Dugan feller didn't express any love for your people, just like the ignorant ass that he is, but Wokana wasn't exactly tossing flowers your way, either."

Red Hand hesitated, eyes wavering while the flood of reality swept through his brain. "We have nowhere to go," he said softly, gazing again across the boundless plains.

47

"You're wrong, Red Hand. Dead wrong," Matt said, gently but firmly. "You will be safe at Outpost Nine until Captain Conway decides what to do with you. Now, your people are tired and we have traveled far today. We'll make camp here tonight to let them rest and give you a chance to bury your brother. By this time tomorrow afternoon we'll be back at the post, but right now we'll move a short distance away and give you some time alone with Standing Crane."

Red Hand gave no indication that he'd heard Kincaid's words, but there appeared to be a softening in the tight lines about his mouth, as though he might have felt a first twinge of respect for the army officer. Matt patted him on the shoulder as he passed by, mounted his horse, and turned the animal away.

"Windy," Kincaid asked as they moved down the line again, "do you think I should have offered a burial party to dig the lad's grave?"

The scout chewed and spat before answering. "Don't think so, Matt. He'll do it his own way. Most likely cover the body with rocks, build a small fire tonight, and pray to his gods for his brother's safe journey to the Distant Place, wherever in hell that is."

"It's really tragic, isn't it?" Matt asked in a distant tone while his eyes swept over the rolling swells of the prairie sea. "All this land, room enough for everybody, but still the killing goes on."

"Yup, and it ain't ever gonna change. Those Bannock ain't following us 'cause they're lost."

"I know. What do you think their next move will be?"

"Hard to say. Obviously they've got more'n a little interest in seeing these Paiute back on the reservation. Might try a little sneaky shit after dark tonight."

Matt nodded his agreement. "That's what I was thinking. Lieutenant Dalby?" he called as they neared the head of the column.

"Yessir?"

"We'll bivouac here tonight. Move these people about three hundred yards away, then set up camp. I want a double guard mount posted to the sides, front and rear of the Paiute. The password is 'dragonfly.' Have a squad standing by to go to Red Hand's defense if necessary. He'll be alone with his brother back there, and I think the Bannock would like to make them a matching set."

"Matching set, sir?"

"Yeah. Both dead. Get on it."

"Yessir."

"Windy?" Matt said, turning to the scout as Dalby moved away. "We haven't got enough food to feed these people and ourselves as well. They're weak, and they've got a damned long walk ahead of them tomorrow. Some fresh meat would sure come in handy."

Windy worked the tobacco in his cheek and squinted at the horizon. "Got about two hours of light left. Give me half of that and then send some men to drag the carcasses back with their horses. You'll know where I am by the shootin'."

"Good. And thanks, Windy."

"No thanks needed, Matt," Windy replied, flicking his reins and turning away at a right angle. "Nothin' to it. 'Sides, I could kinda go for an antelope steak myself."

Kincaid smiled and watched the plainsman adjust the Sharps in the crook of his left arm and press his horse to a gallop.

"Sergeant Olsen?" Matt said, turning toward the platoon sergeant just behind him.

"Yessir?"

"Organize a meat detail. Listen for Windy's shots, then head that direction and bring back whatever he's bagged."

"Yessir."

"Thanks, Sergeant. Corporal Miller?"

"Yessir?"

"Your squad's on wood detail. Dry buffalo chips, logs, limbs, anything that will burn. Try to find some green twigs to use as roasting sticks."

"Yessir."

"Fine," Matt replied while his gaze drifted to the Paiute band moving slowly away under Dalby's direction. They were the most pitiful-looking group of people he had ever seen, and he shook his head almost unconsciously. "It all sounds fine, Red Hand," he said, his voice just above a whisper. "But I really don't know what in hell we're going to do with you."

A low, mournful, singsong chant drifted across the darkened prairie and a single figure could be seen sitting alone, his body silhouetted by the flickering blaze of a fire. To his left, catching the diffuse light, was an oblong mound of stones, and there was a cold stillness about them even in the warmth of the blaze. Red Hand's upper body swayed slowly from side to side and the tone of his voice never wavered from its constant pitch.

The carcasses of four antelope shot by Windy had been divided up among the Paiute, and the smoke rising from several fires was tinged with the odor of roasting meat and hung in a pall above the makeshift camp. The low, excited chatter of Indians seeing their first fresh meat in days mingled with the calls of night birds, and there was an aura of contentment about the campsite that belied the primitive conditions.

Those soldiers not on guard duty lounged about their own separate fires and ate their remaining field rations, with several of them attempting to emulate the Paiute in roasting strips of meat over the open fire. With Windy standing by his side, Matt watched the tranquil scene from a distance and spoke to the scout without looking in his direction.

"Isn't that something, Windy?" he asked, his voice almost mellow. "Our soldiers and their people eating side by side, as though there were absolutely no enmity between them."

"Know what, Matt? The schoolhouse I went to was on the back of a horse, and the schoolmarm was an old gal named Lady Luck, so I ain't real cozy with them ten-dollar words."

"Sorry, Windy," Matt replied with an apologetic smile. "If there are any hard feelings between our two sides, it sure as hell isn't obvious tonight."

"The night ain't over yet, Matt," Windy said, sniffing deeply and holding it as if testing the air.

"No it isn't, but maybe we'll get lucky."

"That's the one thing I learned at that schoolhouse I was tellin' you about. You don't get luck, you make it," Windy drawled, while lifting a finger toward the nearest fire. "See that purty Indian gal over there?"

Matt's eyes shifted in the direction Windy indicated, to find Dark Star bending over the fire with a roasting stick in her hand and an elderly Paiute seated by her side, waiting for the tender morsel.

"Yes I do. I've been watching her off and on all evening. She's certainly beautiful, isn't she?"

"Yup, sure is. And just been raped."

"What?" Matt asked, startled.

50

"For a fact. Her name's Dark Star and she's Red Hand's woman."

"Who raped her?"

"Wokana. Red Hand told me about it. Seems like Wokana would like to have her for his own."

"Is that why he followed them here?"

"Don't know for sure. Could be part of the reason. It's for sure one of the reasons why they quit the reservation."

"Well, if Red Hand will testify to that fact, I'll arrest Wokana and have him stand trial."

Windy spat quietly, smiled in the darkness, and adjusted the Sharps, as was his habit. "No chance of that, Matt. Red Hand don't trust the white man's justice, and his mouth would be tighter than a bull's ass at fly time if you ever put him on the stand. I suspect he'll take care of it his own way, if he lives long enough. Damned ignorant of him to sit out there by himself, with that fire makin' him a better target than most."

Both men looked toward the solitary figure, and Kincaid nodded in agreement. "I know, but he seems determined to honor his brother in death."

"Yup, he does. But he just might go along for the ride if he ain't careful. That's what I meant about makin' your own luck. He's off to a damned poor start in my opinion."

"Well, Windy, I suppose we have to accept their traditions, just as we ask them to accept ours. If Red Hand—"

The first shot rang out in a violent explosion, and they could both see the yellow muzzle blast nearly a hundred yards away while a bullet ricocheted off the rockpile and whined its death cry into the blackness. Red Hand toppled to one side and they could see nothing but the dancing flames where his silhouette had been, while several more rifles fired in a rattling crescendo.

Without knowing why, Kincaid glanced to where Dark Star stood and saw her freeze above the fire, her eyes locked on the place where Red Hand had been sitting. Then, dropping her roasting stick to the ground, she ran toward the glimmering fire now stirred to life by bullets smacking into the coals and sending glowing embers into the sky.

"Stop her, Windy!" Matt shouted, and the scout bolted across the opening between them while Kincaid spun toward the squad arrayed behind him in prone firing positions. "Sergeant Olsen! Lay down a field of covering fire! I'm going after Red Hand!"

"Yessir! Covering fire on those muzzle blasts, men! Keep it high enough so you don't hit the Lieutenant!"

Immediately the Springfields roared to life, and Matt dove to his stomach and began crawling forward, using his elbows and knees in a propelling motion. He glanced once to his right and saw Dark Star sprawl to the grass with Windy's arm around her waist, then his eyes went back to the glow in the distance. The heavy Bannock gunfire had lessened under the withering attack from the troops, and Matt could hear bullets snapping overhead as he crawled beneath the outgoing rounds sailing no more than two feet over his head. Nearing the fire, he could make out a prone figure lying in the shadows just outside the ring of light, but it was motionless and he assumed that Red Hand was dead.

"Damn fool," he muttered, clawing his way forward over the uneven ground. To the rear he could hear the excited cries of the Paiute and he visualized his troops springing away from their fires and deploying themselves in defensible positions previously established. Lieutenant Dalby flashed through his mind and he hoped the young officer wouldn't be stupid enough to attempt a counterattack in the darkness. He stopped and concentrated on the silent form no more than ten yards away. It was motionless, apparently devoid of life, and he wondered briefly if it was worth risking his own skin to save something beyond reclamation. Then he saw the dark object roll onto one side and attempt to sit up, and again it was silhouetted by the firelight.

Springing to his feet, Kincaid covered the intervening distance in three strides and Red Hand sprawled again upon his back, the result of a flying tackle by Kincaid.

"Stay down, damn you!" Kincaid growled as his body slammed into Red Hand's. "If you want to get killed, that's fine and dandy. But I've got another mile or two to go yet before I'm ready to cash in."

Red Hand grunted in surprise and bullets thudded into the ground where his body had been. "My people, I've got to protect my people!"

Kincaid could hear additional rifle fire coming from the rear guard posts, and the shots were punctuated by the bellowing roar of Windy's Sharps. In the same instant a numbing shock jarred his leg; it felt as though someone had slammed a sledgehammer against the sole of his foot. Instinctively he jerked his leg up and rolled in one motion, holding Red Hand clutched in his grasp, and as one they twisted farther into the covering darkness. Matt could feel a sticky, warm substance on his cheek and he knew the Indian was suffering from some kind of head wound that was bleeding freely.

As quickly as it had begun, the firing from out of the blackness ended. Kincaid listened to the faltering shots from the army positions, and heard Lieutenant Dalby give the order to cease fire. A heavy quiet settled over the plains. Feeling the thumping of the Indian's heart against his own chest, he realized he still held Red Hand tightly in his grasp and he rolled away to rise on one knee. The throbbing numbness subsided slowly in his left leg, and when he placed his boot on the ground he realized that the heel had been shot away.

"That was kind of close, Red Hand," he panted as he studied the dark face across from him. "Why did you do it?"

After a pause the Indian said, "Why did I do what?"

"Why did you come out here and sit alone by that fire? You knew you would be a perfect target, and you also knew that Wokana would try to kill you."

"It is the way of my people. If the gods had wanted me to die, I would not be here talking to you now."

"No, I guess you wouldn't," Kincaid allowed. "But your gods can only do so much. I wouldn't push them so hard in the future if I were you."

"You're not me," Red Hand said flatly, and the two men stared at each other in silence for long moments before the Indian spoke again. "I answered your question, now you answer mine."

Kincaid shrugged. "All right."

"Why?"

"Why what?"

"Why did you risk your life to save mine?"

Matt smiled and scratched the back of his head. "Damned if I know. I must have thought your life was worth saving. Is it?"

"The gods have answered that question in their own way. I need add nothing more."

"I suppose not, but I'd sure like to have some gods like yours in my hip pocket when the going gets tough," Kincaid

53

replied, edging forward and reaching his hand up toward the Indian's forehead. "Looks like you've been hit. Here, let me take a look at it."

Red Hand pulled away. "No. It is nothing. I'll take care of it myself."

"Fine with me," Matt replied, standing. "I hope you have better luck with your medicine than your brother did."

Red Hand struggled to his feet, staggered once, then righted himself. "I will have."

"The gods again?"

"The gods."

Shaking his head, Kincaid glanced toward the pile of rocks covering Standing Crane's body, while a thought formulated in his mind. "Maybe we can give those old boys a little help."

A puzzled look crossed the Paiute's face as he watched Matt. "I don't understand."

"You will. Wokana wants you dead, and that's what we're going to give him. Would an Indian, even a rotten one like Wokana, ever remove the stones from a burial site?"

"No, not even Wokana. He would be afraid that the dead one would steal his medicine."

"That's what I thought," Matt replied, turning toward the cooking fires again. "Come on, walk with me to the camp and I'll tell you what we're going to do. I can't guarantee that it'll work forever, but it just might buy you a little time right now."

"Buy me time?" Red Hand asked, falling in step with Kincaid, who was hobbling away on the heelless boot. "I don't understand all white man's talk."

"Sorry, Red Hand. What I meant was, maybe we can get Wokana off your ass, at least until we get back to the outpost."

Red Hand glanced across with a confused look. "Off my what?"

"Off your ass," Kincaid replied with a grin. "Forget it, you don't need to learn that kind of word anyway. You'll see what I mean in the morning. I'll take care of it, but right now I think you'd better get one of your people to clean up that wound. Must hurt a mite, doesn't it?"

The distant look came into Red Hand's eyes again and he stared straight ahead, ignoring the crimson flood of blood now crusting his eyebrow, cheek and jaw.

"The only thing that hurts is my heart, Lieutenant," the

Indian said softly. "And that will never stop hurting until I see my homeland again."

"I can't promise you anything positive, Red Hand, you know that. All I can offer you is my promise to do the best I can by you and your people. Can you accept that?"

Red Hand's head turned slowly toward Matt, and there was something close to a tired smile on his lips. "Yes I can, Lieutenant. But then, as the white man says, promises are made to be broken. I have never seen one that wasn't yet."

"Just hide and watch, Red Hand. All I can tell you is, just hide and watch."

"I haven't any other choice, have I?"

"No, you haven't. And neither have I, apparently."

five

Moving slowly across the prairie and spread out riding side by side, the thirty Bannock warriors approached the abandoned campsite with rifles across their laps and keen eyes searching the vacant ground before them. The sun had barely cleared the horizon, and in its brilliant glare they could see the last of the army troops and their Paiute charges vanish over a distant swell.

Wokana's interest, however, lay not in his receding prey, but in two objects clearly visible beside the remains of a lone campfire. He studied them closely as they drew nearer, and with each step his horse took, the Bannock's cruel grin widened. Instead of the one pile of rocks he had expected to see, there now were two, side by side, with the morning breeze blowing dust from the topmost stones in a twisting swirl. And when their mounts stopped ten feet away from the burial mounds, the grin became a triumphant smile and he thrust his rifle in the air jubilantly.

"*Heya!* We shot well last night, Bannock warriors!" he cried, turning to the brave nearest him. "See there, Hunting Dog! I told you we hit him!"

The smaller Bannock watched the twin piles momentarily. "Do you think Red Hand is beneath the second one, Wokana?"

"Who else would it be?" Wokana replied with a hint of disdain. "He is the only one we were shooting at. I saw him fall."

"Yes, and so did I. But I also saw a blue shirt in the firelight."

"Do you think the white men would cover one of their dead with stones and leave him beside a lowly Paiute?" Wokana asked with a scoffing laugh. "They would not." His eyes narrowed and he watched the other warrior more closely. "Would you care to remove some stones and prove it to yourself, Hunting Dog?" he said, making no attempt to hide the challenge.

"No, Wokana, I would not." Hunting Dog said hastily. "If Red Hand is under there, he can keep his medicine and I'll keep mine."

The other warriors laughed and Wokana glanced up and down the line. "Hear the mighty Hunting Dog, my brothers? If he removes one stone, he will be a Paiute in the Distant Place."

The braves laughed again, louder this time, in full knowledge that their leader would appreciate the gesture, while Wokana edged his horse closer to stare down at the second pile.

"Red Hand is dead," he said with satisfaction, "and now Black Bear will be pleased with us. We will wait for him now and learn what he wants us to do. He should be here before the sun falls tonight, and we will show him the death stones of Red Hand."

Wokana's eyes drifted to where they had last seen the army unit, and his thoughts went to the heated feeling rising in his loins. "And you are mine now," he whispered. "I will not have to take you anymore, because you are mine."

Hunting Dog read Wokana's mind perfectly and he said quietly, "Dark Star will be waiting for you, Wokana. She will warm your bed for many nights."

Wokana's head jerked around and he realized he had been speaking loudly enough for those nearest him to hear. "Heya! We will talk no more of women. Yes, Dark Star is mine, but we are Bannock warriors, Hunting Dog! Get whiskey from our spare pony and we will drink to the death of a Paiute and the birth of Bannock children!"

"Yes, Wokana," Hunting Dog replied, angling his mount toward the brave leading the packhorse. "We drink now, and tomorrow more Paiute will die."

It was well past noon when Dennis Michael Harbert quit the foothills and rode his horse at an easy lope across the open prairie. He was both troubled and pleased in the same instant as he recalled his conversation with Dugan in South Pass City. Yes, his police had caught up with the Paiute, he recalled the foreman as saying, but the army officer had said he was taking them back to his outpost. And he remembered having told McCauley that he would have the Paiute back to work the mine within two days. Now the second day was already upon him.

Damn that lieutenant, he thought. *Why couldn't he just have turned them over to Wokana and been done with it? That way we could have taken them directly to the mine and everyone would have been happy, with the possible exception of the Paiute.* His mind seized upon Red Hand and he knew that the chieftain would have to be killed at the earliest opportunity. And that woman of his. What was her name? Dark Star, that was it. God, but she would be good in bed. *Too damned good for Wokana,* Harbert thought contentedly. *She should be a white man's woman.* "And she damned well will be," he said to himself above the steady thudding of hooves on prairie soil.

It was late afternoon and Harbert's shadow stretched long before him when he topped a rise and saw the band of warriors, some seated in a circle and others stretched out in the grass, with two oblong mounds of stone nearby to the right. The lowering sun glinted off a bottle being raised by the central warrior, and Harbert shook his head in disgust as he reined in to stare down at the scene below. Then, with a vicious jerk of the reins, he lashed his horse's flanks and pounded toward the Bannock, who eventually looked up with a lazy look of disinterest.

Wokana struggled to his feet and staggered through the warriors scattered about him, toward the big horse now plunging to a skittish stop.

"Heya, Black Bear," he said cautiously, his words slurred. "We been waiting for you."

"I can see that, Wokana. Damned lot of good you are to me drunk!"

"We not drunk, Black Bear. Jus' waitin' for you."

"You're drunker than a damned skunk, you ignorant goddamned featherhead! Where the hell are the Paiute?!"

"They go to outpost with Blue Sleeves. We stay here. Wait for you." Wokana blinked his eyes in a futile attempt to focus them, and lurched against Harbert's horse, causing the animal to rear. "We do good job for you," he said as the agent fought to control the animal.

"Yeah, nothin' less than you'd expect from a drunken Indian," Harbert snarled, reining the horse around to face Wokana again. "If you had done a good job for me in the first place, I wouldn't be here right now."

"We do good job for you, Black Bear," Wokana repeated with a flaccid, drunken smile. "You pleased with Wokana."

'Pleased, you rum-gut! What in hell's name vould I have to be pleased with you about?"

The smile faded on Wokana's lips and he closed one eye in an apparent attempt to merge three blurred figures into one. "Because Wokana kill Red Hand."

"What?!" Harbert snapped. "I was told he was in the custody of the army."

"Custody? What that word?"

"Never mind. You say you killed him. When did this happen?"

"One day."

"One day? What the hell do you mean by 'one day'? You mean you plan to kill him one day?"

"No, Black Bear. Wokana kill Red Hand."

"I've heard this threat from you before, Wokana, and to tell you the truth, I'm getting pretty damned sick of it. Did you kill him or didn't you?"

"I kill him."

Harbert was more than a little exasperated by the Bannock's having reverted back to pidgin English under the influence of alcohol, and the contempt raging in his mind was impossible to control, even if he had wanted to. He stepped from the saddle with slow, deliberate motions and advanced on the warrior, his thick legs spread apart and the hamlike hands dangling by his sides slowly clenching into massive fists.

"Wokana, you are nine-tenths ignorant when you're sober and a complete idiot when you're drunk. Now, I'm tired of trading schoolboy English with you. If you killed Red Hawk, I want to see his body."

Instinctively, Wokana backed away, half-stumbled, and pointed hurriedly toward the nearest pile of rocks. "No see body. Wokana say no. Body there. Spirit go, body there."

Harbert's head snapped toward the mound of stones. "Where? There?"

"Yes, body there." He raised his arms to simulate the firing of a rifle and smiled like a boy trying to please an irate parent. "I kill one day."

"What's this 'one day' bullshit? You mean you killed him yesterday?"

"Yes, Black Bear. I no have white man's word. I kill yesterday."

Harbert advanced on the burial mound and propped a foot

on the lower layer of rocks. "All right. If you say he's under here, dig him out and show him to me."

Wokana watched the agent, and in his voice was a mixture of fear and confusion. "I no understand, Black Bear. You say again?"

Harbert's face went dark with rage. Stooping down, he grasped a stone and tossed it aside. "I said dig, damn you! Get some of the others to help you, do it yourself or whatever in hell you want to do, but if Red Hand is under there, I want to see him!"

Now fear dominated confusion and Wokana backed away. "No can do, no can do," he mumbled, eyes fixed on the mound and unguided feet stumbling in their rearward progression. "Paiute medicine not good. Wokana no touch stone."

"Get over here, goddammit!"

Wokana appeared not to have heard the agent's enraged words and continued to back away. Harbert turned and jabbed a finger toward the other Bannock, who watched silently from a distance of some twenty yards. "Hunting Dog! Get two braves and move this pile of rocks!"

Without hesitation, Hunting Dog slowly shook his head while never taking his eyes off the mound at the exact place where the first stone had been removed.

"I said get over here, dammit! Now move it!"

The Indians remained impassive, silent.

"Damned savages!" Harbert growled, glowering at his police for nearly a full minute before stooping again and digging through the stones, throwing them to either side like a bear tearing apart a rotten log in search of grubs. Beads of sweat popped out on his forehead, but he worked even more feverishly, pausing only to mop his brow with a sleeve and digging again. With fingernails broken and the tips of his fingers bleeding, he grasped the last stone in the center of the mound and tossed it away with a mighty heave. Crushed green prairie grass lay beneath his fingertips, and he trailed his hands across the emptiness while rage built in his mind and hatred grew in his heart. Slowly he stood, his massive chest heaving and sweat dripping from his chin, and turned toward the Bannock like a stone statue being laboriously rotated on a turntable.

The Indians watched him in awe, as though he might suddenly disintegrate and vanish into thin air. None of them, including Wokana, had looked at the barren patch of grass, and all eyes were locked on the huge man, whose face was twisted in a grotesque mask of burning rage. Harbert's eyes swept slowly over them until they centered on Wokana.

"So you killed him, Wokana?" Harbert said, the hissed words barely escaping through clenched teeth.

The Bannock nodded, never taking his eyes from the fearsome vision with the bulging eyes and quivering mustache.

"And now you're having a victory party, huh?"

Wokana nodded again, but now there was a weakness around his eyes and lips, and fear that would not be concealed was clearly visible.

"You're a liar, an idiot, a dumb fucking Indian and the most stupid human being I've ever laid eyes on in my life!" Harbert screamed, moving toward his horse with robotlike precision. The blacksnake whip hung from the left side of the agent's saddle horn, and his hand reached for it with slow, ominous accuracy while his eyes never wavered from Wokana's face. "And now you're gonna pay, and pay good."

There was a trembling at the corners of Wokana's mouth as he tore his eyes from the agent's face and forced them to find the hole in the pile of stone. Nothing but grass. Wokana's eyes searched Harbert's face pleadingly, and he stumbled forward to drop to his knees beside the hole. Putting aside his fears, he frantically began tossing other stones aside, searching desperately for what he knew he must find. There came from him a whimpering like that of a bitch dog who had lost her pups. Through the combination of whiskey and fright, tears streamed down his cheeks and he dug even more wildly, as if he could will the body to be there through sheer determination alone.

"It ain't any use, Wokana," a flat voice said from behind him. "Red Hand ain't there."

"He is here!" Wokana shouted, grasping stones and chucking them behind him like a rabid man in search of a miracle potion.

"He ain't there," Harbert repeated, dropping the coils of the blacksnake whip to the grass and slowly coiling it again. "You killed a shadow and they're damned tough to bury."

Wokana ceased his digging, but his eyes continued to search for something not to be found. Then his body froze, and as if he knew what he must face, he rose like a spring plant breaking through frozen ground and turned to face the agent. The whip

61

lashed out with blinding speed, and its tip snapped as the leather bit into Wokana's right cheek. The Bannock's eyes cleared and he sank into a crouch, mindless of the trickle of blood trailing down to his jawbone, while Harbert quickly coiled the whip again. Then, with a bloodcurdling scream, Wokana sprang forward, and the hatred in his eyes was unmasked as his hand pulled the knife from his belt.

With no undue haste, Harbert's wrist went back again. He lashed forward with the whip once more and the coils wrapped around Wokana's legs. The agent jerked back, throwing the Bannock in a sprawling heap upon the ground.

"I sent you to do a job, boy. I paid you to do a job and I expect that job to be done. You're supposed to be the leader of these other Injuns here"—Harbert inclined his head toward the silent braves standing off to his left—"and if you tell them to get drunk, they get drunk. If you tell them to kill, they kill. I'd better see a little less of the former and a little more of the latter in the future."

Unthinkingly, Wokana untangled the whip from his legs and struggled to a standing position with the knife now held before him and his body braced for another lunge. Without bothering to coil the blacksnake, Harbert's hand snapped back and the long lash arced through the air behind his head. Then, with amazing speed, the tip sailed forward again and crackled like a miniature lightning bolt as it sank into the flesh of Wokana's wrist. The knife fell to the ground and the Bannock grimaced in pain, staring at his hand with its fingers locked in an extended, frozen position. Before he could react, the whip sailed forward again, biting deep into Wokana's left shoulder. Instantly a blackish-red welt surfaced on his skin, and blood now ran freely down his cheek, arm and wrist.

The agent's face was cold and expressionless, but his eyes glittered with sadistic pleasure. It was obvious that he could cripple or kill the Indian at will, and as he slowly coiled the loops again, there was no doubt that he was mentally capable of doing either one. With not the slightest indication of emotion, he raised the whip again. Instinctively, Wokana shielded his face with his hands.

"No more, Black Bear," he said with an uncharacteristic plea in his voice. "No more with the snake."

Harbert's tone was even, entirely devoid of compassion. "I want to hear you beg, Injun."

Wokana's hands fell from his face and were held chest-high as he stared silently at the agent. His lips moved but no words came forth. The whip cracked again, and now blood spurted from the Indian's right shoulder and his mouth contorted in a cry of pain.

"I said beg, Injun. I mean to be obeyed."

In desperation, Wokana's eyes darted to his companions, but they stood motionless, watching and waiting to see what their leader would do while the long lash slithered across the ground, retreating toward Harbert's hand once again.

Wokana's head jerked toward the agent and his eyes locked on the blacksnake, coiled now and rising.

"Please . . . Black Bear. No more with the snake."

"I said beg!"

Wokana's entire body was trembling and his hands shook uncontrollably. Harbert seemed not to notice the beseeching look in the Indian's eyes while his lips tried to form the words.

"Please . . . please . . . Black Bear. I beg. No more with the snake."

Harbert smiled in cruel triumph. "That's more like it. And one more thing, Wokana. No more with this 'Black Bear' shit. It's 'Mr. Boss' to you from now on. I am the boss around here and I don't want you or your lads over there ever to forget that little fact. It wouldn't be good for your health, if you know what I mean." Harbert's eyes narrowed to tiny, puffy slits in his face. "Now, say it!"

"Yes . . . Mr. Boss."

"Louder, damn you!"

"Yes, Mr. Boss!"

"That's better," Harbert snarled, turning toward the others. "You've just heard your chief beg for his life—I won't be givin' the rest of you the same chance. Now get to your ponies and mount up. We're going to that damned outpost and take what is rightfully mine—a pack of thievin', lyin' Paiute."

Harbert watched the Bannock warriors move sullenly toward their horses before turning toward Wokana, who continued to stand where he was.

"That means you too, Wokana. Move it out."

The Indian hesitated a moment longer before sucking in a deep breath, pulling his shoulders back and walking away with his dark eyes locked on some invisible object in the distance.

"One more thing, Wokana!" Harbert snapped.

Wokana's step faltered; he stopped, then turned. "Yes . . . Mr. Boss? he asked reluctantly, barely able to control the hatred swelling in his chest.

Harbert held the whip by his side, coiled and ready while he stared at the Indian in silence for several seconds before speaking. "Dark Star is mine from now on. Keep your hands and eyes off her One of the others is good enough for you."

The Indian flinched without knowing it, and his eyes locked on Harbert's. Then he nodded curtly and turned away.

The horizon was tomato-red, with the last rays of the setting sun filtering through a low-hanging cloud bank, as the strange assemblage filed into Outpost Number Nine. The Indians shuffled into the compound with many of them still wearing army blankets draped over their shoulders, and soldiers on either side paced their progress. In contrast to the erect and positive mounted infantrymen, their heads drooped and it was obvious they were both exhausted and weak, with the exception of Red Hand and Dark Star, who walked proudly at the front of the ragged column.

Captain Conway stood beneath the awning above the entrance to the orderly room and shook his head in amazement as he watched the pitiful group walk by. He saw Kincaid turn his horse and angle toward the office; in response, the captain stepped onto the parade and moved forward to meet his executive officer.

Kincaid saluted and smiled slightly. "Mission accomplished, sir." He hesitated. "If you can call if that."

Conway returned the salute, but his eyes were still on the Indian tribe. "Welcome back, Matt. Are these the renegade Paiute who were supposed to be such a threat to the happiness and well-being of settlers in this area?"

Kincaid's grin widened. "The same, Captain."

"They don't look like they're a threat to anything other than themselves."

"My opinion exactly, sir. They've had a pretty rough go of it."

"Obviously. Have they given you any trouble?"

"No, sir. At least not anything that wasn't a product of misunderstanding."

"What do you mean by that?"

Kincaid leaned to his left and stepped down from the saddle, and when he stood on the ground, his body tilted slightly to one side. "Got the heel of my boot shot away last night," he said matter-of-factly, moving toward the captain with the peculiar motions of a man wearing only one shoe. Then he turned by Conway's side and pointed toward Red Hand, who was moving among his people at the far end of the compound. "That's Red Hand, their chief."

"What about him?"

"He is the product of misunderstanding I mentioned. He's absolutely convinced that there's not a white man alive who's drawn one honest breath. He doesn't trust any of us, with good reason I might add, and any trouble he or his people gave us stemmed from their fear and lack of trust in white men."

"What about the agent at their reservation? Hasn't he treated them fairly and honestly?"

"I've never met the man, Captain," Kincaid replied, "and I'm not sure I want to. I'll tell you everything I know in a few minutes, but Windy should be with us when we talk. Right now I'd like to know what you want us to do with them. I promised Red Hand a square shake from us, if you don't mind my taking liberties with your word, sir."

"Absolutely not, Matt. You know that." Conway's gaze drifted back to the Paiute. "To tell you the truth, I don't know what the hell to do with them. For right now, though, let's get them fed and bedded down as best we can. I'll send Sergeant Cohen to tell Dutch to rustle up some grub for them and you go over to the quartermaster and draw whatever blankets, tents and whatnot we'll need to keep them warm. When you've finished, find Windy and both of you come to my office so we can have a little chat about this mess."

"Yes, sir," Kincaid replied, and before turning away he added, "While I'm there, I think I'll see if old Skinflint Wilson has a spare left boot, size ten and a half."

Conway grinned. "Do that. It makes me seasick to watch you walk."

Red Hand watched curiously as the two soldiers expertly erected the first tent and forced the center pole into place before moving away to begin driving pegs for the second one. He peered into the dark enclosure and the unfamiliar odor of musty canvas filled his nostrils. It was the first tent he had ever seen, and when he turned to look at Matt and Windy standing behind

65

him, there was an almost childlike look of pleasure in his eyes.

"It's not as big as a wickiup," he said, gesturing toward the tent, "but it is much faster to build."

"A wickiup?" Kincaid asked, looking at Windy.

"Yeah, that's what they call their traditional home. Kind of like a tipi, but sort of dome-shaped, made from sticks and hides and whatever happens to be lying around."

Matt spoke as he looked at Red Hand again. "Oh, I see. No, they're not intended to be large, merely a place to get out of the cold and rain when we're on maneuvers in the field. It is waterproof, though. Sometimes it looks like the canvas is leaking, but that's just the material sweating. Strange thing, though, you touch one of those beads of sweat and trail your finger down and the damned thing does start leaking."

Red Hand nodded in indication that he understood what the lieutenant had said, and looked upward at the darkening sky. "I don't think we have to worry about rain," he said, his tone cordial.

"Neither do I, but it will get cold tonight. These tents were designed for two men, with each of them carrying half as part of his bedroll. Since we don't have enough to go around, we might have to crowd a few more of your people into each of them than we'd normally like to."

"We have been crowded before."

"I'm sure you have. Our mess sergeant, Dutch Rothausen, is preparing dinner for your people now and it should be ready in a few minutes. I hope you can stomach creamed chipped beef on toast, or 'shit on a shingle' to us, because that's the only thing we have in such large supply."

"We will eat what we are given."

"Good. Organize your tribe into shifts and they will eat in the enlisted men's mess hall. When things are ready, one of my soldiers will show you the way. Windy and I have to speak with the captain now, and I'm sure he'll want to talk with you later. Once the tents are in place, our spare blankets will be distributed and we hope you will be as comfortable as our limited facilities will allow."

"I thank you for my people," Red Hand said with sincerity but without enthusiasm. "If given the chance, we would not need your help."

"Well, Red Hand, everybody needs help one time or another. Maybe someday you'll have a chance to return the favor." Kincaid turned away. "Come on, Windy. The captain is waiting for us."

"Right behind you, Matt," Windy replied, but he looked at Red Hand before lifting the butt of his Sharps from the ground. "With the gates closed and a guard mount posted, I think you can put Wokana and his warriors out of your mind for one night. Tomorrow might be another story, but sleep well tonight."

Red Hand nodded and watched the tall scout move away with effortless strides.

Sergeant Cohen looked up from his desk when Matt and Windy entered. "Good evening, Lieutenant, Windy."

"Evening, Ben," Kincaid replied. "Looks like we're going to have houseguests for a little while. Do you think Maggie would mind organizing a spare-clothing drive among the wives for those people out there? Some of them are as close to naked as you can get without having your ass hanging out."

"Not at all, sir. As a matter of fact, I'm sure she'd be pleased to help in any way she can. Seems like she's got a bigger heart than most when it comes to a situation like this."

The image of Maggie Cohen, full-bodied, buxom, moderately handsome, and fitted with an Irish temper that matched the geniality of her natural mien, flashed through Kincaid's mind. "Yes she has," he said with a warm smile. "If I could find a wife like yours, I might even get married myself some day."

"Talk to me first, Lieutenant," Cohen said with artificial resignation. "That old saying about taking the good with the bad seems to get a little stretched out of proportion when it comes to marriage."

"I'll do that, Ben," Matt replied with a chuckle. "But don't expect me to come callin' on you anytime in the near future."

"One of your better decisions, sir. You might wind up with somebody like old Dutch over there."

"Dutch?"

"Yeah. He's rantin' and ravin' like an Italian looking at his redheaded son for the first time. Seems like he don't much like the idea of fixing dinner for his half of the entire western world. Or, in his words, 'Fuck 'em and feed 'em possum!'"

Matt and Windy laughed. "He'll manage. Serves the old bastard right for going to cooks' and bakers' school just to get out of combat duty," Matt said.

"I think the only combat we're going to see around here tonight is between him and the KPs, Lord rest their troubled souls. The captain is waiting for you, sir."

"Thanks, Ben," Kincaid replied, turning to rap his knuckles against the door.

"Come on in, Matt," a voice called from within, and the two men stepped inside.

Conway stood behind his desk, filled three glasses with brandy, and handed them around before taking his seat again. "Have a chair, Matt, Windy, and tell me about this situation with the Paiute."

Kincaid sank into a chair beside the wall and Windy moved to his usual position next to the window, declining a chair as was his wont.

"Well, Captain," Matt began, "things don't look very promising. At least not for Red Hand and his people. That's why I brought them here."

Conway removed a cigar from the box on his desk, bit off the end, and struck a match. "I know you have a reason for your actions, Matt. Let's hear it. I thought their agent was supposed to come and take them back to the reservation," Conway concluded, touching flame to the tip of his cigar and puffing the tobacco to life.

"I do, sir. Red Hand didn't lead his people off the reservation as part of any uprising, as we were led to believe. They were fleeing for their lives, and I think their agent had a good deal to do with that decision."

"How do you mean?" Conway asked, shaking out the match and leaning back in his chair. "Why would their agent want to kill them?"

"I don't know for sure. But there are a lot of different ways of dying besides the bullet. Windy talked with Red Hand more than I did," Kincaid said, turning toward the scout. "Why don't you tell the captain what Red Hand told you, Windy?"

The scout shifted to a more comfortable position along the wall and sipped his brandy before looking at Conway. "Same song, but a different tune from what we've heard from the Arapaho, Sioux, Cheyenne and the like, Cap'n. The agent doesn't give a shit about his charges. They ain't being given the food they were promised, they're made to live on land that won't support them, and they're plum damned tired of having their women raped and their men killed. Simple as that."

Conway arched his eyebrows over the wisp of smoke drifting from his mouth. "Raped and killed? By whom?"

"In this case, by the agent's special police, Bannock warriors. We talked about them before Matt and I went on this last patrol."

"I remember," Conway agreed, "but then it was mere speculation. Do you have any concrete facts, Windy?"

"Yup. The police are headed up by a genuine asshole named Wokana. The day before the Paiute left the reservation, he and some of his braves raped six women and killed four old men. One of the women raped was Dark Star, Red Hand's fiancee."

"Did the agent know about this?"

"According to Red Hand, he probably ordered it."

"Why?"

"Because he's even a bigger asshole than Wokana, the way it sounds to me. The Paiute get all the shit and the Bannock get all the gravy. Red Hand and his people were damned if they did and damned if they didn't. Dead if they stayed on the reservation and abided by the terms of their treaty, and just as dead if they broke the agreement and left. When we caught up with them, Wokana and his boys were closing in for the kill. Not to mention some shithead named . . . what was his name, Matt?"

"Dugan. Mr. Dugan."

"Yeah, Mr. Dugan."

"Who in hell is he?" Conway inquired.

"Section chief for the Union Pacific over at South Pass City. Seems Red Hand's people were freezin' to death and tried to find some blankets or something to keep them warm. Dugan's hands fired on them and hit one young boy named Standing Crane, who later died." Windy lifted the glass to his lips once more and spoke as the rim neared his mouth. "The boy who died was Red Hand's little brother, Cap'n."

"Jesus Christ," Conway said, studying the cigar in his fingertips. "No wonder this Red Hand hates white men." Then he looked at Kincaid. "Why did they head in this direction, Matt?"

"Because they had nowhere else to go, Captain. They knew that Wokana would come after them and I guess they hoped to pull a little desperation move to try and get him off their trail. Obviously it didn't work. Last night somebody tried to kill Red Hand when he was sitting beside his brother's burial mound. That's when I got my heel shot away. I can't prove it, but I'm damned sure it was the Bannock."

"Sure it was, Matt," Windy put in. "They were on our scent all day, like buzzards circlin' a fresh kill. That ain't no proof either, but it is a fact."

"All right," Conway said, tapping an ash from his cigar while his mind grappled with the situation at hand. "So we've got the agency police, and most likely the agent himself, on one hand and the Paiute on the other. What do we do with them?"

Kincaid swirled the brandy in his glass while saying, "I was kind of hoping you might have the answer to that question, sir."

"Yes, I suppose this business of rank does have its dark side. Windy? Any suggestions?"

"None that the Bureau of Indian Affairs would listen to. Especially from a man who thinks they are the biggest bunch of shit-dealers since the first cow lifted its tail."

"Well put," Conway said, leaning back in his chair, clenching the cigar between his teeth and clasping his hands behind his head. "What about this agent, Dennis Michael Harbert I think his name was. No sign of him at all when you picked up those Paiute?"

"None, Captain. Wokana seems to be his right-hand man, and he said something about his being placed in charge of bringing the Paiute back to the reservation."

"Fat chance of that," Windy snorted. "If I were a Paiute, I'd rather take my chances in a snake pit than risk getting back to that reservation alive with Wokana in charge."

"Doesn't sound like their agent is going to be any great improvement, Windy," Matt said.

"Maybe not, but he's probably just a basic asshole. The Bannock have had years of practice in perfecting the art of hating the Paiute."

Conway leaned forward and tapped the ash from his cigar again. "Either way, those people aren't going to be fed to the wolves if I have anything to say about it—which I do, thanks to that telegram I received the other day. I imagine Harbert will show up here sometime tomorrow, and we'll see what kind of man he is then. I think I have the authority to deny him the right to take Red Hand's people if it's against my better judgment. And if I don't have that right legally, I'll put my career on the line and take the right."

Matt and Windy finished their brandy, placed their glasses on the table and moved toward the door. "I figured you'd see it that way, Captain," Matt said, turning with his hand on the latch. "Do you want Windy and me here when you talk with Harbert?"

"Yes, very much. How about Red Hand? Will he press any charges against either the agent or the Bannock?"

"Don't think so, Cap'n," Windy replied, placing his hat on his head and scratching a sideburn. "Me and him had a little walk-and-talk session yesterday and I don't think he'll say much of anything to anybody, with the possible exception of myself."

"After what he's been through, I assumed as much. You did the right thing by bringing Red Hand's people here, both of you. I guess from here on out it's up to me."

"Not entirely, Captain," Kincaid said, opening the door. "We'll be around if you need us. We've got a little personal score to settle with the other side ourselves. 'Night, sir."

After the door closed, Conway sat in the silence of his office and wondered what he would ever do without the services of his executive officer and chief scout. Then he hooked his hands behind his head again and wondered what in hell he would do with the tribe of Paiute camped out on the parade.

six ————————————

It was midafternoon the following day when Kincaid stopped by the detail digging a new latrine pit near the area that had been set aside for the Paiute band. A burly private named Malone heaved a shovelful of dirt over his shoulder, rested the shovel on the pit wall and wiped the sweat from the back of his forehead with a dust-encrusted hand as he squinted into the sunlight and up at the officer.

"Afternoon to ya, Lieutenant Kincaid," he said in a voice that would obviously never lose the lilt of the land of his birth. "It'd be a bleedin' fine day for diggin' holes in the hot of the sun, I'd be thinkin'."

"How you doin', Malone? Let me guess, you're in Cohen's bad books again?"

"I'd be bloody well pleased to recall the time when I've been out of 'em, sir. 'Tis work for a mole, not a man, what the good sergeant keeps pullin' out o' his bottomless hat."

"I'll admit, you've become quite well acquainted with the uses of a shovel since you've been here, Malone," Kincaid said with a smile. He liked the amicable Irishman, even though he was constantly getting into trouble and was restricted to the post more often than not. "That was a fine thing you did last night."

"And what'd that be, sir?"

"I heard about it. Secrets around here are as scarce as hen's teeth."

"Scarce they do be, Lieutenant. Amongst soldiers, the only secret they keep is the secret that the first man what told the secret don't know that everybody else knows the second man can't keep a secret."

Kincaid allowed himself a chuckle. "I guess I can follow that. Anyway, you were on the detail assigned to distribute blankets to these Paiute, weren't you?"

"That'd be correct, sir."

"And wouldn't it also be correct that, when you realized there weren't enough spare blankets for the last two Indians, you personally took the blankets from your own bunk and gave them away?"

"Well, sir," Malone began, with a slight flush creeping into his cheeks, "I didn't exactly *give* them away, don't ya know. Kinda *loaned* 'em, if ya know what I mean, sir."

"Either way, it was a damned fine gesture. You must've gotten a little cold yourself last night, didn't you?"

"Me, sir? Not on your bleedin' life, if you'll pardon me nasty habit of cussin'. As a wee lad in County Cork, I had nothin' but a nightshirt to comfort away the chill. Here I got me longjohns."

"You're a tough one, all right, Malone, but I still won't forget what you did. Maybe Sergeant Cohen can—"

"Lieutenant Kincaid!"

Kincaid turned toward the sound of the voice coming from the guard posted beside the front gate. "Yes, Corporal. What is it?"

"Got somebody out here who wants to talk to the officer in charge, sir! Says his name is Mr. Harbert! And you might want to know, sir, he's got about thirty armed Indians with him."

"Be right there, Corporal!" Kincaid replied, glancing down at Malone once again before moving away. "As I said, Malone, I won't forget what you did. I'll have a little chat with Sergeant Cohen."

"Naw, don't do that, sir. Diggin' kinda grows on ya after the first two or three years. 'Sides sir, I'd be needin' me exercise. Thankin' ya just the same."

Kincaid smiled with a shrug of his shoulders and walked quickly across the parade, then climbed the steps near the front gate and moved along the walkway atop the wall. His premonitions about Harbert proved entirely true, and when he looked down at the thick-bodied man with dark, heavy eyebrows and a thick mustache, with a black hat pulled low on his forehead, he knew immediately that he didn't like him. Even though Harbert was smiling pleasantly, there was something in his eyes that told a different story as he tilted his head up toward Kincaid—something cold, ominous and lacking sincerity.

"May I help you, sir?" Matt asked, leaning forward and placing his hands on the ledge. "My name is Lieutenant Kincaid."

Harbert continued to smile and tilted his hat back a notch. "If you're the man in charge, you can. I'm Mike Harbert, Indian agent over at the Sand Ridge Reservation. I think you have taken some of my charges into custody."

"The officer in charge is Captain Conway," Matt replied with neither cordiality nor hostility. "I'm his executive officer. And yes, we do have a tribe of Paiute currently under our protection."

"Protection? Sounds to me like you've got it all wrong, Lieutenant. They don't need protection, it's everyone else that does. I thought I explained that in my telegram." Harbert laughed innocently while his smile widened. "I'm here to relieve you of that little problem. You just turn them over to me, and my police here will see that they get safely back to the reservation. Sorry to have put you to this trouble."

Kincaid's eyes swept over the Bannock, and he had little trouble picking out Wokana, sitting his horse to Harbert's right. He noted the sullen expression on the Indian's face, the welts on either cheek and the dark, swollen bruises on both shoulders. When Matt looked toward Harbert again, he saw the blacksnake whip coiled beside the agent's right leg and he thought he knew the source of the Indian's injuries.

"And I'm sorry too, Mr. Harbert, but I don't have the authority to release them to you. You'll have to talk with Captain Conway."

A hint of animosity flickered across Harbert's face and he shifted impatiently in his saddle. "All right, whatever the procedure is, let's get to it. We've got a long ride ahead of us and I can't be away from the agency too long. Where is this Captain Conway?"

"In his office."

"Fine. Open the gates and show me to him."

"One moment please, Mr. Harbert. I have substantial reason to believe that there is no love lost between the Paiute and your Bannock police. To avoid any complications, I would ask you to have your police retreat from the walls a hundred yards and wait for you there. Strictly a precaution, you understand."

"Precaution! What the hell do you mean by that, man? These people were deputized personally by me through powers vested

74

in me by the Bureau of Indian Affairs." Harbert's face was flushed with instant anger and he quickly forgot the guise of cordiality. "I'll not have some damned army lieutenant tell me what to do with my—"

"Yes you will, if you wish to gain entry into that lieutenant's post," Kincaid said evenly. "This time I won't ask you, I'll tell you. Have your police move away, or you can all ride out the way you came in."

"Your captain will hear about this, Lieutenant, mark my words on that."

"Consider them marked. Now move 'em out."

Harbert looked across at Wokana while jabbing a thumb over his shoulder. Turning their mounts, the Bannock retreated onto the plains before stopping the specified distance away.

"Is that far enough?" Harbert asked icily, glaring up at Kincaid.

"It'll do," Matt replied, turning and leaning over the inner wall to call down to the guard posted there. "Open one gate, Private. Show Mr. Harbert in, then close it again."

"Yessir."

While Harbert maneuvered his horse inside, Kincaid moved down the stairwell and led the agent across the parade in the direction of the orderly room. He could hear the excited chatter coming from the Paiute on the far end of the compound and he saw Red Hand standing before his tent with arms folded across his chest and staring at Harbert impassively.

The agent nodded cordially and tipped his hat toward Dark Star with a leering smile before stepping down and tying his horse to the rail. He followed Kincaid into the orderly room and waited while the lieutenant paused to speak to the first sergeant.

"Ben, go and find Windy and send him here, will you? Also, tell Red Hand we'll be wanting to talk with him in a few minutes."

"Sure, Lieutenant," Cohen replied, rising immediately and moving toward the door. "Go on in, sir. The captain is waiting for you."

"Thanks, Ben," Kincaid said, opening the door to Conway's office and standing to one side for Harbert to enter first.

Conway looked up from the telegram he was reading and nodded politely while Harbert removed his hat and moved inside.

"Captain Conway, this is Mr. Harbert, the agent from the Sand Ridge Reservation. Mr. Harbert, meet Captain Conway."

The two men exchanged handshakes, and Harbert's expression again showed only innocent cordiality.

"Pleased to meet you, Captain Conway. I'm sure I'll get more satisfaction from you than I got from your lieutenant here. I won't take up much of your time, sir, and if you'll just release—"

"Excuse the interruption, Mr. Harbert, but I don't think it's going to be quite as easy as you seem to assume. Whatever Lieutenant Kincaid told you, I concur with it entirely. Won't you have a seat?"

A dark look wiped the innocence from Harbert's face while he lowered his bulk into a chair near the desk.

"Care for a cigar?" Conway asked, drawing one for himself and offering the box.

"Don't smoke."

"Good for you. Nasty habit." Conway made overly long his ritual of moistening, nipping and lighting the cigar while saying, "My wife is constantly after me to quit. With the odor and whatnot, I suppose—"

"I didn't come here to discuss your family problems with you, Captain," Harbert said, his voice a low growl. "When can I take custody of my Paiute?"

Conway's eyes narrowed while he leaned back in his chair and exhaled a stream of smoke. "When I say you can, Mr. Harbert. And not one minute before."

"What the hell's going on around here? On direct authority from the Bureau of Indian Affairs, I have sole responsibility for the protection and welfare of those Indians. I demand that they be turned over to me."

"You're in the wrong place to be making any demands, Mr. Harbert. This is United States Army Outpost Number Nine, not the Sand Ridge Reservation. You would do well to remember that. And as for that responsibility you mention," Conway continued, taking up the telegram again, "this telegram, which I assume originated with you, negates that entirely."

Harbert glanced at the document. "What do you mean by that?"

Conway smiled. "It's this part near the end. Do you remember what it says?"

"No, not exactly."

"I thought not. Just to refresh your memory I'll read it to you. It says: 'Again, consider them to be hostiles and take whatever means necessary to rectify this breach of the legal treaty between the United States of America and the Paiute nation.'" Conway lowered the paper and looked again at Harbert. "Do you remember that?"

"Of course I do," Harbert snapped. "But that has nothing to do with my legal right to return those Paiute to their reservation."

"It has everything to do with it, Mr. Harbert. Everything. I am empowered by the BIA, through this telegram, to take whatever means necessary to rectify this breach of the legal treaty between the United States of America and the Paiute nation. And that is what I intend to do."

A defensive wariness crept into Harbert's eyes and he said slowly, "I don't know what in hell you're trying to pull off here, Captain, but I do know I'm getting damned sick and tired of it. Those Paiute broke the treaty and they damned well have to be punished for it."

Conway relaxed in his chair and smiled easily. "No they didn't."

"Then who the hell did?!" Harbert snapped, lurching forward.

"The United States of America."

"What! You're out of your goddamned mind, man! How in hell did our government break the treaty?"

"By assigning you as its agent at the Sand Ridge."

"What! By God, I'm not going to sit here and—"

The agent's tirade was interrupted by two quick raps on the door and the entrance of Windy Mandalian. Harbert glowered at the scout and Windy returned a look of absolute indifference.

"Windy," Conway asked, "do you know Mr. Harbert here?"

"Well enough."

"I thought so. Mr. Harbert, this is Windy Mandalian, our chief scout."

"I don't care who the hell he is," Harbert snarled. "And you, Captain, are going to be busted back to bone-assed private just as soon as I can get to a telegraph office."

"Fine, there's one in town and I'm sure it's at your disposal. We have one here at the outpost that you would be welcome to use, but unfortunately it seems to be inoperative at this time."

"Yeah, sure, in a pig's ass!"

"That could be the problem. We'll look into it." Conway glanced at the scout. "Windy, on the strength of what you and Matt have told me regarding your conversation with Red Hand, I am assuming full authority and responsibility for the safety and welfare of those Paiute. I am declaring a breach of treaty on the part of the United States of America per the testimony of Red Hand regarding the actions of Mr. Harbert while acting as agent at the Sand Ridge Reservation. I'll be leaving this afternoon for regimental headquarters to have orders cut to that effect. Right now, though, do you think Red Hand would come in here and tell us what he told you as a statement of his allegations?"

Windy tilted his hat forward and scratched the back of his head. "Does that mean you want him to come in here and lay it on the line with Harbert?"

Conway grinned. "Yes, Windy, that's what it means I should have said it that way myself."

"Could save yourself several deep breaths, Cap'n. I brought him with me when I came. He's waitin' outside. I don't think he'll have much to say, but you want me to bring him in anyway?"

"Please."

There was an uneasy silence in the room while Windy went for Red Hand, and when the Indian walked in he looked directly at Harbert. His face was a stoic mask, completely expressionless.

"Thanks for coming, Red Hand," Conway began. "I have heard accounts on good authority of the abuse of your people by Mr. Harbert here and his Bannock police. Would you care to make a statement to that effect?"

The Indian's burning eyes never left Harbert's face, and he remained totally silent, as though he hadn't heard Conway's words.

"Excuse me, Cap'n," Windy said laconically, "but old Red Hand ain't no Philadelphia lawyer. Mind if I try?"

"Please do, Windy."

Mandalian turned to the Paiute. "Red Hand, the captain here is a fair and honest man. He wouldn't steal an egg from a chicken and he wants to hear what you think about your agent. Want to give it a try?"

With what appeared to be great effort, Red Hand tore his

78

eyes from Harbert's face and his gaze shifted slowly to Windy.

"I have told you, I will speak to no white man. You and the lieutenant are different. I will speak to no one else. If the captain wants to help my people, let him show me, not tell me."

"He does want to help your people," Kincaid said softly, "but he just might need a little help from you to get that job done."

Red Hand fell silent again, crossing his arms over his chest and turning to stare at Harbert once more.

"See there!" Harbert yelled, leaping to his feet and jabbing a blunt finger at Red Hand. "He's nothing but a lyin' Indian and he wouldn't tell the truth if his life depended on it!"

"I think it just might in this case, Mr. Harbert," Conway replied calmly.

"He isn't gonna talk and you know damned well he won't. Without him you've got no case against me, which you never had in the first place. You'd better cut this bullshit right now and release those people to me, or your ass is gonna be in a sling like you've never seen!"

"It's been there before, Mr. Harbert," Conway replied. "From what I've been told, I don't blame Red Hand for not wanting to speak with or trust any white man. I can get all the information I need from him through Matt and Windy. Who knows, Red Hand might change his mind and be willing to testify against you by the time his statement is needed. Until then, those Paiute are completely under my authority and you are free to leave anytime you wish."

Harbert slammed his hat on his head and his jowls quivered in barely controllable rage. "You're damned right I'll leave. But I'll be back with a telegram in hand and you're gonna be hauled before your regimental commander for tryin' to use authority you ain't got."

"There is no reason for me to be hauled, Mr. Harbert. I'm going of my own accord."

Harbert glowered at the captain for long moments. "You're gonna pay for this, Captain. And you're gonna pay dear."

"I doubt it. Good day, Mr. Harbert."

Harbert spun on his heel and stomped to the door. Then he stopped and his withering gaze fell on Red Hand. "And you, Injun, will regret the day you ever set foot off the Sand Ridge. You'll be mine again in a day or two, and when you are, you'll learn a little lesson about bad-mouthin' white men who are tryin' to help you."

Red Hand's lips curled, his tongue worked, and he spat viciously toward Harbert. The spittle smacked the agent's right cheek.

Stunned, Harbert only stared at the Indian for several seconds before a bellowing roar escaped his throat and he lunged at Red Hand. Instantly, Matt and Windy were on him, throwing the agent against the wall, with Windy's knife point pressed against Harbert's wide neck.

"Swallow, and you're a dead man," Windy said calmly, but his eyes indicated more than an empty threat.

Harbert's cheeks puffed out and he strained his head backward in a futile attempt to escape the razor-sharp steel.

Kincaid reached out with one hand and opened the door. "As the captain said, Mr. Harbert, you are free to go. I suggest you take advantage of that opportunity."

Simultaneously, Windy withdrew the knife, leaving no more than an inch of space between it and Harbert's throat. "Everybody gets two chances, Harbert. You just used up your first one."

Harbert eased along the wall until he was clear of the blade, then he lunged for the doorway.

"Mr. Harbert?"

The agent turned and stared sullenly at Conway. "Yeah?"

"Don't bother bringing me a telegram. Any communications directed to me from the BIA will have to be received over our own telegraph."

"Thought yours was broken."

Conway smiled. "We'll have it fixed by that time, I'm sure."

"Fuck you and all you blue-bellied sons of bitches!" Harbert snarled, stomping through the orderly room and slamming the door hard enough to make the windows rattle.

Windy sheathed his knife and looked at Kincaid. "Think we should open the gate, or just let him ride right through it?"

"I'd prefer the second choice, Windy, but wood's too hard to come by. That wasn't a real smart thing our friend Red Hand did, was it?"

"Best damned move he ever made. Should have kicked him in the balls at the same time."

"Well, Matt," Conway said, rising from behind his desk, "looks like the ball's rolling and we'd better keep it headed in the right direction. Have two squads prepared immediately for a ride to Regiment. I probably won't get back until tomorrow sometime, so you're in charge of things here until I get back."

"Consider it done, sir. Do you think your interpretation of that telegram will hold up?"

"I haven't got the slightest idea," Conway replied, buckling on his gunbelt. "But it might. At least it's going to buy us enough time to try and get a sensible decision out of the BIA. It would be kind of nice to think Harbert hung himself by his own hand with his wording of that telegram, don't you think?"

"That it would, sir. But I'd rather see it done with a real rope instead of words."

"Words are the ammunition with which bureaucrats kill, Matt. Let's just hope they don't backfire on us." He winked and added, "Now that the telegraph is fixed, send a wire to Regiment and tell them I'm on my way. Tell the colonel not to make any decisions on anything he may receive from Washington until I've had a chance to talk with him personally."

"It will be done immediately, sir."

"Thanks." Conway adjusted his hat and stopped by Windy on his way to the door. "You could hurt somebody with that thing, you know that, Windy?" he said, nodding toward the big knife.

"That's the point, Cap'n. It's an old mama bear, she don't come out of her cave 'less she's got a reason to be in the sunlight. Have a good ride."

Conway grinned and pulled his gloves on as he walked through the office.

It was late afternoon when the captain and his detachment passed through the front gates of regimental headquarters, and the shadow of the flagpole stretched long across the vacant parade. Conway returned the guard's salute while wondering why there never seemed to be any activity around the headquarters command. Pencil-pusher types must have something against fresh air, he decided, or they are too damned busy screwing everything up to get out from behind their desks. Reining in before the main office, he stepped down and turned to the two squad leaders.

"Have your men care for their horses, and then arrange accommodations for them for the night. We'll be leaving early tomorrow morning, unless I get thrown out before that."

"Yessir," the corporals said in unison.

"Very good. I think you might find a little three-two beer over at the sutler's after supper. Feel free to down a couple if you like."

"Thank you, sir. We will."

Conway waved off their salutes and stepped toward the door. He experienced conflicting emotions as he reached for the latch, one being slight consternation and the other a sense of satisfaction for doing what he knew to be right and humane.

He had only met Colonel Wainwright, the new regimental commander, once, at a formal reception, and he had thought about the colonel's reaction to his decision during the ride in from the outpost. He remembered Wainwright as being tall and slender with an erect military posture and given to a penchant for placing his right fist in the small of his back and pacing the room while thinking. His straight black hair was slicked back, and a pencil-thin mustache graced his upper lip. His eyes were close-set, which, in combination with his lean and jutting jaw, gave him the appearance of a harsh man who was hard and unforgiving.

The colonel had lived up to his physical reputation at that reception, Conway remembered, when he had taken the officers aside from their wives and detailed what he expected from his subordinates. They would adhere unwaveringly to the chain of command, no decisions were to be made beyond each man's individual level of authority, and all communications received from, or sent to, army headquarters would pass through his office first. As Conway opened the door, the thought occurred to him that he had violated all of the colonel's edicts regarding the behavior of subordinates.

An elderly sergeant looked up from the paperwork strewn across his desk, adjusted his spectacles, and peered up at Conway.

"May I help you, sir?"

"Yes, thank you. My name is Captain Warner Conway, commanding officer of Outpost Number Nine. I wish to speak with Colonel Wainwright, please."

The sergeant cleared his throat nervously as he rose. "What was that name again, please, sir?"

"Captain Warner Conway. Outpost Nine."

Now the sergeant studied Conway more closely. "So you're the one."

"The one what, Sergeant?"

"Never mind, Captain," the sergeant replied with a wan smile. "I'm sure Colonel Wainwright will be more than happy to fill you in on what he thinks you are. Just one moment, please, sir. I'll see if the colonel is in."

"Thank you, Sergeant."

Conway thought about the sergeant's words while he waited what seemed an extraordinary length of time, and an inner resolve built in his chest—a commitment to purpose and to hell with a military career that seemed to be bogged down at captaincy in the first place.

Finally the sergeant reappeared and held the glass-paneled door to one side. "The colonel will see you now, Captain."

It seemed to Conway that the aging noncom had put undue emphasis on the word 'captain,' but then he pushed the notion aside as a product of his imagination.

"Thank you, Sergeant," he said, passing through the opening and hearing the door close behind him.

Colonel Wainwright stood at the window with his back to the door, and appeared as though he hadn't heard Conway enter. His posture was ramrod-stiff, his shoulders thrown back. Conway stood several feet away from the desk for several seconds with hat in hand before clearing his throat.

"Captain Warner Conway, Outpost Number Nine, to see the colonel, sir."

The colonel continued to stare out the window in silence for nearly a minute before saying in a surprisingly low voice, his back still turned toward Conway, "Military life is an unusually restricting thing, isn't it, Captain?"

"In what way, sir?" Conway asked, feeling more uncomfortable than at any time he could remember.

"Basically in the fact that there is no room for individualists here."

"That's true, sir. Unless honesty and integrity are at stake."

Wainwright hesitated as if studying the captain's words. "Honesty and integrity?" he finally asked. "They are one and the same, are they not, Captain?"

"No, sir, they aren't. Honesty applies to a man's dealings with others. Integrity applies to his dealings with himself."

Another pause. "Very good, Captain. But that's enough philosophizing on the human condition." The colonel turned very slowly to face Conway. His outward mien betrayed no emotion, but his eyes held a strange glitter. "Now, Captain," he said, unconsciously brushing the corner of his mustache with his free hand, "would you mind answering one question for me?"

"Certainly not, sir."

"Just what the hell do you think you're doing?"

"Regarding what, sir?" Conway asked, although he knew the question was unnecessary.

"You know what I'm referring to." Wainwright reached out and lifted a pair of telegrams from his desk. "I received two of these today. One from your outpost, telling me not to make any decisions, and the other from the Bureau of Indian Affairs, telling me I damned well better make one."

"I'm familiar with what mine says, Colonel, but not the other one."

"No, you wouldn't be. So I'll read it to you, forgetting all the extraneous nonsense. This is the part that applies to you:

"'You are instructed to order Captain Warner Conway to relinquish his illegal authority over the Paiute Indians presently quartered at Outpost Number Nine and turn them over to one Dennis Michael Harbert, duly appointed agent at the Sand Ridge Reservation. Additionally, you are instructed to take whatever disciplinary action you deem necessary to ensure that Captain Conway will never overstep his authority again.'"

Wainwright laid the papers ceremoniously on the desk and looked up at Conway. "Now I'll repeat my original question, Captain. Just what the hell do you think you're doing?"

Conway thought for a moment before answering. "So, he already got to town. Must've ridden his horse to death to get there so quickly."

"What? Speak up, Captain Conway. I can't hear you."

"Sorry, sir, I was just thinking out loud. The agent mentioned in that telegram, Harbert, was at Outpost Nine this morning. I'm just a little surprised to see that he's beaten me to the punch."

"And what is that supposed to mean?"

"What it's *supposed* to mean amounts to nothing, sir. It's what it *does* mean that counts. Harbert is a vicious liar, cruel beyond comparison, and if those Paiute are turned over to him they will be dead just as surely as if they were hung."

The intensity in Conway's voice and the absolute finality

84

of his tone took the colonel by surprise. "How do you mean, Captain?" he asked.

"It's kind of a long story, Colonel, and most of my information is based on facts relayed to me by two men not directly involved. But there are no two men in this world to whom I would credit a higher level of believability. They are Lieutenant Matthew Kincaid, my executive officer, and Windy Mandalian, my chief scout. They are the only two with whom the Paiute chief, Red Hand, will speak, and any information I have regarding Harbert's value as an agent, or lack thereof, comes directly from them."

"Well, Captain," Wainwright began with a new respect in his voice, "if you place such tremendous faith in those men, then I would appreciate your relating their information to me. I happen to be a firm believer in hearing both sides of a story, and yours has yet to be revealed. Won't you have a seat, Captain?" the colonel concluded, slowly lowering himself into the swivel chair behind his desk, as if any sudden movement might cause him to break in half, while indicating the chairs arranged throughout the room with a sweep of his hand.

"Thank you, sir," Conway replied, taking a seat and placing his hat over a knee. "The whole thing begins with a telegram I received from the BIA three days ago."

Conway related all he knew about what had happened at the Sand Ridge Reservation, including the background information Windy and Matt had given him on the ancient Paiute-Bannock hatred for each other. He mentioned the flight of Red Hand's people, their physical condition, and the unsuitable environment in which they were being forced to live. He placed particular emphasis on his own personal reaction to the agent named Harbert, Red Hand's hatred of the man, and Harbert's implied threats of reprisal. The colonel listened intently, with his fingertips pressed together across his chest. Nearly half an hour had passed before Conway fell silent and absently turned the hat on his knee before looking up at his superior.

"Well, sir, that's about it. I honestly feel that I am within my authority, from both a legal and a humane standpoint, for taking the actions I have. I came here personally to explain the plight of the Paiute to you and ask that you use the powers of your position to aid them in this moment of their continuing crisis."

Wainwright stood, poured two glasses of brandy, handed one to Conway, then assumed his normal posture when thinking, and paced the room.

"I guess you know, Captain, that what you have done is highly irregular."

"It was a highly irregular situation, sir."

The colonel nodded. "You are also firmly aware of my belief in the necessity of a working chain of command."

"I am, Colonel. I am also aware that decisions made in the field often derive from the demands of the situation at hand and do not always lend themselves to the luxury of a second opinion."

"True. Very true." The colonel pursed his lips in thought before taking a sip of brandy and reversing his course toward Conway again.

"My reputation is one of unbending military propriety, Captain. Be that good or bad, it is self-earned. I will brook no insubordination from my commanders in the field, and under no circumstances will I tolerate one man thinking he is bigger than the entire system."

The colonel stopped beside Conway's chair and looked down at the captain. "On the other hand, I will not tolerate ignorance or a lack of flexibility from those same officers. It takes guts to stand up for what is right even in the face of the possible ending of one's military career. I respect that, and if I am going to demand that from the men serving under me, I must also expect that of myself."

"What do you mean by that, sir?"

"That I'm going to back you one hundred percent, Captain. In doing so, I will be in violation of direct orders, but as you have taken a chance, so will I. What do you suggest we do with your Paiute?"

"To tell you the truth, Colonel, I really haven't got any idea. But they should be relocated somewhere in the vicinity of their native land, and somewhere as far away from the Bannock and other horse cultures as they can get."

"Sounds like a logical place for them to be," Wainwright agreed, narrowing his eyes in thought. "I wonder why they weren't located there in the first place."

"Because the big minds back East don't know their asses from a load of hay, if you don't mind my saying so, sir. To them, Indians are Indians, plain and simple. I'm sure they didn't place the Bannock and Paiute side by side for any malicious reasons. Their decision merely reflects their ignorance of the situation out here."

The colonel chuckled. "Ass from a load of hay, huh, Captain? I'll have to remember that. It's pretty good." Then his face turned serious again. "All right, we both know I have been ordered to order you to turn those people over to this Harbert fellow. Well, I'm not going to do that. They are standing by in Washington right now, waiting for my response to their telegram, and as soon as I finish this brandy I'm going to send them one."

Wainwright downed the drink in one gulp and placed the glass on his desk. "Consider the first factor of the equation in place. Now, the second. Would you care to walk to the telegraph shack with me, Captain?"

"Certainly, sir. May I ask what your response will be?"

The colonel smiled. "It won't be *my* response, Captain. It will be yours, with my name on it. We are going to paraphrase what you've just told me and emphasize the fact that those Paiute should not be forced to return to the Sand Ridge Reservation. The BIA people seem to be pretty keen on this Harbert fellow, so I don't think we'll have much luck in ousting him. But if I have to, I'll go to Washington personally, as you've come to me, to plead the case for your Paiute. Nothing less could be done in good conscience."

Conway felt a surge of genuine admiration for the colonel. "Thank you, sir. And thank you for your confidence in me."

"Nonsense, Captain. At first, I'll admit, I was going to chew your butt good. But a good officer is like a good horse—both prove themselves within the first few minutes. I'm sure we won't get a response tonight, so may I invite you to dinner with my wife and me?"

"Thank you, sir, if it isn't an inconvenience."

"Not at all. Do you play gin rummy, by any chance?"

"I couldn't have lived as a bachelor second lieutenant years ago if I didn't, Colonel," Conway replied with a grin.

Wainwright arched his eyebrows in feigned surprise. "So, we both went to the same school. Excellent. Shall we say a penny a point?"

"Penny a point. And the winner donates his accumulation to the widows' and orphans' fund."

Now the colonel smiled with genuine warmth. "You, Captain, are a man after my own heart. Now, if you only smoked cigars, we'd—"

"Havanas, when I can get them."

"I just got a fresh box in. Let's get the hell out of here and get on with it."

seven _____

The following morning, Conway was again seated in Wainwright's office, waiting for the colonel to return from the telegraph shack, where he had gone minutes before to await the incoming message from Washington. His two squads were mounted and prepared to move out when the final decision had been made, and Conway had concluded from the bleary look on several faces that they might have had more than two beers at the sutler's the night before.

He wondered what the response would be, and hoped that the actions taken by Easy Company would not put the regimental commander in an unhealthy situation with his superiors. The colonel had proven to be a most cordial host, as was his gracious wife, and their evening together had been a pleasant one. And when Conway had announced that he would be pleased to donate his five dollars in winnings to the widows' and orphans' fund in the colonel's name, the colonel had laughed heartily and offered the traditional "things will be different next time" threat. Before Conway had left for the bachelor officers' quarters late that night, the colonel and his wife had both made him promise to bring his wife for a weekend visit soon, and the captain had agreed.

Nearly two hours had passed before Conway heard the glass pane rattle in the door behind him and turned to watch the colonel step inside with a message in hand, which he continued to peruse as he took a seat behind his desk.

"I'm sorry this took so long, Captain Conway," he said, flipping over the top page of the two-page communique. "That Bradly Warington fellow doesn't seem to be an easy man to convince."

"I hadn't assumed he would be, Colonel. Did you have any luck?"

Wainwright glanced up from his reading with a wan smile.

"I don't know if you are going to consider it luck or not, Captain. But we did get a positive response."

"Great. Let's hear it."

"As a precaution last evening," the colonel began, laying the telegram down, resting his elbows on the desk and folding his fingers together, "when I sent that telegram to the BIA, I also sent one to an old friend of mine with some clout in Washington, General William Blackburn. The general has absolute confidence in my decisions, and in that telegram I outlined what you had told me of the plight of this particular Paiute band. I included your suggestion for relocation to another reservation, preferably in a region with which they are historically familiar. The general talked personally with Warington and he finally agreed to a transfer."

There was a brightness in Conway's eyes and he nodded vigorously. "Good, Colonel. Excellent. Where will this new reservation be?"

"It's not exactly a new one. As a matter of fact, it's been in existence for some time, and there is another tribe of Paiute already assigned there. It's known as the Skull Valley Reservation, which, from its name, doesn't sound particularly appealing to me. The agent in charge is said to be a good man, a Mormon named Hiram Young. The reservation proper is located south of the Great Salt Lake on the fringes of the Great Basin in the Utah Territory."

"South of the Great Salt Lake?" Conway asked in surprise. "Hell, Colonel, that's got to be more than three hundred miles from here as the crow flies, and probably almost five hundred on horseback or afoot."

Wainwright allowed an easy smile to spread across his face. "I'm aware of that, as are Blackburn and the BIA. I told you when I came in that you might not consider their decision to be necessarily good luck."

"Just as long as they're properly taken care of, I don't care where they're located. Obviously, since they have no horses, they're going to have to walk, but they'll need an escort of some kind to protect them from those Bannock police. Who's going to provide that?"

"We are, Captain. Or, more specifically, you are. The general consensus back in Washington seems to be that if you, as commanding officer of Easy Company, are going to take such a personal interest in this particular tribe, then they are your

90

'charges until the matter is settled to everyone's satisfaction."

"Good God, sir," Conway said in hushed tones while he calculated rapidly. "Even if we could make twenty-five miles a day that's a twenty-day march, and counting the return we're looking at better than a month in the field. That's going to create some real logistical problems."

"That it is." Wainwright watched the captain closely. "Are you up to it?"

"Of course I am, Colonel."

"Good. I thought that would be your response. Before you leave, I will give you the necessary papers authorizing you to draw rations from any government installation or federally financed private corporation, such as the railroad, and any other private parties willing to outfit you, with promise of payment for their contributions. Additionally, a field kitchen with supplies and personnel will be sent from Regiment to your outpost to assist along the way."

"Thank you, sir. But we've got one major problem to confront the first two days out: the Rocky Mountains. Those Paiute damned near froze to death coming this way, and it won't be any warmer going back."

"Any suggestions?"

"Yes, I have one. Do we have an adequate supply of blankets here with the regimental quartermaster?"

The colonel arched an eyebrow. "That depends on what you mean by adequate. If enough blankets placed end to end to run from here to Washington and back is considered adequate in your opinion, then we have an adequate supply. Blankets, Captain, are the one thing we have in surplus around here."

"And we'll need every damned spare one we can get our hands on, sir. They'll serve two purposes: the first and most obvious is bedding, and the second, less obvious, is for warmth while crossing the Rockies."

"How do you mean, Captain?"

"We'll cut a head-hole in the center of each blanket and the Paiute can wear them sort of like capes or ponchos. It won't be pretty, but warmth is what we're after."

"Very good," Wainwright replied. "Can you think of any other supplies you'll need?"

"Yes. I'd like to draw some extra rounds of ammunition. When those Indians showed up at Outpost Nine, they were armed with approximately forty Springfields, but damned little ammunition. I'd like to re-arm them for the return trip."

"Isn't that a little risky, Captain?"

"Not in my opinion. They have a lot more at stake in this than we have. Those Bannock police of Harbert's number around thirty, and there may be more. They're armed with repeating Remingtons, and I wouldn't be surprised if we got a little harassment from them on the way to Salt Lake. I can spare two platoons for this mission, but even at that, we're going to be spread a little thin in trying to protect over a hundred Paiute. Seems to me those Indians can take part in their own defense if it comes to that."

"The Paiute aren't much noted for being fighters, are they?"

"No, but neither is a fox until it's cornered. They'll come around when it comes time to fight or die."

"You've got the extra rounds, Captain," Wainwright said, pursing his lips and drumming his fingers on the desktop in thought. "Anything else?"

"Yes, sir. Extra medical supplies, and we could use a wagonload of beans, dried beef, flour, any type of foodstuffs that can survive the journey. If we're going to make good time, those Indians will have to be healthy and well fed."

"Fine. On your way out, stop by quartermaster stores and leave the sergeant a list of what you'll need." The colonel paused as though making a final decision, and then said, "There's one more thing I'd like for you to take along, even though you might not need it."

"What's that, sir?"

"A Gatling gun. Ever used one?"

"No, sir. I've seen it used in demonstrations, but never under actual combat conditions."

"Same here. I'd like to have a report on its effectiveness. You may not have occasion to use it, but if it's all that they say it is, it might come in handy."

"Thank you, sir. I've got a feeling we're going to need all the help we can get."

"I hope not, but you could be right. Will you be leading the expedition yourself?"

"No. I couldn't be away from the outpost for more than a month at one stretch. Lieutenant Kincaid and Windy Mandalian are more than qualified to handle whatever comes up."

"Well, I guess everything is settled then, Captain," Wainwright said, rising and extending his hand. "I admire you for your actions taken regarding this matter."

Conway shook the commander's hand firmly. "Thank you, sir. And thank you for the confidence you have placed in me and the men of my command."

Wainwright smiled warmly. "Good luck with this mission, Captain, and don't forget that invitation. You might brush up on your game a little bit for our next encounter," he concluded with a wink. "I do not take defeat lightly."

"I'll do that, sir," Conway replied with a chuckle. "But next time watch out for the diamonds. I killed you with them last night."

"Consider your advice noted and duly recorded. Good day, Warner."

"Good day, sir," Conway said, saluting. "And thanks again."

Conway, Kincaid and Windy Mandalian stood beside the supply wagon and mobile field kitchen parked near the center of the parade, and Kincaid lifted the tarps to inspect their contents.

"Have you talked with Red Hand and told him of the BIA's decision, Windy?" Conway asked.

"Yeah, I did, Cap'n."

"What was his response?"

"Well, in the first place, he can't believe that he could actually be going back to his homeland. In the second place, he won't believe it, till he gets there."

"Certainly he's aware of the difficulties that lie ahead?"

"Better'n you and me, I reckon. When do you want 'em to start makin' those blanket-coats you mentioned?"

"As soon as possible. The more quickly we can get this show on the road, the better off we will all be. Matt will head up the first platoon and Dalby the second. You, of course, will be the eyes of the expedition."

"The eyes, Cap'n?" Windy asked, rolling the lump of cut-plug in his jaw. "Hell, I can't see from here to the main gate 'less I'm squintin' down a rifle barrel."

"And that you may well be, Windy," Kincaid said, gingerly pulling back the tarp on the supply wagon and touching the cosmolene-coated, cylindrical barrel of the Gatling. "The way it looks, Regiment must think we're going up against the entire Dakota Confederacy."

"Just an experiment, Matt," Conway responded. "Colonel

Wainwright wants to see if the damned thing works. Let's keep it under wraps, though, until it's needed. Could be just the one little surprise that Wokana and his Bannock aren't expecting."

"Anybody know how it works?"

"You will this afternoon. Sergeant Rikker, from Regiment, is going to take you, Windy, Sergeant Olsen and Private Malone out onto the prairie and away from the outpost and give you a little briefing on the weapon. That way, in case of a fight, there will always be somebody in the chain of command who knows how to use it."

"Looks ominous enough," Kincaid allowed, lowering the tarp and coming around the end of the wagon. "But I'd still prefer to have our two escort platoons armed with repeaters. Any word from the Colonel on upgrading our weapons?"

"None. I thought I'd pressed my luck to the breaking point as it was, and I didn't want to push it by asking for anything more than I got."

Windy spat, and a tiny puff of dust rose from the worn earth of the parade. "We'll make do with what we've got, Matt," he said, wiping his mouth with the back of his hand. "You and me could handle thirty Bannock ourselves without having that coffee grinder along."

"Yeah, you old bastard," Matt replied with a grin, "if you handled twenty-nine of 'em." Then his face turned serious as he looked at Conway. "When do we leave, Captain?"

"Tomorrow morning. That should put you into the foothills of the Rockies by nightfall. In a few days you should be on the other side. Draw what you need from Dugan at the Union Pacific when you get there, and be on your way."

"Captain, do you honestly believe that Dugan is going to cooperate in any way with us? He's not overly fond of Indians."

"I don't give a damn where his fondness lies, Matt. You have orders from the United States Government giving you authorization to do whatever is necessary. Your job is to see that they are carried out by whomever you confront along the way."

"Well, it'll be an experience, if nothing else," Kincaid allowed. "And you can bet your last brass button that we're not leaving here with the intention of taking any shit from anybody, including Dugan, or Harbert and his Bannock."

Conway looked at his executive officer. "Remember, Matt, your first responsibility is to see that these Paiute get safely to the Skull Valley Reservation. No personal vendettas against Harbert or his Bannock. Personally, I'd like to see you kick the shit out of—"

"Captain Conway!"

The captain turned toward the sound of the guard's voice originating from near the main gate.

"Yes, Corporal?"

"Looks like that same fellow's comin' back again, sir! Him and that bunch of Indians he's got with him! They're about a hundred yards away right now, sir!"

"Speak of the devil," Conway said almost to himself. "Thank you, Corporal! Same rules as before! Mr. Harbert comes in, his police stay a hundred yards from the walls!" Then he glanced at Kincaid. "Show him in, would you, Matt? I'll be waiting for you in my office. I've got a little surprise for Mr. Harbert that we all might enjoy. You're welcome too, Windy."

"Thanks, Cap'n," Windy replied, moving toward the office in stride with Conway. "Anything that might piss Harbert off just tickles the hell out of me."

So cold and haughty was Harbert's greeting when Kincaid met him through the opening gate that one might have thought Matt was merely a bootblack.

"I'm here to talk to your captain," Harbert said curtly as the gate swung closed behind him.

"Excellent, Mr. Harbert. The captain wants to talk with you. Won't you follow me?"

"I know the way."

"Such a keen memory," Kincaid said dryly. "But you won't be seeing the captain until after I've announced you."

Harbert glowered down from his horse. "All right, smart boy. Play your little military games. I'll go along with them for now, but after you've seen the telegram I've got in my pocket, you'll all be singin' a different tune."

"Only know one tune, Harbert," Kincaid replied, moving across the parade. "And nothing your telegram has to say is going to change that."

Once they were inside the orderly room, Kincaid paused beside the captain's door, saying over his shoulder, "Wait here, Harbert. I'll ask if the captain has time to see you now."

"He damned well better," Harbert growled.

Kincaid rapped twice and opened the door a crack. "Sorry

to bother you, Captain, but Mr. Harbert is here to see you again."

"Oh, really? I'm kind of busy right now, Lieutenant."

Kincaid could almost hear the Indian agent stiffen behind him.

"He says it's urgent, sir."

"Urgent? Well, by all means, show the man in."

"The captain will see you now, Mr. Harbert," Matt said, smiling as he stepped aside.

Harbert's face was livid with rage as he brushed past Kincaid and stomped into the office. Conway looked up from some paperwork spread across his desk and smiled cordially, while Windy leaned against the wall and stared at the agent with hawk-eyed coldness.

"Good day, Mr. Harbert," Conway said. "How may I help you?"

"Cut the bullshit, Captain. This isn't a social call. I want those Paiute turned over to me immediately."

"Want, Mr. Harbert? There are many things in life that we may want but ultimately don't receive."

"Yeah?" Harbert snarled, jerking a telegram from his pocket and tossing it onto the desk. "Well, that ain't gonna happen in this case. Read it."

Conway unfolded the paper and read the telegram with an expressionless face before looking up again. "So? What about it?"

"What about it! That telegram came straight from Bradly Warington himself! And in case you didn't understand it, you are directly ordered by him to turn those renegades over to me. Now, dammit! Now!" Harbert raged, slamming his huge fist down on the desk and causing the captain's cigar box to jump.

"Don't do that again, Harbert," Conway said evenly but coldly. "And as for your telegram, it's outdated and nothing but a piece of paper to be crumpled and tossed in the waste-basket."

"What do you mean by that?"

The captain opened his top desk drawer, drew out the telegram that Colonel Wainwright had given him, and shoved it across the desk. "This is what I mean. Read it. You'll notice it was issued on the authority of both Mr. Warington from the BIA and General Blackburn from the War Department. Also, please note the date and time. I believe you will find it was sent at least fifteen hours after the one in your possession."

The agent picked up the telegram angrily and slowly read the message detailing the transfer of the Paiute band to the Skull Valley Reservation in Utah Territory. After reading it a second time in total shock and disbelief, he threw the telegram onto the desk with a whipping motion of his hand.

"That's a forgery. If Mr. Warington had changed his mind, I would have been notified."

"Yes, you would have, and probably were. Did you check at the telegraph office in town before leaving there this morning?"

"Well . . . no. I, uh, was kind of in a hurry."

"Slow down, Mr. Harbert. You have all the time in the world now. You and your Bannock can go back to Sand Ridge and share the misery of each other's company."

"No, sir, Conway. Not on your life! Until I am duly notified by the BIA, those Paiute are still in my charge."

Conway smiled as though weary of the entire scenario, while glancing at Kincaid. "Lieutenant? Would you be so kind as to show Mr. Harbert to our telegraph shack? I rather suspect he would like to send a telegram to Washington." Then he glanced again at Harbert. "Our telegraph is fixed now, Mr. Harbert, and thank you for suggesting the problem. Seems it did have something to do with the posterior portion of a pig's anatomy."

"I don't need to use your goddamned telegraph, 'cause I ain't sendin' no message," Harbert snapped, his voice menacing and his dark face an ominous glower. "If they have something they want to tell me, they know where to find me. And until that time, like I said before, I will continue to consider those Paiute to be legally mine."

"Yours? Aren't you clouding the distinction between representation and ownership just a little, Mr. Harbert?"

"You know what I mean."

"Yes, I'm afraid I do. Now, I've got other matters of importance that require my attention. Like preparing two platoons of Easy Company for an escort ride to the Skull Valley Reservation."

"Then you really are going to go through with this charade?"

Conway watched the agent closely. "I am going to carry out my orders to the letter. It is my responsibility to see that those Paiute are safely transferred to a new reservation. No one—I repeat, no one—will stand between me and that goal."

Harbert's lips curled back into a cruel, defiant smile. "Well, good luck, Captain. It's a damned long ways you've got to travel, and who knows what the hell might happen between here and there. I'd better leave now and let you get on with your job."

The agent seemed almost pleased as he turned toward the door and stopped beside Kincaid. "Good luck to you, Lieutenant. And your half-breed friend over there. You're going to need it."

"Is that a threat, Mr. Harbert?" Kincaid asked, staring into Harbert's eyes."

Harbert smiled again, innocently this time. "Me? Threaten you? No way, Lieutenant." Then his face turned cold again and he stepped through the doorway. "Just tellin' you the facts like they are, soldier boy. Just tellin' you the facts."

Windy pushed himself away from the wall several seconds later and turned to look out the window. He saw Harbert mount up and angle across the parade toward the Paiute tents, and watched the agent lean down and jab his finger angrily toward Red Hand's chest before pointing at Dark Star, who stood some distance away. Finally the agent threw his head back and laughed while jerking his horse's head around and slamming his heels against the animal's flanks. The gate swung open before the galloping mount, then closed again, and Harbert was lost from view.

Windy turned away from the window and looked at Conway. "Wouldn't be surprised if that miserable scum's got some shit up his sleeve, Cap'n. Might be best to kill him right off and be done with it."

"No doubt, Windy," Conway agreed. "But unfortunately we can't do anything to him or his Bannock unless they give us sufficient cause. If they do, though, you may react to the fullest extent of your authority."

"That Gatling gun probably packs quite a bit of authority, Captain," Kincaid said. "Is that the kind of authority you have in mind?"

"We are not sending it with you on this mission to see how well it survives transport, Matt. The colonel wants to know how well it works. I can't give you any orders beyond that."

"Don't need any, sir."

"I didn't think you would. Now, why don't you and Windy

98

get started with the preparations that have to be made? I'll see you later on, when we test out the gun."

"Come on, Matt," Windy said, moving toward the door. "I'd like to find out what little gem of wisdom Harbert passed along to Red Hand."

"Sure. I'm kind of curious myself."

When they stepped onto the parade, they saw Red Hand standing with arms folded across his chest and staring at the closed gate, as though he could look through it and out over the plains. He had not moved since Harbert departed, and neither had Dark Star, who continued to watch him with a sad, sympathetic smile. The Indian gave no acknowledgment when Windy and Matt approached to stand beside him.

"How's it goin', Red Hand?" Windy asked.

There was no response.

"We're gonna be leavin' at first light in the mornin'. You know that, don't you?"

Again, no response.

Windy tilted the corner of his hat upward and scratched the back of his head. "This conversation seems to be just a mite one-sided, Red Hand," the scout said with an easy grin. "You know I'm your friend and I'd like to help you if I can. What'd Harbert have to say?"

Red Hand's eyes never left the gate and he continued his silence for nearly a minute before speaking in a low, controlled voice. "He said I would never live to see my homeland again. He said I would be tortured and killed for leading my people away from the Sand Ridge."

"Well now, ain't that just like old Harbert? Always stretchin' the truth, talkin' when he should be listenin', and lyin' every time he opens his mouth. Don't you worry none about gettin' to the Skull Valley, friend. Me and Matt here aim to see that you do."

The Indian's lips were tight in silence again, but he nodded his acknowledgment of Windy's words.

"I was watchin' out the captain's window and I saw Harbert say something to you and then point at Dark Star. What was that all about?"

"He said that once I was dead, she would be his. He said he would make love to her on my grave."

"I wouldn't worry none about Harbert takin' your lady away

from you, Red Hand," Windy said. "In the first place, you ain't gonna have any rocks on your chest for quite a spell yet, if me and Matt can help it, and in the second place, Dark Star would kill herself before she'd let Harbert touch her."

"She would."

"That's settled, then. Dark Star is gonna live long enough to have lots of beautiful Paiute babies, and you will most likely have a little somethin' to do with that, I suspect. Now, what say we quit all this jawin' and get on with ruinin' army blankets? We've got lots to do and damned little time to get 'er done."

Red Hand continued to stare at the gate for several moments longer, before breaking off his gaze and striding toward the supply wagon.

"See any holes burned in them gates over there, Matt?" Windy asked, squinting toward the gates to confirm his suspicions.

"I don't even see any gates," Kincaid replied with a chuckle.

"Damned if I do, either, now that you mention it. Told the Cap'n I couldn't see worth a damn. Come on, let's help out old Red Hand."

eight

The noonday sun rode at its zenith in the hard blue sky and beat down upon the strange caravan slowly working its way across the plains. The band of Paiute, with the women and children and old people in the center, surrounded by armed tribesmen, was flanked on either side by a platoon of mounted infantry, resplendent in their blue uniforms and mounted on well-groomed bay horses. Several packhorses brought up the rear, and behind them rumbled three wagons, the rearmost having two soldiers up on the seat and two more riding close by. The strange lump in the center of the wagon was covered with canvas, and it was obviously the only article of baggage being transported.

In the combined interest of making maximum headway and conserving supplies, the decision had been made to eat only two meals a day: a late breakfast and an early dinner. And when they did finally stop for the evening meal, the magnificent Rocky Mountains loomed before them.

Lieutenant Kincaid forked in a last mouthful of beans before carefully laying his tin plate on the pile beside the fire and looking toward the mountains. "Looks like we've got about two hours before dark sets in, huh, Windy?"

"Yeah, about that," Windy replied, not bothering to look up. "Should be able to make the foothills by that time."

The scout laid his plate on top of Kincaid's and wiped his mouth with the back of a sleeve. "Reckon we'd better move out if we're gonna make any headway before dark."

"Yeah. Looks like everybody's about finished." Kincaid glanced toward the range again. "If those Bannock are going to take a crack at us, where do you think would be the first place they'd try?"

"Same place you think," Windy replied as he moved toward his horse, lifted a stirrup and adjusted the cinch strap. "Sometime after we leave the foothills, so they can cut the Paiute off from escape into the mountains."

"Yeah, that's what I thought too. You remember the captain's giving me that telegram authorizing me to requisition whatever supplies I'd need from any federally financed private enterprise?"

"I remember he said to take whatever you need and fuck 'em if they don't like it. Or words to that effect."

"Words to that effect. If I left now with two squads, how long do you think it would take me to get to South Pass City?"

"You've got good horses. Should be there around midnight. You got some kind of plan brewin' around in that dark brain of yours, Matt?" Windy asked, lowering the stirrup again and reaching for his plug of tobacco.

"Yes, I think I do. At any rate, wait for me at the foothills until eight o'clock tomorrow morning. Then, if I'm not back, start up the grade."

Kincaid turned to search out Lieutenant Dalby. "Lieutenant?"

"Yes, sir?" Dalby asked, leading his horse toward the commanding officer.

"I'll be gone until tomorrow morning, taking two squads with me. You're familiar with the Gatling. Use it if necessary. I'd like to save that for a future surprise a little farther down the trail, if we can. You're in charge here, but make no decisions without consulting Windy first."

"Fine, sir. May I ask where you are going?"

"To pay a short visit to Mr. Dugan. I think I might requisition a little equipment from the Union Pacific."

"What kind of equipment, sir?"

"If I'm not successful, you'll find that out soon enough, Lieutenant. Bivouac in the foothills tonight with double guards posted. If the Bannock are going to hit us, I don't think they'll try until we're well into the pass tomorrow, but I don't want to take any chances."

"Consider it done, sir. Do you want me to select two squads to accompany you?"

"Yes, do that. Have them prepared to move out immediately."

"Yes, sir."

Windy watched the young lieutenant move away before looking at Matt again. "I think I know what you've got up your sleeve, Matt. I'd give ten pounds of good chawin' tobacco to see the look on Dugan's face when you tell him."

"Save your tobacco, Windy. I'll tell you about it," Kincaid replied, swinging into his saddle. "Keep an eye on things for me while I'm gone, and don't let Dalby do anything stupid."

"He won't. And you stay on your toes going over the divide tonight. Wokana won't be expecting you this early, but then you never know."

"I will. See you in the morning. You'll know what to do when you see me."

Windy lifted his hand and Kincaid cantered away to head up the two columns of soldiers forming to the right of the Paiute, who were now standing and prepared to move out.

The moon was a brilliant silver disc in the black, star-sprinkled sky, and Kincaid buttoned his coat up to the collar in defense against the bitter cold. White puffs of steam escaped from the horses' mouths as they strained upward, and the divide was silent except for the sound of iron-shod hooves striking stone. The crest of the pass loomed before them as a ragged, dark line outlined against the heavens, and Kincaid searched the narrowing divide for any indication of hostile presence. He knew they were passing through the perfect place for an ambush, and he mentally thanked the near-freezing temperature in awareness that the Bannock would not want to spend any more time on the crest of the mountain range than necessary. They too were ill-equipped for its hostile climate and very likely would not prepare their ambush until early the following morning.

After they crested the summit and started down the other side, he allowed a sigh of relief to escape his lungs and pulled the watch from his pocket to check the time. Ten-thirty. The lights of South Pass City winked below them, and for the first time his mind went to the day of the week.

"What day is this, Corporal?" he asked, turning toward the squad leader riding beside him.

"Saturday, sir. At least I think it is."

"I think you're right. That means those railroad hands will have tomorrow off. I imagine the first place to look for Dugan would be in one of the saloons."

The corporal smiled in the darkness. "That's where I'd be, sir, if I had tomorrow off and a dollar in my pocket. Neither of which I've got, by the way, sir."

"I don't know about the dollar, Corporal. But you sure as hell don't have tomorrow off. I'll see that you and the other men are taken care of when we get back to the outpost. You've got a month or better to think about it."

"Wish in one hand and shit in the other, and see which hand gets full faster, Lieutenant," the corporal sighed. "The story of my life."

Matt chuckled and leaned back in the saddle as his mount started downward.

Unknown to Kincaid, that particular afternoon had been payday, and South Pass City was filled with drunken railroad men staggering every which way, making the rounds from one bar to another. As he led his twin squads down the wide central street, Kincaid saw two locomotives quietly venting steam in the switchyards off to the left, and he could make out the dark silhouettes of several cattle cars and passenger coaches parked on the siding.

"Pardon me," Kincaid said, reining his horse in beside a group of four men. "Could you tell me where I might find Mr. Dugan?"

The tallest of the four had been telling a joke; he broke off in mid-sentence and looked up at the lieutenant.

"What?"

"I asked if you might know where I could find Mr. Dugan. He's the section chief here for the Union Pacific."

"I know who he is, soldier. I happen to work for him." The man's words were whiskey-slurred and he closed one eye in an attempt to focus on Kincaid and the others. "What the hell do you want with him?"

"Nothing that concerns you, friend. Just tell me where I might find him."

"I ain't got much use for the army, mister. I had enough of you smart-mouthed lieutenants during the War."

"I'm sure you did, and I'm not asking you to dance. I only want to know where to find Dugan," Kincaid replied dryly, but with a hint of irritation. "Any of you other men know where I might find him?"

"Don't tell the son of a bitch nothin'!" the tall man snarled. "Dugan ain't got no more use for the army than I have."

Kincaid leaned down swiftly and his hand shot out like a striking snake. His fingers closed around the man's throat. "And I haven't got time for any bullshit from you. It's going to be a lot less difficult for you to tell me where Dugan is with your throat in one piece, friend. Now, where the hell do I find him?"

The railroad man's eyes bulged in his face and he turned his head from side to side in an attempt to escape Kincaid's grasp. Matt's viselike grip closed ever more tightly. "Talk or I'll break your goddamned neck," he said in a low, menacing tone.

"All right, all right," the man managed to croak, while clawing at Kincaid's wrist. "Just let go of my goddamned throat!"

Kincaid released his grip, shoving at the same time, and the man staggered backward to massage his bruised neck, while saying sullenly, "He's over at the Iron Horse Saloon."

"Where's that?"

"Down the street. Left-hand side."

"Thank you for your cooperation."

Kincaid heard the man's shouted insult behind him, but he was already moving down the street with his eyes fixed on the two yellow globes illuminating a sign proclaiming the Iron Horse Saloon.

Swinging down, he looped his reins over the hitching rail and looked toward the soldiers behind him at the same time. "Corporal, you stay out here, but be ready to come in if I need you. I'll want two men to go with me."

"Yes sir. Higgins. Jones. Go with the lieutenant!"

The two soldiers immediately stepped from their saddles, but by the time their boots hit the street, Kincaid was already pressing his way through the batwing doors.

Even though the room was crowded, he easily spotted the foreman sitting at a table with his back turned toward the door. Kincaid worked his way through the press of bodies and stopped behind Dugan.

"I'd like to talk with you, Mr. Dugan. Alone, if possible."

The foreman swiveled in his chair and looked up. "Well now, if it's not the Injun-lovin' lieutenant. What brings you this far from the safety of your little outpost?"

"Business. Business of a nature that requires privacy."

Dugan grinned coldly. "You were on your own ground the last time, Lieutenant. Now you're on mine." He made a sweeping gesture to indicate the others seated at the table. "Whatever you've got to say, these boys can hear."

"Have it your way. I want two of your locomotives and however many cars you can spare."

"You what?"

"You heard me."

"Maybe I don't hear so good. Besides that, all the equipment I've got is already spoken for."

"You've got two engines and several cars parked on that siding that don't seem to be doing anything."

"They will be. Gotta help the westbound over the pass tomorrow."

"That's tomorrow. I'm talking about now."

Dugan picked up his glass and studied it in the dim light. "They might not look like they're doin' much right now, Lieutenant, but we happen to be doin' maintenance on 'em, and their boilers and fireboxes are empty."

"When will they be ready?"

"Sometime tomorrow morning."

"Fine. I'll wait until then."

"Sorry. Like I said, they're spoken for."

"Well, that'll just have to wait," Kincaid said, moving around the table to look Dugan squarely in the eye. "Upon authority given me by the War Department, I am hereby requisitioning those two locomotives and whatever rolling stock I deem necessary."

"Like hell you are. I run this show around here, not you."

"And you're welcome to it. I have no wish to question your authority, just as I don't intend to have mine questioned. Those two locomotives and rail cars are hereby conscripted for use by the United States Army. How quickly can they be made ready to roll?"

"Not so fast, soldier boy," Dugan said, slapping his palms onto the tabletop. "Just what makes you think you have authority to bust in here and commandeer my company's property?"

"The Pacific Railway Act of 1862. Your Union Pacific company was given land grants and federal loans through the issuance of bonds at that time. A stipulation of those loans was the availability of this railroad for military use in times of crisis. Additionally, you are bound by the terms of that agreement to the movement of government property and personnel at reduced rates." Kincaid reached into his pocket and drew out a silver dollar, which he tossed onto the table. "Now, Mr. Dugan, your train has been both conscripted and hired. I don't wish to press charges against you for a seditious act against this government, so please answer my previous question. How quickly can that train be made ready to roll?"

The lieutenant's complete knowledge of the Pacific Railway Act and its workings stunned Dugan. A hush fell over the saloon as the foreman absently toyed with the coin before him while the other railroad men watched their hard-bitten boss in quiet expectation. Dugan was not ready yet to concede that he had been trapped, and he squinted up at Kincaid once more.

"All right, so you know a little something about our agreement with the government. Well, friend, so do I. I have to see written authorization issued by the proper authorities before I release any of my equipment to you." A cunning smile crossed his face as he concluded, "I haven't seen that yet, Lieutenant."

Kincaid reached in his left breast pocket and produced the telegram sent by the War Department. His expression had not changed throughout the entire conversation, and it remained constant as he unfolded the document and laid it before Dugan.

"I think you will find that the contents of this telegram satisfactorily meet that requirement, Mr. Dugan. Please read it and then let's get on with the business at hand."

The foreman reluctantly took up the slip of paper and his eyes skipped over the words. His lips pressed more tightly together as he read, and finally tossed the telegram to one side.

"All right," he said without looking up. "You have proper authorization. What is it that you want to haul?"

"Two platoons of mounted infantry, three wagons and a complete complement of horses." Kincaid paused. "There is also a matter of property aside from field equipment."

Now Dugan looked up. "What would that be?"

"You'll see when we get there. That property will require at least four extra cars."

"And where would that property be located, and what is its destination?"

"In the foothills on the east side of the pass. It is to be transported here, to South Pass City."

Dugan watched Kincaid closely. "And you can't tell me what we'll be haulin'?"

"No I can't. Now how quickly can you be prepared to move out?"

"That maintenance is scheduled to be completed by six

o'clock tomorrow morning. Isn't that right, Leroy?" the foreman asked, turning toward a potbellied man wearing bib over-
alls and a visored, floppy cap.

"That's right, Harry. At least old Number Twelve will be.
Twenty-one might take a little longer."

"What do you do?" Kincaid asked, glancing at the middle-
aged man.

"Engineer. I handle the throttle on Number Twelve."

"Good. You're just the man I want to talk to. Make sure
both engines are ready to go by six, or as close to it as possible.
Can you back over the divide?"

"That's the way we do it for the westbounds."

"With several cars attached?"

"Piece of cake."

"All right. I want to be prepared to move out the instant I
get that property loaded. I'm not sure if there's going to be
any trouble, but expect it just the same."

"Trouble?" Dugan asked. "What kind of trouble?"

"I can't tell you that, either. Just expect it, and if nothing
happens, neither one of us will be disappointed."

"Just a minute now, mister. I'm not about to send a crew
out to get their asses shot off. If you think I—"

"You won't be sending any crews out, Mr. Dugan," Kincaid
said softly.

"What do you mean by that?"

"Because you'll be going with them."

"What the hell!" Dugan exploded. "I've got work to do. I
haven't got time for playing army games."

"This isn't a game, far from it. I'll be back in one of the
cattle cars with my troops; I've got two squads standing by
outside right now. I'll need you up in the lead engine to coordinate my signals with the engineer. Both he and the foreman
are going to be pretty damned busy, I think, once we start
back."

The foreman stood and jabbed a finger toward Kincaid's
chest. "I ain't likin' this one damned bit, Lieutenant. Not one
damned bit."

"I'm not asking you to like it, Mr. Dugan. I'm merely telling
you to do it."

"Oh, we'll do it all right, mister. But the second I get off
that train I'm going to wire a complaint to company head-

quarters, and they'll report you to your superiors."

"You do that, sir. In the meantime, I'll need quarters for my troops. Do you have any suggestions?"

"Yeah," Dugan snarled. "You can all hang from the trees like the baboons you are."

Kincaid smiled. "I think we'll explore other options, if it's all the same to you. And don't forget, Mr. Dugan, I am just as familiar with the process of sending complaints as you are. I'd wager I'll have a lot better luck in having you removed as foreman here than you will in having me removed as government representative and commanding officer of this military region." Ignoring the silent hostility emanating from the men surrounding him, Kincaid matched Dugan's stare. "Now would you care to try another suggestion as to possible quarters for my troops?"

After several long moments, Dugan's gaze faltered and he looked away. "There's some crew quarters down by the switchyard," he replied in a lowered voice. "Should be enough bunks for all of you." The foreman jerked his head toward the door while glancing at another man. "Show him, Charlie."

"Thanks. I sincerely appreciate your cooperation, however reluctantly it's given," Kincaid said, moving toward the doorway behind the man named Charlie. Just as his hand touched the swinging door, he heard his rank called out.

"Lieutenant?"

"Yes?" Matt replied, stopping and turning.

The silver dollar sailed toward him, ricocheted off a table, and clattered to the floor in the silent room. "I don't want your goddamned money. Pick it up and spend it on one of them Injun squaws you're so much in love with. I ain't for sale."

Kincaid looked down at the coin, stooped to retrieve it, and flipped in onto the bar. "There, bartender, buy the foreman a drink, compliments of the United States Army. I doubt he's ever drunk in company that good before. Good night," he concluded, pushing through the twin doors and stepping into the chill of the mountain night.

A light drizzle was falling across the divide when Kincaid stepped from the crew quarters at five-thirty the following morning. The maze of tracks in the switchyard glinted weakly in a dull gray dawn that was made even more bleak by a low-hanging cloud bank. The brisk wind sweeping down from the divide pierced through his clothing and drove the cold into the very marrow of his bones.

Kincaid turned up the collar of his sheepskin coat and pulled on his gloves while stepping over the first set of tracks and walking in the direction of the engine shed. The two engines he had seen the night before had been moved into the big building, and he could hear the clatter of metal on metal. The voices of two men drifted out to him on the damp, cold air. When he stepped inside, Matt saw two hostlers replacing a grease seal on the lead locomotive, and he stopped just behind them.

"Good morning."

One man wiped his hands on a greasy rag and looked up while the other continued to pack the bearing. "Mornin'."

"How's it going?"

The man shrugged. "Same old sixes and eights. Too much to do and not enough time to do it in."

Kincaid pressed his hands against the boiler and felt the warmth of the heated metal spread through his gloves. "Kind of cold this morning, isn't it?"

"Nope. Come by around January."

"No thanks," Kincaid replied, smiling. "Will these engines be ready to roll by six?"

"Hell no. Already told Dugan that." The hostler inclined his head toward the rear of the building. "That one back there is, but this one won't be."

Kincaid looked toward the second locomotive and frowned. "If that one's ready to go first, why isn't it in the lead so we can start lining out the cars?"

By this time the hostler had resumed his task and spoke without looking up. "I asked Dugan that same question, but he said he wanted it this way. Go on over to the cookshack and talk to him. We should be done here in a couple of hours."

"Thanks," Matt replied, moving away from the warmth of the huge engine and stepping into the cold once more. He felt a twinge of anger rise within his mind as he realized that Dugan could play mechanical games with him for as long as he wanted to. Resolve quickly replaced anger, however, and Kincaid walked briskly toward the low-silhouetted building with a column of white smoke rising from its chimney.

The pleasant aroma of fried meat, fresh bread and hot coffee

110

touched his nostrils as he stepped into the cookhouse and closed the door behind him. The room was filled with railroad men, and their chatter died instantly as the army officer entered their presence. Kincaid's eyes swept over the room until he found Dugan seated at a corner table, a checkered napkin tucked into his shirt front, munching contentedly on a mouthful of salt pork. With a knife in one hand and a fork in the other, his clenched fists rested on the table while he watched Kincaid walk toward him.

"Morning, Mr. Dugan," Matt offered with as much cordiality as he could muster.

The foreman nodded, glanced down at his plate and began sawing at his salt pork again.

"I just talked with your hostler. He said one of your engines wouldn't be ready for another two hours yet."

"That's right," Dugan replied as the fork moved toward his mouth.

"Why wasn't the repaired engine left out front so we could use it to switch the cars?"

Now Dugan looked up again, and there was a look of triumph in his eyes. "To learn you a little lesson."

"And what lesson would that be?" Kincaid asked, feeling the heat rising in him again.

"That I run this show around here and you don't. True, you can requisition my equipment, but you can't requisition my cooperation. You'll get your rolling stock, but only when I say so and not one damned minute before."

Kincaid could feel the ominous silence surrounding him while he continued to stare at the foreman. "And when will that be, Mr. Dugan?" he asked, his voice low and even.

"When I get damned good and ready!" Dugan snapped, squinting one eye and pointing the fork at Kincaid's chest.

"You are good and ready right now, Dugan," Kincaid replied.

"You don't say?"

"I do say. You are under arrest for obstructing an army unit on patrol in the field. This entire Union Pacific facility is now under the control of the United States Government. There will be guards posted at every building and no one will be allowed to leave or enter without my permission and until the equipment I requested is ready to roll."

Kincaid turned and surveyed the silent, sullen faces. "You

111

men have exactly five minutes to finish your breakfast and return to your quarters. Your foreman will be taken to his office under armed guard, and any questions you might have will be directed to me. Now eat and move out."

He looked back at Dugan. "I'll be back in two minutes with sixteen armed soldiers. Forget about my having to requisition your cooperation, Mr. Dugan. I have taken it."

Kincaid spun on his heel and crossed the room with long, angry strides. In less than two minutes he returned, and the soldiers filed into the room behind him, loaded Springfields held at port arms across their chests. They were hard-looking men, seasoned veterans of numerous Indian campaigns, and the look on their faces left no doubt that they were prepared to do whatever their commanding officer ordered them to do.

The railroad men watched sullenly while the soldiers spread out around the room and Kincaid stepped toward Dugan's table once more.

"Please don't take me or my actions lightly, Mr. Dugan. There are many lives at stake in this matter, on the other side of the divide as well as here. If anyone dies as a result of your truculent attitude, I will personally see that you are prosecuted to the fullest extent of the law."

"I think you're bluffing, Kincaid."

Matt turned to the nearest squad leader. "Move these men out of this room and to their quarters, Corporal. If they resist, use force. You are authorized to shoot any insurgents. Have two men assigned to Mr. Dugan here."

His gaze returned again to the foreman. "It starts right now, Mr. Dugan. If you think I'm bluffing, call it. One man injured or killed, and you go to jail."

Dugan heard the corporal pass along Kincaid's orders, and saw the soldiers move forward to roust his men from their chairs while two privates circled to stand behind him at the table. He looked up at Kincaid in weary resignation.

"Looks like you win this hand, Lieutenant. Go with them, boys," he said to his crew. "We'll get a chance to even the score when this thing's over."

Chairs scraped on the floor amid low grumbling, and the railroad men filed silently from the room with soldiers surrounding them on either side and to the rear. One soldier behind Dugan touched the foreman's shoulder and he violently threw the hand away. Instantly a Springfield slammed sideways across his chest and was then drawn tightly against his neck. The foreman's eyes bulged in his face and his mouth contorted in response to the pain. The soldier holding the weapon asked casually, "Do you want his neck broken, sir?"

"Only if he resists further, Private. It should be readily apparent to you at this point, Mr. Dugan, that I am playing no bluff. I want the equipment I've asked for made available to me at the earliest opportunity. I'm giving you one more chance to cooperate. Either you will be taken now to your office and be held under house arrest, or you will go with me and those two guards to the engine shed and supervise the preparations for this endeavor. Your choice, but make it now."

The pressure of the rifle barrel was neither lessened nor increased, and the foreman's face turned even redder with each passing second. Finally, Dugan nodded his head and Kincaid waved his hand to indicate that the private should release his captive.

Dugan massaged his throat while Kincaid asked, "Did that nod indicate your intention to cooperate?"

"Yeah. I'll cooperate, but—"

"No buts, Mr. Dugan. You will do exactly as you are instructed to do."

A long hesitation, then, "All right. My day will come."

"And I wish you well when it does. In the meantime we've got some work to do. Escort Mr. Dugan to the roundhouse, Private. Treat him as a captive, but not as a hostile."

With those words, Kincaid left and stepped into what was now a driving rain. He turned his face up to the lashing storm and smiled almost imperceptibly. He knew he had been right in making his decision to commandeer the train, but he was pleased with himself even beyond that; he had won the game on a bluff, even though the cards were stacked against him.

nine _____

At exactly seven-thirty that morning, the two engines were backed from the engine shed, their pistons slowly pumping as steam curled around the drive wheels with ghostly swirls in the punishing wind. Another hour passed while the necessary switching of cars was completed, and at eight-thirty the twin engines sat on the main line, venting steam, with four passenger coaches and five cattle cars stretched out behind them.

Kincaid shielded his eyes from the storm and looked up at Dugan, who stood in the doorway of the lead engine while the fireman and engineer manned their seats.

"All right, Mr. Dugan," Matt said, speaking loudly and taking his hat from his head with his other hand to demonstrate, "if I wave my hat crosswise, like this, I want you to stop immediately. If I wave it in a forward, circular motion, I want you to go ahead. Backward means reverse. When I've gotten that property loaded, I'll use a pumping up-and-down motion; that means 'full speed ahead and stop for nothing or no one.' Have you got that?"

"Yeah, I've got it. We're scheduled to pick up a westbound at exactly noon. For your own sake, you'd better hope this is over by then."

"It will be," Kincaid called back, working his way to the rear, where his two squads and their mounts had been loaded into a cattle car. "Just do exactly as I told you and you'll have your train back in plenty of time. Otherwise the other train will just have to wait."

Then Kincaid was gone and the two guards climbed the ladder to take up positions inside the engine. Drive wheels spun on slick rails and the train slowly ground toward the divide, obscured by clouds in the distance.

When they were nearly halfway down the backside of the divide, Kincaid checked his pocket watch and a feeling of

114

apprehension passed through him. It was nine-thirty, and Windy had quit the foothills nearly an hour and a half before. He studied the terrain as they moved downward, searching for just the right place to do what had to be done. Then the crackling of faraway rifle shots reached his ears. Moving quickly, he climbed the grab-rails on the cattle car and clung to the uppermost board for support against the swaying, lurching train. They continued backing downward, and with each turn of the wheels, the sound of firing became more intense, with countless rifles blasting away in the gloom.

As the grade began to flatten out toward the foothills, Kincaid could determine from the alternating muzzle flashes that the remainder of his two platoons and the Paiute were pinned down to the south and west by attackers forted well in the high ground. There was an opening in the canyon wall where a stream fed into the main divide, and Kincaid rose up and waved his hat with a sideways motion. Brake shoes set up a squeal against the huge iron wheels and the train came to a jolting stop. Kincaid leaped down from the cattle car and called the two squad leaders to him while the heavy pounding of weapons fire continued incessantly off to their right. He pulled the man nearest to him up close and shouted in his ear to be heard above the din.

"Corporal Butterfield! You are in charge of these combined squads. Have the men mount up while I lower the ramp. We'll need you to provide flanking cover while I take the train lower to pick up the rest of the company. By going up that creekbed you can get behind and above them and lay down a field of fire. Leave one man posted to watch the tracks. When we come back, break off the counterattack and run for the tracks. We'll pick you up, but we won't have much time. We'll cover you from here as best we can."

"Yessir! *Squaaads! Mount up!*"

The soldiers swung into their saddles, and seconds after Kincaid had lowered the loading ramp, sixteen horses clattered down the wooden planking and plunged up the draw. Kincaid raised the ramp again, scaled the grab-irons once more, and waved his hat in a rearward motion. The train lurched like a drunken man struggling for his balance while the first shot from the attackers' position thudded into the wooden planking of the car's side. Kincaid ducked, pulled out his Schofield and fired three quick shots in the general direction from which the first round had come. From his vantage point he could see the massed Paiute huddling near where the mounts were being held by handlers. Blue uniforms were scattered across the upper foothills, close to the ground in prone positions and firing at the targets up above. He saw a tall man in buckskins moving among the armed Paiute and arranging them in defensive positions, and at a point where the left bank lowered to the approximate height of the doors of the cattle cars, he waved his hat frantically above his head. The train stopped with a shuddering quiver while Kincaid raised himself up again, heedless of the weapons firing in his direction.

"Windy! Over here, Windy!" He could hear the new fire coming from the two flanking squads, now raining down from above, and he cupped his hands to his mouth as the scout turned toward the tracks some seventy-five yards away. "Over here, Windy! Get the Indians and our horses loaded as fast as you can! Have our troops continue to fire until everyone's aboard and then have them fall back in covering stages!"

"Right, Matt! They're layin' it on us pretty good!"

"I see that! Let's get the hell out of here!"

With those words, Kincaid pulled out an iron pin, dropping the ramp on the car in which he was riding, then leaped to the ground and dropped the gates on all the following cars. He opened the doors on the passenger cars as he passed by, then climbed on top of the rearmost vehicle.

Crouched low, the Paiute were running toward the train. Handlers were trying to control skittish mounts while leading them toward the cattle cars. Whinnies, excited shouts and the continuing roar of exploding weapons filled the air. Kincaid glanced toward the army weapons and his heart leaped into his throat. Lieutenant Dalby was struggling with little success to get the canvas off the Gatling, while to the rear and off to his right, four Bannock warriors worked their way through the scattered boulders and were nearly in position to spring.

Kincaid scrambled down the ladder and raced across the opening to meet Dark Star at the forefront of the running tribe.

"Where's Red Hand?" he yelled, pausing only long enough to grab her by the shoulders and scream the question in her ear.

"He is with the young ones!" she shouted back, her face flushed with excitement and fear.

"All right. You are in charge of getting your people into

116

the enclosed cars! Tell them not to be afraid. I'll have them out of here in a few minutes!"

"I understand, Lieutenant! I will do my best!"

"That's good enough," Kincaid said, snatching the Scoff from his holster once again and running toward the three wagons.

Dalby, unaware of the Bannock closing on his rear, continued to throw canvas about in a desperate attempt to bring the Gatling into action. Kincaid's boot skidded off a rain-slick rock and he tumbled to the ground before rolling onto his stomach and raising the pistol in his hands. The four warriors had quit the safety of the rocks and were sprinting toward the wagons when Matt fired his first shot, followed quickly by two more. Three Bannock spun and twisted to collapse in the mud, and the fourth continued to run as Kincaid lined up his sights and heard the hammer fall harmlessly on an empty chamber.

Neither Matt nor the Indian was more than twenty yards from the wagon, and Kincaid sprang to his feet while the warrior fired on the run, his shot skipping off a boulder to Kincaid's left and screaming harmlessly into the rain-soaked sky.

"Behind you, Lieutenant!" Kincaid screamed, while the Bannock paused to jack in another shell.

Dalby dropped immediately to the wagon bed, pulled his revolver and rested the weapon on the side board. A round ripped into the wood inches from his face, and yet the lieutenant did not fire, even though the warrior was bounding toward him once more. Kincaid had managed to slip one bullet into his Scoff. Having no time to position the shell directly under the hammer, he pulled the trigger and heard only the dull snap of spring-loaded steel colliding with cold metal. The horses hitched to the wagon were plunging in their traces, and now they lunged forward, revealing to Kincaid the dead driver lying on the floorboard and his companion stretched out beside the far front wheel.

The Indian leaped onto the tongue of the wagon and Kincaid drew the hammer back again while watching the warrior frantically pump another shell into his rifle. Dalby remained frozen in place with his revolver aimed at his assailant, but he seemed incapable of pulling the trigger.

Kincaid's finger tightened once again on the trigger, and the big revolver belched flame and bucked upward in his hand.

117

The slug crashed squarely into the Indian's chest, picking him up and throwing him onto the ground, while his rifle clattered into the wagon bed.

Matt ran to the wagon, calmed the team, and then crouched down long enough to reload his pistol before peering over the railing.

"Are you all right, Lieutenant?"

Dalby's head slowly turned toward the sound of the voice behind him. "What?"

"I said, are you all right?"

There was a blank look in his eyes, and Dalby held the revolver loosely in his grasp. "I . . . I guess so."

"Why the hell didn't you shoot that son of a bitch?" Kincaid demanded.

"I did, sir. It took several shots, but I finally hit him," Dalby replied, glancing down at his weapon.

Kincaid rested his forearms on the railing and allowed his head to slump slightly as he looked down at his boots. He had seen it before: an untested man, frightened and stunned in battle, never firing his weapon but thinking he was shooting all the time.

"Check your weapon for rounds, Lieutenant."

"Why, sir?"

"Because if it's not empty, you never pulled the trigger once."

"I'm sure, sir. It's not empty, but—"

"Check it."

Dalby broke the weapon open and peered at the cylinder, and a touch of crimson crept into his pale cheeks. "It's fully loaded, sir," he said just above a whisper.

"I knew it would be. You just suffered a little case of what we call 'first fight fever' out here. You'll do better next time." Kincaid was speaking almost gently when he asked, "Have you ever killed a man before, Lieutenant?"

"No . . . no, sir, I haven't."

"Well, your record is still intact. I think you've found out that learning how to shoot and knowing how to kill are two different matters. It's one of the things they don't teach you at the Point." The firefight continued to rage farther up the trail and Kincaid glanced sharply in that direction before looking back at Dalby. "Can you handle a team?"

118

"I don't know, sir."

"Do it. Get this wagon and those other two over to the train on the double. I'll send a detachment down here to help you load them aboard. I'll also send Red Hand and his people down, so you make sure that all the Paiute are safe in the passenger cars. I'll bring our troops down in stages, and you have the first ones give us covering fire from the tracks after they've got their horses loaded into the cattle cars. Do you understand what I want you to do?"

"Yessir," Dalby replied, scrambling onto the seat.

"Just a minute. Let me load our dead in the back."

Kincaid dragged the two soldiers individually to the wagon, hoisted them up and lowered them gently onto the canvas, then slammed the tailgate and latched it. "Move it out, Lieutenant!"

He watched momentarily while Dalby turned the team with some difficulty and rattled away in the direction of the rail line, then he sprinted forward in a crouched position. Using rocks and boulders for limited protection, he worked his way upward and knelt beside Red Hand.

"Chief, get your braves loaded on that train back there! We'll cover you from here! Dark Star should have the others aboard by now!"

Red Hand nodded and shouted some commands to his warriors, who slipped quickly toward the rear. Kincaid could see Windy sending the troops rearward, one squad at a time, taking their dead and wounded with them.

"How's it goin', pardner?" Matt asked as he laid a hand on Windy's shoulder.

The scout spat, wiped his mouth and grinned. "Just like all ambushes are supposed to go, Matt. They hit us just about where we thought they would."

A shell whined off a rock to their left and both men ducked instinctively. "Yeah, I see that," Kincaid replied, squeezing off two quick rounds at the pall of smoke from above.

"Not a bad hat trick, Matt, bringin' that train when you did."

"Dugan doesn't see it that way. Let's fall back with this last group. I've got two squads firing down on them from the high ground."

Windy squinted down the barrel of his Sharps, pulled the trigger, and a Bannock flipped to the ground above and to the

119

left. "Too bad we got them Paiute with us, Matt," Windy said, lowering the rifle and ejecting a spent cartridge. "I'd like to take these bastards right here and now."

"So would I, but our first responsibility is to Red Hand's people. I think we'll get another crack at Wokana before this is over." Kincaid glanced over his shoulder. "Looks like everybody's aboard except us. That's the only train out of here that I know of, and I'd kind of like to be on 'er when she leaves. Let's go."

They backed down the hill side by side, firing when a target was visible. Kincaid heard the shrill screech of the engine's whistle, mixed with the grinding of wheels and steady chuffing of the locomotive as it strained to get under way.

"That son of a bitch!" he shouted, turning and breaking into a run. "Come on, Windy. We'll have to catch it on the fly."

Their boots hit the cinders just as the last car rolled by, and Windy leaped for the grab-irons while Kincaid ran along beside. After the scout had scrambled up the first rungs, he hung on with one hand and, leaning down, extended the Sharps to Kincaid, who was losing ground as the train picked up speed.

"Here, Matt! Grab on to my rifle and I'll pull you aboard!"

Kincaid grasped the barrel and nearly lost his balance, then, with Windy's aid, managed to get one boot on the lower step and hoisted the boot dragging in the cinders aboard. Kincaid was panting heavily when they lowered themselves down the ladder and into the car. He rested an elbow on a horse's rump before straightening.

"You take care of things back here, Windy," he said between gasps. "I'm going to have a little chat with Dugan up in the lead engine."

"Got it handled, Matt. That bastard would have left us if he could have."

"I know."

Kincaid worked his way forward past the soldiers firing through the slits in the car's side walls. He was exposed to enemy fire each time he went to the top of one car and leaped to the next, until he got to the passenger cars, which he entered through the rear door and exited through the front. The Indians jabbered excitedly at him, but Kincaid forced his way through them and finally he was on the coupling between the cars and the second engine. After crawling across the tender, he worked his way along the catwalk on the far side of the engine. When he climbed onto the lead locomotive, he pulled out his revolver and slithered on his stomach across the coal piled high in the tender.

He could see Dugan standing with his back to Matt while the fireman shoveled coal into the blazing opening of the boiler section. The foreman held a pistol on the two soldiers assigned to the engine, and his face was rigid with determination. Matt stood and leaped to the steel plates on the floor of the cab and instantly shoved the barrel of his Scoff into Dugan's neck just below the hinge point of his jaw.

"Drop it, Dugan!" he shouted at the startled foreman.

The foreman's hand wavered before his pistol clattered to the floor.

"I want this train stopped in the exact place where we let those two squads off!"

"No, we have to keep going! We might not get started again on this slick track!"

"Either this train stops or you'll be minus one head!" Kincaid snarled. "Now tell your engineer!"

"No! I—"

"Do it!"

Dugan's jowls quivered in fright and his mouth hung open as though frozen while Kincaid pulled the hammer back with a solid, unmistakable click.

"Now, Dugan! You have five seconds!"

"Leroy! Stop . . . stop the train."

The engineer glanced once at his foreman, hesitated, then his hand went to the throttle and the train immediately began slowing down. The two soldiers had retrieved their Springfields and Matt nodded toward the nearest man.

"Get over here, Private! I want the muzzle of that rifle right down this bastard's throat! Kill him if he even blinks an eye!"

As soon as the gun was in place, Kincaid withdrew and sprang to the doorway on the left side. He could see the Bannock racing along the trail leading toward the creek while his two squads pounded along the narrow ravine. Kincaid grasped the grab-irons and leaned out, looking back and judging the exact point at which the ramp of the first cattle car would reach the bank.

"Now! Cut the throttle!"

The train shuddered to a stop on squealing brakes and Kincaid could see the ramp lowering even before the train's forward motion stopped. The lead rider reined in and his horse's hooves clattered on wood as it disappeared inside, to be followed by the others. In less than two minutes the ramp rose behind the rear hooves of the last mount and Kincaid turned toward the engineer.

"Move it out! Full speed!"

Bullets splattered against the side of the locomotive and sang their screeching, dying song into the flooded sky while iron wheels spun wildly. The engineer crouched low and worked the throttle in a desperate search for traction. A stray bullet ricocheted through the cab and slammed into the fireman's left shoulder, and he slumped to the floor, his coal shovel clattering on the steel plates.

"Private!" Kincaid shouted at the second soldier. "Grab that shovel and get to it!"

"Yessir!"

The train inched forward with grunts and groans. Finally they were gaining speed and the sound of rifle shots receding behind them were lost to the gloom of the South Pass. Kincaid knelt beside the fireman and quickly examined his wound.

"You're not hurt bad," he said after a brief inspection. "That bullet didn't have much in it by the time it got to you."

Kincaid patted the man's leg, then rose and turned toward the soldier guarding Dugan. "What happened, Private?"

"He got the drop on us, sir. We didn't know he had a gun under his coat. Sorry, sir."

"Sorry isn't good enough, soldier. Who blew the whistle?"

"I did, sir. I thought he'd shoot me, but I had to take that chance. He was going to leave you and Windy behind."

"I'm sure he would have. I'll forget your mishandling a prisoner this time, but never again. Is that understood?"

"I understand, sir."

"Good. Thanks for risking your life to save mine."

Now Kincaid's blazing eyes fell on the foreman. "You, Dugan, are a miserable, low-life son of a bitch. If it weren't for my training as an officer and a gentleman, I'd bust you up like a dry twig."

A surly look crossed Dugan's face. "If I'd known you wanted us to risk our lives for a bunch of thievin' Injuns, I'd never have let you have this train, no matter how many telegrams you had in your pocket."

"Those Paiute back there are innocent human beings. If it

122

hadn't been for this train, do you realize how many of them might have been killed?"

"Injuns ain't human beings, and as far as innocent goes—"

Kincaid's fist reared back and his knuckles cracked against the foreman's jaw, and Dugan cowered against the wall with a whimper.

"As a decent man, Dugan, you wouldn't make a pimple on Red Hand's ass. And as for hitting you just now, that 'officer and gentleman' shit only goes so far. If you've got enough guts to pursue the matter further when we get back to South Pass City, I'd be more than happy to oblige you."

Kincaid stared at the silent man, who turned his head away to gaze out the window at the rugged ground rushing by.

"Just as I thought," Matt said icily. "Yellow to the god-damned core. Word of what happened here will get around among your men, and that will do you more damage than anything I could do to you."

Kincaid spun away and reached for the ladder on the tender. "Keep an eye on him, Private. I'm going back to check our casualties. If he gives you any shit from now on, I won't expect to find a certain foreman with anything less than a broken jaw when we get back to his switchyard."

The private grinned. "You won't, sir. He owes me one."

"Then collect if the situation warrants, soldier," Kincaid said as his boot hit the first rung. "I'm sure that bastard's got debts like that out all over the High Plains."

ten _____

Bill McCauley looked at the dark mine shaft one last time before placing a foot in the stirrup and swinging onto his horse's back. His three partners were already mounted, and they watched him turn his horse to face them.

"Harbert said two days and we're workin' on the third one now. I think it's time we paid a visit to our friend and take a little look at that money we advanced him."

"We're losin' valuable time, Bill," one man offered. "The equipment's all in place, but it ain't worth a damn without them featherheads to drive iron. We can't play that vein out by ourselves before the old man gets back."

"Shit! With just the four of us workin', we couldn't even pay expenses, let alone cover what we already gave to Harbert." McCauley's face took on an even deeper look of resentment. "I done warned him about me turrible dislike for double-crossin'. I hate to have to remind a man twice."

A second man crossed his hands on his saddle horn and adjusted his weight. "This whole thing is set up around having those Paiute to work the mine, Bill. What happens if Harbert don't deliver? Havin' him dead isn't goin' to make us a goddamned nickel."

"I'm aware of that, Logan, dammit! We'll just have to make sure he delivers, that's all. That's why a little visit to his agency is called for right now. We're just gonna have to remind him of a contract we agreed to. Them Indians should have been back by now. Let's go."

"Hey, Mac?" asked the third man. He was tall and slender, with a neatly groomed mustache, and wore a long duster over tailored clothes. A heavy Colt .44 hung around his hips, resting in silver-studded leatherwork.

"Yeah, Reno? Spill it."

The man named Reno smiled and adjusted the razor-brimmed sombrero atop his slicked-back, jet-black hair. "What have you got in mind if Harbert went south on us? Most of that money we advanced him came from my, uh, enterprises."

"You don't think I remember that, Reno? You've killed more men than most with that gun of yours. Maybe you'll get a chance to add one more."

"What's killing him going to do for this mine, Bill?" Logan protested. "Sure, Reno is damned handy with his gun, but Harbert dead ain't gonna put any gold through that crusher over there."

"You're soft, Logan," Reno said, his hand resting on his thigh, fingers spread apart. "In this business, if a man doesn't deliver, he gets delivered. Same goes for you."

"Aw, fuck you, Reno. Don't threaten me. With me dead, there ain't a damned one of you who'd know how to operate that equipment in there. You might get your fingernails dirty."

Reno's face went stone cold. "Only way I'll get 'em dirty is draggin' your filthy butt to a grave."

"What the hell's going on around here?" McCauley demanded, jerking his horse's head around once more. "There ain't one of us more important than the other. I organized this deal. Jenkins there rigged the assays. You, Logan, are supposed to know how to run the equipment, and Reno's got most of the money invested. We all get a quarter split, but a quarter's all we're gonna *have* to split if we start fighting among ourselves! We've got a problem right now and we're going to get it straightened out. Now, what say we all calm down and go and hear what Harbert has to say." He made a point of studying each man's face individually before speaking again. "Are we agreed on that?"

Jenkins and Logan mumbled their agreement, but Reno only smiled and allowed the duster to fall free of his elbow. "You know what does the talkin' for me, William. When the time comes, it'll talk loud enough."

"Yeah, sure," Logan grumbled. "All bullets and no brains."

"I'm tired of your shit, Logan," Reno said flatly to the man, who was wearing a high-belted, short-barreled gun and was dressed in typical engineer's clothes of khaki, derby hat and high brown boots with the pants legs tucked inside. "You might be fast with the figures, addin', subtractin', dividin' and all

125

that, but I'll bet your mouth isn't fast enough to catch a bullet in your teeth."

"I'm not afraid of you, Reno," Logan said with something less than absolute confidence as he adjusted his derby nervously. "You've been bellyaching since we started this project, and I'm a little sick of it. I repeat, without me—"

Reno pulled the duster away again. "We'd be better off."

McCauley kicked his horse and steered the mount between the two men. "That's enough of this shit! To make this work, we've all got to depend on each other. You, Logan, keep your educated mouth shut! You, Reno, keep that gun covered up or I'll kill you with my bare hands! If I hear one more word out of any of you, you can pack your gear and ride. I'm still in charge of this goddamned deal, and I will be until it's over!"

With those words, McCauley wrenched his horse's head around so hard that the animal almost lost its footing, but a pair of boots lashing against its ribs sent the mount into a hard gallop instead. Jenkins and Logan followed quickly, and after a lighting a thin cigar, Reno shook the match out and allowed his horse an easy lope nearly a hundred yards behind the others.

The westbound train arrived at Culver Junction at exactly two in the afternoon, only one hour behind schedule. A diminutive, frail-looking man stepped down with a carpetbag in one hand and a briefcase in the other. He wore gold-rimmed glasses, a derby hat and an overly large three-piece suit made of now-rumpled material, sagging from his somewhat emaciated frame. A watch chain dangled across his lean stomach, and as he glanced in both directions, his hand, more from habit than from curiosity, dug the watch from his vest pocket. He might have been in his late thirties, but his sunken eyes and the shadow of whiskers on his cheeks added years to his physical countenance. After snapping open the watch and checking the time, he closed the lid and returned the watch to his vest pocket while signaling a station attendant with the other hand.

"Pardon me, sir?"

The station attendant, who sported a paunch indicating years of inactivity behind a desk, stopped and turned. "Yeah, friend? What can I do for you?"

"My name is Isaiah Rosenfeld. I would like two things from

you if you would be so kind, sir. First of all I would like a hot bath, and secondly I would like to know where I can hire a carriage to convey me to the Indian reservation at Sand Ridge." He unconsciously tugged down his coat and cleared his throat. "I am to be the new agent there."

"You?"

"Yes, me. Why, if I may be so rude as to ask, do you apparently find that so strange?"

The attendant could only stare. "You?"

Isaiah glanced around with a hint of nervousness. "Why, yes. I happen to be the only one standing here."

The attendant tried to control it, but his chuckle became a laugh and then transformed into a rumbling roar. He crossed his arms across his bulbous stomach and gave himself over to mirth.

"I'm afraid I have missed the humor here, sir," Isaiah said, clearing his throat again. "I asked you two questions, neither of which I consider either unreasonable or humorous."

When the attendant finally brought his laughter under control, he wiped his tear-laden eyes with the back of a hand and tried to hide the grin on his face. But he had little luck; each time he risked a glance at Isaiah Rosenfeld, he chuckled.

Isaiah clutched his bag more tightly in his hand. "I've had quite enough of this, sir. I am a representative of the United States Government, and if you can't provide me with assistance, then I will find someone who can."

"Just...just a minute...Mr. Rosenfeld," the attendant managed. "It's just that every time I look at you, I see a vision of Big Mike Harbert."

"Ah, yes. Mr. Harbert. He is the man whom I have come to replace. I assume he is a cooperative and decent person?"

"Big Mike?" the attendant asked with another chuckle. "Oh, hell yes. He's gonna like being replaced, no doubt about that. You just go on over to the hotel there across the street, get your bath, and I'll send a buggy and team around from the livery for you in about an hour. Would that suit your time schedule, Mr. Rosenbloom?"

"Rosenfeld," the little man corrected him.

"Whatever. It ain't gonna matter anyway, I'm thinkin'. Be ready in one hour."

Isaiah smiled cordially and hefted his carpetbag.

"Thank you, sir. You are a gentleman."

"That's all right, friend," the attendant said as Rosenfeld walked primly down the station platform in the direction of the hotel. "Save your thanks for when you get back." He turned into the station office and said under his breath, "If you do."

eleven ─────────────

Dennis Michael Harbert sat in the white frame house of the agency and stared at the flag hanging limply from its staff in the absence of afternoon breeze. He was thinking about the ambush in the South Pass and was confident of its success. For his own purposes he had chosen to take no chance of being seen near the site, but had instructed Wokana on both the place of ambush and the intended result. The entire army command was to be annihilated, their remains hidden from view and their equipment and mounts brought to the agency under cover of darkness. Then, in an abandoned, worthless shaft in the vicinity of the would-be "glory hole," the horses would be slaughtered and any evidence of the army unit burned.

Harbert was pleased with his overall plan. If Wokana was successful, there would be no way that he or the Bannock could be linked with the disappearance of the troops. And even more satisfying, no one would know of their fate or suspect foul play for more than a month, the approximate time it would take to escort the Paiute to the Skull Valley Reservation. By that time the Paiute would be moved to the mine site, and he would tell anyone posing questions that as far as he knew, the Paiute had been transferred to another reservation, on orders from the Bureau of Indian Affairs. As a matter of fact, he would tell them, he had seen the orders personally.

The agent leaned back and crossed his boots on the desk to contemplate the only problem confronting him: Bill Mc-Cauley. He knew that McCauley and his partners were becoming impatient, and he was hoping they could restrain themselves for one more day. That would give Wokana plenty of time to return with the Paiute and transfer them to the mine. Once that was accomplished—

Harbert sat up sharply and cocked an ear toward the door. He had heard the pounding of shod hooves on the hard ground and he rose, reaching for his revolver at the same time. With careful, silent steps, he crossed the room to part the curtain only slightly and peer out. Combined relief and consternation passed over him when he saw McCauley and the others step down from their horses.

Moving quickly now, Harbert hid the gun in the top drawer of his desk and sat down with the weapon still partially in view. He had just spilled a sheaf of papers on the desktop to indicate work in progress when a sharp rapping came at the door.

"Yes? Who is it?"

"It's me. McCauley."

"Hey, Bill! You're just the man I want to see!" Harbert exclaimed cheerily, rising again and rushing to open the door. "Come on in. I was just thinking about you," he said to the big miner while extending his hand.

"Yeah? We've been thinkin' about you too," McCauley said, ignoring the proffered hand and brushing past, with his three partners following close behind.

Harbert's face reddened in response to the rebuke and the hard stares he received as they entered the room. But he recovered quickly and, managing to hide the sudden burst of anger, smiled amiably as he crossed to the closet where he kept a full bottle of whiskey for just such an occasion.

"Damn, it's good to see you lads," he said, opening the door and reaching in. "What say we have a little drink? Throats must be dry from the ride."

"Didn't come here to drink with you, Mike. Came here to get some answers."

"Come on now, Bill. We can drink and talk at the same time, can't we?" the agent asked, hurriedly popping the cork and splashing whiskey into five glasses.

"Guess a drink wouldn't hurt. In your case, it might even ease the pain."

"Pain? What pain?" Harbert asked innocently as he passed the glasses around. "Things couldn't be better, as far as I'm concerned."

"Then that's one thing we ain't got in common," McCauley observed sullenly as he raised his glass. "Where's them Paiute?"

"The Paiute? Is that what's troubling you?" Harbert asked, easing himself into his chair and pulling the desk drawer out an inch farther.

"Yeah, that's what's troublin' us, Harbert," Reno replied from where he stood beside the closed door.

The agent's glance went to the cold-eyed man who held his drink in his left hand while his right dangled within easy reach of a Colt exposed by a pulled-back duster.

Harbert leaned forward to place his glass on the desk and allow his other hand to close over the butt of his revolver. "Well, Reno, your troubles are over."

"My troubles are never over. Answer the question. Mr. McCauley here wants to know where those featherheads are, and so do I."

"They'll be here sometime after sundown tonight. My police are bringing them."

McCauley's bushy eyebrows arched in surprise. "Your police? I thought you were going to get them from that army outfit. How come you're here and they ain't?"

"Well, some minor complications arose," Harbert said, smiling.

"Don't want to hear about many more of your complications, Mike. What the hell happened this time?"

"There seemed to be some kind of simple mixup about who had authority over those Paiute, me or an army captain named Conway. At any rate, the whole matter was supposed to be straightened out over the wire, and the captain assured me that they would be released to my police once the government bullshit was cleared away. I'm sure they're on their way here right now."

McCauley watched the agent closely. "We're already behind schedule on this project, Mike, and we ain't got a whole passel of time to waste. You said two days and I gave you three. Now you're askin' me to wait again." McCauley jerked a thumb over his shoulder toward the door. "I saw a whole damned bunch of Injuns out there when we rode in. What the hell's wrong with them? They can dig rock as well as the others can."

Feeling the tension pass, Harbert withdrew his hand from the drawer and leaned back in his chair. "That's why I'm an agent and you're not, Bill. All Indians are not the same."

"What do you mean by that?" McCauley demanded, snatching the bottle and filling his glass as well as the others' before thumping the container down again. "A featherhead's a featherhead."

"Not quite. The people I am contracted to deliver to you

131

are Paiute. Those out there are Bannock."

"So?"

"There's a world of difference between them, Bill. The Paiute are shiftless digger Indians who are used to getting pushed around. They haven't got a mean bone in their bodies and we can easily force them to work for us. The Bannock, on the other hand, would fight us every step of the way. There's nothing they like better than to kill, especially white people and Paiute. We couldn't turn our backs on them for one second. And even if we did subdue them and drag them to the mine, they wouldn't lift a finger. They would rather be killed than put to work of any kind, especially the sort of thing we have in mind. No, those Bannock are out of the question and that's why I made them my police. They like to ride around on their horses and act tough, and they wouldn't stoop to roll a rock out of the way, even if they thought there was a hundred-dollar bill under it."

"Sounds like they're even more worthless than the Paiute to me," Logan said with obvious disgust.

"For our purposes, they are. Except for making damned sure the Paiute do all the work."

McCauley propped a boot on a nearby chair and turned the glass in his fingertips. "So those Bannock are worthless as tits on a boar pig. When do I get my Paiute?"

"Tomorrow morning at the latest," Harbert replied with forced confidence. "You boys just go on back to your cabin and leave everything to me. In the morning I'll—"

"Nope. Don't think we're gonna do that, Mike. I don't want you out of my sight till I see nothing but assholes and elbows in that mine back yonder. Looks like you've got company till that time, which had damned well better be tomorrow."

"Fine, Bill. That's fine. You boys are welcome—"

They all heard it at the same time, and Reno held up his hand for silence. The rattle of buckboard wheels continued for a few more seconds before being replaced by the creaking of leather springs as a passenger stepped down.

Reno opened the door a crack while drawing his revolver and pressing an eye to the light.

"Who is it, Reno?" Harbert asked in a harsh whisper.

"Don't know. Looks like some dude from back East. Funny-lookin' little feller carryin' a grip of some kind."

"Is he armed?"

"Can't see that he is."

"Good. Put your gun away and we'll find out what he wants," Harbert said, folding his fingers confidently and watching the door. "Could be he's just lost and wanting directions."

Reno closed the door and holstered his gun while moving away to stand in the rear with his back to the wall. A gentle, almost timid rapping came from the door.

"Yes? Who is it?"

A throat was cleared, then a relatively high-pitched voice said, "My name is Isaiah Rosenfeld. I wish to talk with a Dennis Michael Harbert."

A puzzled look came over Harbert's face as he tried to recall the name. Failing, he shrugged as he looked at the others. "Speaking! Come on in!"

The door opened and Isaiah stepped inside, taking his derby off with one hand and offering the other around the office. "Which of you is Mr. Harbert?"

"He is," McCauley growled, ignoring the hand and inclining his head sideways toward the desk.

"Ah, pleased to meet you, sir," Isaiah said, adjusting his glasses and stepping forward. "I've had a long journey, and this should be a welcome day for both of us."

Harbert half rose out of his chair, accepted the handshake and sank down again. "Pleased to meet you, Mr. Rosenfeld. What can I do for you?"

"It's not what you can do for me, sir," Isaiah replied, opening his briefcase on the desk. "Rather, it's what I can do for you."

The pleasant smile melted from Harbert's face as he stared at the sheaf of official documents. "What's that supposed to mean?"

"What it means, sir, is that I am here to officially relieve you of your duties."

"What?!" The word snapped from Harbert's mouth like a crack of lightning.

"Oh, please don't misunderstand, Mr. Harbert. This has nothing to do with your record of service. Mr. Warington, our mutual superior, only felt you had served in this lonely post long enough. From what I've seen traveling here, he is absolutely correct. As of this moment, you are no longer the agent here at Sand Ridge." Isaiah offered a boyish smile and added, "I am."

133

There could not have been a more complete silence than that which now spread through the room. Isaiah's head slowly swiveled from one man to the next until his gaze finally returned to Harbert.

"You are pleased, aren't you, Mr. Harbert?"

"Tickled shitless. Let me see some documentation."

Isaiah took a sheet of official stationery from the top of the pile, glanced at it briefly, then handed it across. "Of course, sir. Here it is, signed by Mr. Warington and bearing his official seal."

Harbert snatched the paper from Isaiah's hand, causing the little man to jerk back and adjust his glasses unnecessarily. A worried look crossed his face and he glanced at McCauley while Harbert read the document.

"Do you live in the area, sir?"

"Yeah."

"Excellent. We'll have to get to know each other better. What is your line of work?"

"What?"

"Ah . . . er . . . what do you do for a living?"

"Raise cow turds."

"Oh, I see. Unusual occupation."

"Yeah."

A terribly uncomfortable feeling swept through Isaiah's body and he cleared his throat again as he turned back to Harbert. "I trust you have found everything in order, sir. I had rather thought this change of administration might please you."

"Shut up," Harbert snarled, crumpling the paper angrily and tossing it over his shoulder before leaning forward to rest his massive forearms on the desktop. "You fell into the wrong nest, little fella."

Isaiah gripped his hat before him as if it might provide some protection. "I don't understand, sir. And if you don't mind my saying so, I object to your destroying Mr. Warington's personal letter. I had intended to save it as a souvenir for my children."

"You ain't gonna have no children."

Isaiah offered a weak, apologetic smile. "Well, not right away."

"Never."

"Marriage, of course, comes first," Isaiah muttered with a nervous smile. "And finding the proper mate isn't always a simple task."

134

"Neither is taking over this agency."

"Sir, this is not a takeover, let me emphasize that. It is a legal transfer of positions, and I hope this transition can be both expeditious and cordial." Isaiah reached into his briefcase with one hand and produced a packet of folded papers. "Now here are some documents for you to sign, which I will witness, and—"

Harbert's hand came out of the drawer and he cocked the Colt as his hand rested again on the desk. "There is only one thing you're going to witness, friend, and that's the workin' end of this gun."

Isaiah's hands clutched the hat again, which he jerked up to his chest. Instinctively he lurched backward and his glasses slipped down on the bridge of his nose.

"What is the meaning of this, Mr. Harbert?" he asked, failing to control the twitch at the corner of his mouth while his eyes widened at sight of the gun. "I am an agent of the United States Government and you are legally bound—"

Harbert's finger closed on the trigger and the booming explosion rattled the room while the gun bucked in his hand. The bullet pierced through the center of Isaiah's derby hat, smashed into his chest and spewed flesh, blood and bits of bone out the hole in his back. The frail agent was lifted off his feet and slammed against the wall. He slid slowly downward, his glasses dangling from one ear. His eyes remained open and he sat on the floor with legs extended before him, like a common drunk propped against a wall.

Without the slightest hint of emotion, Harbert returned the gun to the drawer, then looked up at McCauley. "That's one minor complication I won't have to explain to you."

The dead man was of no more concern to the four partners in front of the desk than an overturned chair. "Good riddance," McCauley said, sipping his whiskey. "He would have been even a worse agent than you are, Mike. How you gonna explain his sudden departure?"

"I'm not. I'll have one of my Indians take his buckboard back to town so old Harry at the livery doesn't get suspicious. Those Bannock can't read English anyway, so I'll send a message along with him to take to the telegraph office and have wired to Warington. I'll sign his name and say that I arrived safely and that everything is fine and in order." Harbert grinned and added, "I'll also mention that Mr. Harbert gracefully accepted his request for resignation and has departed the agency."

"You're a cold bastard, Mike. I like that, but I don't like all these loose ends popping up."

"What loose ends?" Harbert asked, showing his palms in innocence. "Even though we're a few days off schedule, we're still right on track. I'll get somebody to drag that fucking idiot out of here and bury him, then we'll have another drink and wait for Wokana. He should be here in a few hours."

"No, he *shouldn't* be here in a few hours," McCauley corrected with narrowing eyes. "He'd *better* be here in a few hours."

"However you want to say it, Bill. Excuse me a second while I get rid of that thing over there. Have a seat at my desk and help yourself to a drink."

It was nearly eight o'clock when Wokana and the other Bannock turned their weary mounts in before the agency's main building. McCauley had declined a seat behind Harbert's desk, and now the agent rose and walked quickly to the door.

"See? I told you he'd be back tonight," Harbert said with a satisfied smile. "I'll go out and make sure everything's all right."

"Go ahead," McCauley replied. "I've waited this long, I can wait a little longer."

After Harbert stepped out the door, the big miner looked at Reno and inclined his head toward the window. Reno nodded, stepped to the window and opened it a crack before stooping to hear what was being said outside.

Harbert stood just beyond the front door, his hands on his hips, and watched Wokana slip from his pony's back. In the brilliant moonlight he could see that his police had returned alone, and fury flared in his mind.

"Where the hell are they?!" he raged as Wokana drew near.

"We didn't get them, Mr. Boss. They went away in the Iron Horse."

"What the hell do you mean by that? They bought tickets to Chicago?!"

"Wokana not know Chicago," the Bannock replied, making sure to stay several feet away from the agent. He searched his mind for something that might please Harbert and added, "We kill many Blue Sleeves."

"Did you kill all of them?"

"No. They go away in Iron Horse too."

"You simpering idiot!" Harbert screamed. "What's this shit about the Iron Horse?"

Wokana explained how the ambush had gone, that he had lost five warriors and killed as many as ten army troops. He told of the arrival of the train, the flanking maneuver by the two squads from above, and how they would have accomplished their mission if it hadn't been for the trick played on them by the lieutenant. He concluded by saying, "The Paiute have a long way to walk. We have much time to get them."

Uncontrollable anger and frustration swept over Harbert and he lunged forward to knock the Indian down with a backward lash of his fist.

"Time is the one thing I haven't got, damn you!" Harbert bellowed as Wokana sprawled onto his back in the dust. "This is the second time you've failed me and the second time you've let Red Hand and his tribe get away! I should kill you right where you lay, damn your red hide!"

Wokana rolled away an instant before Harbert's heavy boot sailed past where his head had been and he scrambled to his feet. "Wokana get him for you, Mr. Boss," the Indian said, crouching with legs braced apart as he backed away. "Wokana get him for you tomorrow."

"You damned well better!" Harbert said, glaring at the Bannock and shaking his fist in the air before turning away and walking toward the office. "I want you in front of my desk at dawn tomorrow morning."

"Yes, Mr. Boss."

After the door closed behind the agent, Wokana shook his fist in a similar manner and said, *"Kah Saltu!"*

Reno stepped away from the window when he saw Harbert approaching, and quickly filled McCauley in on what he had heard. "They didn't get the Paiute. They killed ten soldiers and Harbert is sending him after the Paiute in the morning."

McCauley nodded and the movement of his shaggy head resembled a bear sniffing the breeze while his eyes locked on the door like the same animal finding a scent.

"Well, they didn't get 'em," Harbert growled as he stomped toward his desk. "Ignorant sonsabitches anyway!"

"I'm beginning to wonder who's ignorant around here, Mike, them or us."

Harbert spun, glaring, while his hand moved inside the top

drawer again. "What's that supposed to mean?"

Reno's hand dropped instantly to the butt of his revolver "Get your hand out of that drawer, Harbert!"

Harbert smiled disarmingly while slowly placing both hands on the desktop and leaning forward. "Is that better, Reno?"

"Yeah. Keep it that way."

McCauley concentrated on pouring the last of the whiskey into his glass and spoke at the same time. "What's that supposed to mean, Mike? I'll tell you. Reno heard your conversation with your little featherhead friend out there. If getting those Paiute back was simply a matter of sending a few telegrams, why'd they have to kill ten soldiers in the process and still show up empty-handed?"

"Well, Bill, maybe I didn't tell you everything exactly the way it happened."

"Is that the same thing as lying to me?"

"Not exactly. I just didn't want to cause you unnecessary worry, that's all."

Now McCauley glanced up from his pouring. "I *am* worried, Mike. Damned worried. And you should be too."

"I'll get those Paiute, just like I promised. Don't worry, I'll get 'em tomorrow or the next day."

"We're runnin' out of tomorrows and next days. In fact, we're runnin' out of *nows*. I want the gold out of that mine and I want it out quick. You've got a whole bunch of our money that's supposed to pay for that little chore. I've got a mind to let old Reno there blow a hole in your guts right now."

The agent gave no show of emotion. "What's that going to accomplish, Bill? Sure, I've got your money, but I've also got it hidden where you and no one else can ever find it. With me dead, you're out both your investment and those Paiute to pull this thing off."

"The pleasure might be worth the loss," McCauley mumbled, taking a drink to buy time for thought. "Besides that, you're in up past your ass with the federal government on a hangin' charge for your police killin' those soldiers. I ain't hankerin' to get myself in the same fix."

"You already are, Bill," Harbert said softly.

"Like hell I am!"

"Like hell you're not. You don't think I'd be fool enough to deal with you people without some protection, do you? I've got a letter on deposit with a certain banker, to be opened only on my death. He thinks it's a will, but I know otherwise. In that letter I detailed this whole operation, and just yesterday I amended it to include what I thought would be the deaths of two platoons of United States Army. You and the others are in this thing as deep as I am, like it or not."

"You son of a bitch! I should kill you myself!"

"Fine, go ahead. But if you do, you're putting a noose around your own neck. You have no way out but to give me time to take back those Paiute. You said you weren't going to let me out of your sight until I turned them over to you," Harbert concluded with a wan smile. "If that's the case, it looks like you'll be riding with us when we go."

"Us? Who's us?"

"Me, my Bannock police and every other damned Indian we can find who loves to shoot Paiute. Tomorrow morning I'm going to send Wokana to bring back the biggest goddamned war party you've ever seen. There are only two platoons of mounted infantry escorting those Paiute over two hundred miles of open plains. We can wipe them out with little effort, and no one will be the wiser. You'll have the bodies to work your mine and all of us will quit this goddamned stinkhole rich men."

Harbert paused for effect. "Or you can shoot me now and we'll all be dead men before two months are out. Your choice."

"I say shoot the son of a bitch!" Reno snarled, flexing the fingers of his gun hand.

"I think he's got us by the short hairs, Bill," Logan threw in with a disgusted glance at Harbert.

Jenkins stepped forward and glanced at all five men. "I don't like this any more than you fellers do, but Logan's right. We've come too damned far to quit now. We'd better play along with Harbert for the time being."

McCauley sucked in a deep breath and exhaled slowly while turning toward the agent. "Looks like we gotta go along with you, Mike. But if anything else goes wrong I'm gonna shoot you myself and damn the consequences."

"Nothing else is going to go wrong, Bill," Harbert replied, grinning as he retrieved another bottle of whiskey from the cabinet. "Trust me. I know what I'm doing."

"I trust you as far as I can throw a pair of plow mules,

Harbert," McCauley replied, holding his glass out for a refill. "and I ain't thrown one out of sight yet."

Harbert laughed. "We've gone beyond a mere question of trust, my friend. Now it's a matter of mutual survival."

He raised his glass and extended it in a toast. "To your health, gentlemen."

twelve ═══════════

With the Rocky Mountains looming majestically behind them, the Paiute, shielded on either side and to the rear by the two platoons from Easy Company, worked their way slowly across the rolling prairie swells. Tawny grass, often lush, other times sparse and scattered, provided the image of a green carpet stretching before them in seemingly endless undulations to the horizon and beyond.

Perhaps it was the monotony of the landscape, or the constant marching from sunup until sundown, but the Paiute seemed to be losing interest in their journey, with the exception of Red Hand, who walked erect at the head of the ragged formation. Often he would fall back and offer words of encouragement to his people, exhorting them to continue the march to that "great land of our fathers where the sun always shines and the pinyon trees grow."

He was returning from one such effort, trotting now to regain his place at the head of the caravan, while Matt Kincaid and Windy Mandalian watched him from their position in front and to the left of the strange pilgrimage.

"He's a man cut out of whole cloth, ain't he, Matt?" Windy asked.

"That he is, Windy. That he is. Strange how his tribe has such a reputation for slovenliness while Red Hand, if he were mounted, could easily be the chief of any of the most proud, warlike and noble tribes we've ever encountered."

"Yup. He reminds me of a man I used to know, old Judd Hawkins. He wasn't big, didn't talk much and usually drank alone when he was in a saloon, which wasn't often. Every time, almost like it was an unwritten law or somethin', some damned fool would think that because he kept to himself, he was yellow. Old Judd used to say, 'If they push me once, shame on them. If they push me twice, shame on me.'"

Windy chuckled and spat contentedly. "Yeah, that's what he used to say. And that's the way he felt deep down. I never yet saw a man get in that second shove."

Matt nodded his agreement. "I've never seen a quiet man yet that didn't have the hide of a lamb and the heart of a grizzly bear."

"Yeah. Maybe he'll get a chance to prove that to that bastard Wokana before this parade is over."

"Speaking of Wokana, do you think he's given up the fight? We're five days out from South Pass City now, and haven't seen hide nor hair of him."

Windy squinted, rose up on his stirrups and searched the surrounding prairie before offering a reply. "Don't think so, Matt. Whoever's behind this whole thing, and that's gotta be Harbert, wants those Paiute awful bad. Can't figure out why quite yet, but it sure as hell ain't to make sure they eat their morning porridge. They'll be back, I ain't real positive just when, but I'd make it damned soon."

"Sure, Harbert's a prize asshole," Kincaid said, shaking his head, "but I can't understand why he would go to such lengths to keep these people on his reservation."

"Like I said, I ain't got that figured out either. Workin' on it, though."

"He's in the shit up past his neck now. We suffered three dead and four wounded in that last ambush. I wired the captain from South Pass City, and he'll send an escort out to bring them back to the post, but he isn't going to settle for a maybe answer when we get back. Harbert and his Bannock will be hunted down, and killed if necessary, to put an end to this goddamned mess."

"'Course he will. Hope we have a hand in it. The cap'n don't take lightly to dead men, particularly when they're on his company's payroll." Windy paused to study the angle of the sun. "We've got less than an hour till dark. What say I take a little sashay over to them hills yonder. Should be about where we'll lay it down for the night, and it wouldn't hurt to make sure we're the only ones spreadin' a bedroll there."

"Sure, go ahead, Windy. That's where we'll make camp. Those Paiute, especially the older ones, seem to be playing out a bit. Couldn't make it much farther than that anyway."

"One foot in front of the other, that's the Indians' motto,

Matt. Never count 'em out till the countin's done. See ya in an hour or so."

Riding in a southerly direction, the scout's shadow stretched long to his left, with the sun nearing the horizon, as he slowed his big roan and approached the intertwined humps of ground that passed for hills on those northern plains.

Call it an inexplicable sixth sense, a premonition heeded, or just the uncanny wariness of a man who had survived so long by his wits; whatever it was, there was something about the area that triggered a precautionary signal in Windy Mandalian's mind. He turned the horse to the right, skirting the broken ground and staying just out of rifle range while maintaining open ground between himself and the platoons to the rear.

Four sets of eyes watched the scout angle westward, his horse walking slowly while he studied the earth below.

"We take him now," Wokana whispered to the man beside him.

"No!" Harbert snapped, conscious of the need for secrecy. "We could never cut him off, and that would alert the others."

Wokana fell silent and watched Windy with hate-filled eyes. The scout pulled his horse in abruptly, leaned down, and studied something that had caught his attention. Then, after a cautious sweep of his eyes in all directions, he stepped down to run his fingers through the grass. After nearly a minute of close scrutiny, he rose, glanced sharply at the low hills, then swung onto his horse's back and galloped away in the direction from which he had come.

Kincaid watched the scout angling toward them. From the way he rode, Matt knew Windy had found something. He urged his horse to a canter and met Windy some fifty yards in front of the remainder of the group.

"What have you got, Windy?"

"Nothin' you could hold in your hand, Matt. I think we'd better steer clear of them hills, though."

"Did you pick up some sign?"

"Yeah. The tracks of four horses, three bone and one iron. Real fresh, like maybe an hour or so ago."

Kincaid studied the hills in the settling twilight. "Think it's Harbert and some of his police?"

"Hell, I don't know. Could be some damned buff hunter

and his guides for all I know. Then, it could be Harbert and his Bannock."

"Try a hunch."

"The second guess."

"Me too," Matt replied, reining his horse around. "Think they'll hit us tonight?"

"Yup."

"Lieutenant Dalby!"

"Yessir?" Dalby responded, riding forward.

"Veer to the west maybe a quarter-mile, then set up camp. Try to find a depression or draw of some kind so we can't be hit by long-range fire. Post double guards tonight and tell them to be extra alert. Have the cooks prepare a hasty meal, and then I want all fires out."

"Why the extra precautions, sir?"

"For the same reason you don't lift a skunk's tail to find out if it's a stud, son," Windy threw in laconically.

Kincaid grinned slightly. "We have sufficient reason to believe that the Bannock have caught up with us again. We'll follow that same procedure every night the rest of the way. Now get on with it, Lieutenant. It'll be dark soon."

"Yessir!"

Harbert had been watching the brief meeting, and he saw the columns turn right and finally vanish into a draw. "Bastard must have picked up our tracks," he said softly, concentrating now on Kincaid and Windy, who had not yet moved.

"Will we attack tonight, Mr. Boss?" Wokana asked.

"No, but we're not going to let them get much sleep, either. How many warriors have we got now?"

"Forty Bannock and thirty Shoshone."

"Good. Are there any more coming?"

"We told everybody that we will kill Paiute, just like in the Grandfather Times. More will come."

"Excellent. We'll play it this way until we have enough guns to take them in an all-out attack. Split your warriors into two groups. When it's dark tonight, have those groups separate into twos and threes and circle that camp over there. Have them alternate shots, firing just enough to draw return fire. In four hours the second group will replace the first. We'll keep that up all night, and I'll guarantee you there'll be a red-eyed bunch of Paiute in the morning. The less rest they get, the slower they'll go and give us more time to gather strength." Harbert smiled at the cleverness of his plan. "Them soldier boys won't be so hot in a fight, either, if they haven't slept for a few days."

"You think good, Mr. Boss."

"I don't need any compliments from you, Wokana. If you'd done your job right the first time, I wouldn't be crawlin' around here on my belly like a damned snake right now. Get to your ponies and get on with what has to be done."

Wokana's jaw tightened and he stared at the agent for several seconds before rising into a crouched position and trotting away. Even though he had been trained to show no emotion, there was nothing his father had taught him regarding control of his inner feelings. Those inner feelings were now concentrated on his hatred for Paiutes, Red Hand in particular, and on his hatred for white men in general, with Harbert rapidly becoming the focal point of that sentiment.

"You think good, Mr. Boss," he grunted as he swung onto his pony's back and jerked its head around with the hackamore in his hand. "Wokana thinks good too. You will find that out after we get Red Hand." He thought again about the agent's threat of taking Dark Star away from him, and the blood pounded in his temples. "She will be mine, *Saltu*," he said through gritted teeth as he lashed his pony's flanks with moccasined heels. "For her I will kill you."

It was nearing nine o'clock when the first shot rang out, followed by scattered fire erupting in the darkness. The army guards at their posts returned the fire and the night was filled with orange bursts of flame. After a few minutes the firing from the outer ring died, and an uneasy calm settled over the plains. Nearly half an hour later, the same pattern began again: one shot, followed by staccato blasts from the other rifles, which continued for several minutes until all firing stopped.

"What do you make of it, Windy?" Kincaid asked, lying beside the scout on the lee side of the depression. "Surely they wouldn't be stupid enough to try an attack on our positions tonight."

Windy, immersed in thought, chewed a blade of grass in silence. Then he said, "Don't reckon that's what they've got in mind, Matt. From the way things look, they just want to keep us jittery, and they'll consider themselves lucky if they pick somebody off."

"That's pretty much the way I see it. They're firing just often enough to keep us on our toes, but not enough to cover an assault."

"I'd guess their plan is to try and wear us down. Keep those Paiute awake all night and then watch them walk all day tomorrow."

Kincaid turned on one side to look down at the mass of people huddled together in the draw. "The lambs surrounded by wolves," he said quietly. "Ever heard of an Englishman named Chaucer, Windy?"

"Nope. Knew a feller named Howzer. Trapped beaver with him up in the Wind River country a few years back."

Kincaid chuckled in the darkness. "Not the same person. Chaucer was a writer, and I read some of his stuff in school. One of the things he said was, 'The shepherd is weak when the wolf shits wool.'"

"Catchy little number, all right," Windy commented dryly, forsaking the blade of grass for a chew of tobacco. "Man could never forget somethin' as brilliant as that."

"You've got a fine taste for literature, Windy."

"Me and books never been real close," the scout replied, squinting into the darkness. "Saw a feller prop a door open with one, one time. Seemed like the best job for it. Did purty good, too."

"You old bastard," Kincaid muttered, turning again onto his stomach. "Anyway, I never really thought much about that saying until now. Those are the sheep behind us, we're the shepherds, and the wolves are out there."

Windy raised his head slightly to spit, then lowered it again. "I might've figured that out on my own, Matt. 'Cept the wolves you're talkin' about are a little more interested in shittin' feathers than wool."

"I don't intend to allow them the pleasure of either. What was that, about half an hour between volleys?"

"About that."

"Let's wait and see what happens in the next half-hour."

Twenty-five minutes later the pattern was repeated a third time, and when the firing died, Kincaid nudged Windy's ribs. "Right on schedule. Good. I'm going down to talk to Red Hand. You sneak out to all our guard posts and tell our people to fire at, but just below, those muzzle flashes. A bullet tends to rise when it leaves the barrel, and I think we're shooting over their heads. They should pretty well have them pinpointed by now, and even if we don't hit anybody, we should throw a little dirt in their faces."

Windy crawled forward with the Sharps cradled in his elbows. "You might have to fill me in a little bit on who some of them English fellers are, Matt," he said, slithering through the grass, "but I don't need a hell of a lot of help when it comes to bullets. See ya in a while."

Kincaid waited until the scout was gone before moving to the bottom of the swale in a hunched-over trot. "Red Hand?" he said to the mass of people huddled there. "Where's Red Hand?"

"Here, Lieutenant," a tall, dark figure replied, stepping forward.

"How are your people doing?"

"They don't like the dark. They wish for the light of the sun. They think we will be killed tonight."

"I agree with them on the first two, but not on the third one. They'll see another sunrise. The Bannock are just trying to keep them from resting, but I'm pretty sure they won't attack. If they do, it will be mass suicide. Tell your people to lie down and rest, to sleep if they can. They need their rest for tomorrow. They will hear firing at spaced intervals, but they should get used to that. I think they'll be hearing a lot of this sort of thing before we get to Skull Valley."

"I will tell them."

"Also, Red Hand, you've got approximately forty armed braves. Have those without weapons sleep in the center and the armed ones sleep on the outside, in a sort of circle around the others. It's just a precautionary thing in case Wokana's warriors do attack, get lucky and break through."

"I will."

"Fine. Get as much sleep as you can," Kincaid said, turning away.

"Lieutenant?"

Kincaid stopped. "Yes?"

"I have not told you this because Dark Star asked me not to."

Kincaid moved closer again. "What is it, Red Hand?"

The Paiute hesitated, undecided, then said, "You know of what Wokana did to her?"

"I do."

147

"She has been bleeding from her woman place, and now she gets weaker with every rising sun."

"How long has that been going on?"

"Since the day we left the reservation."

"Oh Christ," Kincaid said, almost under his breath. "If I'd known that when we were at the post, Maggie and Mrs. Conway would have been able to help. They'd know what to do."

"I did not understand, Lieutenant."

"Do you . . . do you want me to take . . . a look at her?"

"No. Dark Star would say no. But she cannot walk much farther."

"Of course not," Kincaid said, feeling a bond growing between himself and the Paiute. "She'll ride in one of the wagons. How badly is she bleeding?"

"It gets worse. The Dream Singer has talked with the gods. She will die."

"No she won't. I'm not saying your friend is wrong, but then again, I think he's proven he's not always right either. We'll make a bed for her in the back of the wagon. Maybe if she doesn't move much, the injury will heal itself. To tell you the truth, I don't know a damned thing about that kind of stuff, but we'll get her through somehow."

"We have far to go, Lieutenant."

"And we'll get there. Maybe we can find some help for Dark Star along the way. For right now, though, I've got some disinfectant in our medical kit, along with some clean bandages. I'll give them to you, show you how to use them, and maybe we can keep things from getting worse. She can administer them to herself without any embarrassment."

Kincaid could read the hesitation on Red Hand's face, and he remembered the death of Standing Crane. "Our medicine did not kill your brother, Red Hand. A bullet did. I'm asking you to trust me and let me try and help you to save Dark Star's life."

The fourth volley of weapons fire shattered the stillness, and lead snapped and sizzled over their heads. Neither Red Hand nor Kincaid ducked, and Matt studied the resigned look on the Paiute's face.

"They are a different kind of people from you and me, Red Hand. They know only death, killing and destruction. They don't know compassion and have no feeling for their fellow man. I'm sure as hell not asking you to forgive them, because

148

I don't, either. I'm just asking you to understand that we are different. And we will never change, just as they won't."

"It has been this way since I was a boy. We wish only to live in peace in a land where we can survive," Red Hand said, his tone almost wistful. "No one, white or Indian, will give us that chance. I have failed my people. They follow me because they think I will lead them to a place where we can live without fear, but I know we will never find that place."

"Just hang on a few days longer," Kincaid said, touching Red Hand's arm for the first time without the Indian pulling away. "Just hang on. You are a great leader of your people, and they have no choice but to trust you. I pray to God that when we get to Skull Valley, things will be different for all of you. And I damned well plan to see that you get there."

The Paiute smiled tiredly. "Things will never be different, but we have no other way than to trust you."

"Does that mean you'll give the disinfectant to Dark Star?"

"Yes. That is what it means."

"Good," Kincaid replied, turning away again. "Wait here, I'll be right back."

For all of Kincaid's entreaties, the Paiute obviously were not adjusting to being constantly under fire every night, and judging from their increasingly weary trek across the plains, sleep had been the exception instead of the rule. Even though they continued to put forth their best effort, it became necessary for the Indians to rest more each day, decreasing the number of miles covered and lowering a pall of depression over them.

On the afternoon of the fourth day after Dark Star had been confined to the wagon, Kincaid fell back to turn his horse in beside the rocking, jolting conveyance and look at the young Paiute woman. Her eyes were closed like those of a nesting dove, and her long black lashes resembled those of a princess resting comfortably on a feather bed.

"How are you feeling, Dark Star?" Kincaid asked, just loudly enough to be heard over the rattling of the wagon.

Dark Star's eyelids fluttered and she opened them to look up at the officer, bathed in strong sunlight. She lay upon a cushion of blankets, beneath which was a bed of tawny grass that had been prepared for her by the Paiute. But there was a pallor about her face.

"I am fine, Lieutenant. Thank you."

"Is there anything I can get for you? Water, perhaps?"

Dark Star smiled weakly and shook her head. "No thank you. I am not thirsty."

"Have you eaten anything?" Kincaid asked, reining his prancing horse in to stay in pace with the wagon.

"No. I do not feel hunger."

"Has the bleeding stopped at all?" The question embarrassed him and he cleared his throat. "I don't mean to pry, but I have to know."

Dark Star watched him with emotionless, ebony eyes. "It has stayed the same. It could be worse."

"I'm sorry. Look, we'll be in Mormon country in about four days, maybe five. There are women there who know about these things, and we should be able to get you some help. Can you hang on that long?"

"Hang on, Lieutenant?" she asked, not understanding the term.

"I mean, can you make it? Four or five more days?"

Dark Star closed her eyes and smiled patiently. "The gods have called for me. I will go when they speak again."

Dammit, Kincaid thought. *We've got to step up the pace if she is going to have any chance at all.* He watched Dark Star a few moments longer before lifting his reins and riding again to the head of the column. The young Indian woman didn't appear to notice his departure, and Matt wondered if she had merely gone to sleep or if she had lapsed into a coma.

"Windy," he said, catching up with the scout and riding alongside, "we've got to do something. We're losing more ground every day, and those people back there are getting damned tired. Hell, they haven't had a decent night's sleep since Wokana caught up with us, and I don't know how much longer they can go on. Dark Star's looking pretty bad, and the slower we go, the less chance she has of making it."

"I've been studying on that, Matt," Windy replied, "but I ain't come up with any answers yet."

"Neither have I. But do you remember when I requisitioned that case of dynamite from Dugan back at South Pass City?"

"Yup. I've been thinkin' about that too. From the way old Dugan acted, you'd think he'd lost about a ten-mile stretch of track."

"To hell with him."

150

"Don't think they'd let him in. Know anything about dynamite?"

"Not much, but Sergeant Olsen does. When I took that stuff, I didn't really know what I'd use it for, but I thought I might need another ace along the way somewhere. Before I get into that, though, why, in your opinion, haven't the Bannock attacked us in daylight? Do you think they know about the Gatling?"

Windy adjusted the Sharps in the crook of his arm and looked across at Kincaid. "Don't reckon they do. Seems to me like they must be waitin' for something. Reinforcements, maybe. When I backtracked this morning and crossed their trail, I made 'em out to be about sixty, maybe seventy strong. Counting the Paiute, we're about equal in number as far as rifles go, and we're in wide open country, so they'd have a tough time takin' us on face to face. My guess is they're wantin' a little bigger advantage than they've got before they bring this thing out into the open."

"Well, we've got to do something before then." Kincaid turned his horse to cross a dry wash and reined in beside Windy once again. "Every night for the last four in a row, they've used the same tactics. Think they'll do the same tonight?"

"Yup. Not much else they can do. Whatcha got in mind?"

"It may be desperation, but we've got to do something to take the offensive away from them. I want you to ride ahead and find us someplace to camp tonight—something like we've used in the past, but someplace where we arrive right at dark. Can you do that?"

Windy dug the moist wad of tobacco from his jaw and cast it aside. "If it's there, I'll find it. If it ain't, you'll be the first to know."

"That's reassuring as hell, you know that?"

"Didn't come along to be the padre, Matt."

"You insufferable old bastard," Kincaid said with a grin before sobering again. "Leave about an hour and a half before sunset. Take two squads with you for protection."

"Don't need no protection, Matt."

"Take them anyway. I can't afford to lose you. I'm going to parcel the dynamite into packets and...hell, I don't even know what I'm talking about." Kincaid turned in the saddle and looked back toward his command. "Sergeant Olsen? Front and center!"

151

Windy chuckled as he wiped his mouth with the back of a hand. "Sounds like a hell of a plan, Matt. 'I'm gonna parcel the dynamite into packets and Sergeant Olsen front and center.' Those Bannock would be crazy to go up against a stacked deck like that."

"I told you I didn't know anything about dynamite."

"You called for me, sir?" the battle-scarred veteran asked when his horse came even with Kincaid's.

"Yes I did, Sergeant. You know something about dynamite, don't you?"

"Yup. I got farmed out to the Corps of Engineers for one hitch, sir."

"I thought you had. How's it work?"

"Fuse, cap and match. Pretty simple."

"How fast does the fuse burn?"

"Three feet a minute, sir, if it's the right kind of fuse."

"Let's hope I've got the right kind. I want several big blasts. How many sticks would that take?"

Olsen pursed his lips in momentary thought. "Four sticks will give you a pretty big hole in the ground, Lieutenant."

"That's what I want. Rig up the packets and load them on a packhorse, then—"

"Beggin' your pardon, sir. You never keep dynamite and caps in the same place. I'll carry the caps in my saddlebags and the dynamite can stay with the packhorse." The sergeant allowed a gap-toothed grin. "I'd like to live long enough to decide whether or not I want to reenlist again, sir."

"I'm all for that, Sergeant. Do it however you want to, but we'll need at least ten packets with varying lengths of fuse. How much fuse have we got?"

"More fuse than dynamite, sir."

"Great. I finally did something right. Can you rig those packets so one fuse will set them off in succession?"

"No problem, Lieutenant."

"Good. Now, as we all have noticed, the Bannock have been setting themselves up about one hundred and fifty yards from our bivouac area. I want you to bury those packets—" Kincaid hesitated. "Will that fuse burn underground?"

"Sure will. Even underwater."

"Forget the water. Bury the packets within that range and connect the entire damned mess to one fuse and bury or hide that too, if you can. Leave enough fuse sticking out so I can find it tonight."

Windy turned away and spat, then turned back and said, "Hell, you ain't gonna find nothin', Matt. I'm the one who does the findin' around here."

"Not this time, Windy. It's my harebrained scheme. Might as well be my harebrained ass that blows up with it."

"We're partners, ain't we, Matt?" Windy asked, squinting across at the commanding officer.

"Always have been. Why?"

"Thought so, and I'd kind of like to keep it that way. I'll know where Olsen hides the fuse, and it'll be a hell of a lot easier for me to find it in the dark than you. Hate to pull brain rank on ya, Matt, but I'm gonna have to. You're needed around here a damned site more'n I am. If brains was a chicken's ass, I couldn't pucker up one damned egg."

"Windy, your tobacco chewing is a bad enough habit. Don't take up lying to go along with it," Kincaid said, smiling. "But you win. We'll go together."

"Sir, I'll volunteer—"

"Thanks, but no thanks, Sergeant. I need you to make sure Dalby doesn't fuck up again if something happens to me. Besides, I've never touched a match to that stuff before. Should be a real pretty sight in the dark."

Olsen turned his horse away, saying, "It is, Lieutenant. As long as you don't get too close a look at it. I'll go back to the supply wagon and get things prepared."

"Thank you, Sergeant. Let us know when you're ready."

"Right, sir."

They rode in silence for nearly a full minute before Windy looked at Kincaid again.

"Tell me somethin', Matt."

"Sure. What's on your mind?"

"First the train and now the dynamite. How the hell do you come up with damfool ideas like that?"

Kincaid grinned openly now. "There are brave men, stupid men and desperate men, Windy. I'd have to put myself in that last category right now."

"Sounds to me like the first two are one and the same, Matt. But the last one, now I kind of like that." Mandalian scratched the back of his head as if trying to remember. "On the whole, though, it sounds like somethin' old Hawzer might have said when that grizzly chased him into the middle of the creek back in the Wind River country. Damned near froze his balls off, but kept his bacon out of the fire."

Matt threw his head back and laughed. "What do you think Chaucer would have said?"

"Chaucer? Can't rightly remember him, but I might have met him up in Canada one time. I think a skunk had him stumped, and..."

thirteen _____

Matt Kincaid lay beside Windy Mandalian in a shallow, dry creekbed that fed into a wide depression that might have been a winter lake at one time. Behind them, the Paiute were clustered in a group toward the center of the low ground, with the guards of Easy Company posted around the perimeter. Brilliant moonlight bathed the land, but there were alternating periods of complete darkness as huge clouds drifted across the sky, riding southward on the prevailing north wind.

Windy was watching one such cloud now as it drifted toward the silver sphere that dominated the night sky, while Kincaid rolled onto one side to check his pocket watch.

"Just about nine o'clock, Windy," Matt said, closing the watch with a muffled click and shoving it into his pocket again. "Should start up any minute if they're going to follow the same pattern."

Windy's attention remained with the cloud. "They will. Should be just about right, too. That big old cloud up there'll cross the moon in less than two minutes."

"You say the fuse is buried along this creekbed?"

"Yeah. That's why I chose it. The Bannock will want to fire from the highest ground they can find, so we shouldn't have any surprises right in front of us. The fuses are about a hundred and fifty yards away, one on my side and one on yours. Sure you've got the matches?"

"Yes, I have them. We'll go just as soon as—"

Kincaid's words were cut off by the first shot, which was then followed by an encircling volley of fire. Muzzle blasts winked in the darkness.

Windy watched the cloud sweep across the sky, and he pressed one hand against Matt's arm until blackness engulfed them as if a lamp had suddenly gone out.

"Now, Matt. We've got about five minutes, no more. Let's go."

Kincaid immediately squirmed forward with a pistol in either hand, and Windy followed close behind with his revolver drawn but not cocked. They could hear the army weapons firing behind them and could tell from the placement of Bannock positions that one group was no more than fifty yards from the creekbed, off to the right, with another group seventy-five yards away to the left.

The booming crack of rifles grew louder the farther they crawled, and both men were secretly happy about the Indians' preoccupation with laying down a field of fire on the depression. Their shots obliterated the clatter of dislodged stones as Matt and Windy scrambled hurriedly along the ditch.

"There. Just in front of you, Matt," Windy whispered. "Right by that big rock on the bank."

"I see it," Matt replied, snatching the wooden matches from a breast pocket. "Here." He passed several back as he spoke. "We'll light 'em both at the same time."

The first match broke in Kincaid's hand as he scratched it against the stone, and he hurriedly produced another. The second one broke as well, but he could smell the sulfur and see the sheltered light of the match in Windy's hand, and he held out the third match.

"Touch yours to this one, Windy. All I'm getting out of mine is kindling."

The third match flared instantly, and simultaneously both men touched flame to fuse. There was a hesitation, a splutter, and then the sizzling crackle of powder spewing sparks and inching along the fuse on a trail of whitish blue flame and smoke. Suddenly the firing from the Bannock positions stopped completely, and there was no mistaking the alien sound of burning fuse.

"How far away is the first one, Windy?" Kincaid asked, pressing his body against the shallow ditch.

"Fifty yards. One on each side."

Kincaid did some swift calculating. "Hell, at three feet a minute, it's going to take at least five minutes for those things to go off."

"Yup. Could be a long five minutes."

They could hear excited chatter coming from Indians on

either side, and after two minutes the first testing shots slammed into the creek banks.

"I think they've got us figured, Windy. They'll be on us before the first one blows."

"Yeah, probably will. That's why I brought these along," Windy replied calmly as he reached into his coat. "Light another match, will you, Matt?"

Slightly confused, Kincaid struck another match and Windy touched two single sticks of dynamite to the flame. "There's only about three inches of fuse on these, so we'd better get rid of 'em damned quick. Here." Windy pressed one stick into Kincaid's hand. "This one's yours."

Hearing the Indians crawling cautiously toward them on either side, they held the dynamite until there was no more than an inch of fuse showing, before lobbing them out of the ditch with looping tosses. Then both men rolled onto their stomachs and covered their heads with their hands.

No more than ten seconds passed before twin explosions ripped the night sky with dirt, pebbles and tiny rocks cascading down over the creekbed. Screams and startled yells filled the air. Drawing his pistols, Kincaid turned around to fire. The trailing edge of the cloud slithered beyond the moon, and the prairie was again flooded with an ethereal light. He could see several braves staggering to their feet to rush forward, and he fired four times and saw three of them fall. Windy's revolver was barking its deadly commands behind him, and Kincaid took careful aim on the fourth warrior and dropped him cleanly with his next shot.

Then a massive explosion shook the ground with an ear-splitting blast, and there was a brief flash of yellow fire. The second charge went off instants later. Windy watched the Indians who had left their position to crawl directly over the charge as they were thrown into the air in twisting, broken fragments. Dazed, one survivor lurched to his feet and raised his rifle to fire, but a bullet from the scout's gun ripped into his forehead and he flopped over backward. The third and fourth charges went off in rapid succession, and Kincaid could see in the angry flashes of light that the Bannock were fleeing toward the security of the darkness beyond.

"I think we've bought enough time to get back to the command, Windy," Kincaid said, rising to a crouched position and turning away. "Let's get the hell out of here."

Windy fired one last shot at a brave streaking past a bush that had been set afire by the blasts, and watched him sommersault to his death.

"We're just startin' to have a good time, Matt," Windy replied, searching in the darkness for another target. "Hate to be the first one to leave a good party."

"Come on, damn you. We've done what we came here to do."

Windy raised his revolver, aimed, then changed his mind and lowered the weapon. "I'll let you go till next time," he muttered, turning reluctantly to follow Kincaid down the ditch.

Several more charges went off before they tumbled into the depression, and Kincaid gulped in several deep breaths as he pressed his shoulders against the bank. He glanced at Windy, who was methodically ejecting spent cartridges from his revolver and replacing them with new ones.

"What the hell's the matter with you, you old bastard? You and me wouldn't have stood a chance against them out there in the dark."

"They're scared plumb shitless, Matt," Windy said, snapping the loading gate closed on his revolver and returning it to its holster. "Only reason for leavin' was 'cause there wasn't anybody left to shoot."

"Speaking of being scared shitless, I wasn't too pleased about having the stick of dynamite in my hand."

Windy smiled. "Did surprise ya a little bit, didn't it?"

"Hell yes. Didn't Olsen say something about not having caps and dynamite together at the same time? Did you crawl all the way out there with those damned things under your arm?"

"Nope. Had 'em in the top of my pants."

"Wasn't that a little crazy?"

"Stupid maybe, but not crazy." Windy drew the cut-plug from his pocket and carefully cut off a chew before looking at Kincaid. "Worked, didn't it?"

"Sure it did. But if one of 'em had gone off while we were crawling out there, we'd both be singing hymns and playing harps right now."

"You maybe, but not me. I plan on stayin' warm next to a great big fire." The scout squinted toward the mess wagon.

"I wonder if old Dutch's got any of them biscuits left. I'm feelin' a mite hungry myself."

Kincaid couldn't help but chuckle. "You're a strange son of a bitch, Windy, that's all I can say."

"What's strange about being hungry? Come on, I'll buy."

There was no more sniper fire from the Bannock that night, nor for the next four in a row. The Paiute could sleep, gaining their strength once more and stepping up the pace of the daily march. Not knowing how much dynamite Easy Company had, Harbert had abandoned his nightly harassment and switched to a series of swift daylight strikes. Whenever the terrain would afford sufficient coverage, the Bannock would suddenly materialize in separate groups, fire on the columns from a safe but mostly ineffective range, then disappear once again. Their raids netted one soldier killed and three wounded, and five Paiute dead. According to Windy's count, at least four and maybe five Bannock had toppled from their horses as a result of defensive fire from Easy Company.

On the morning of the fourteenth day, Kincaid and Windy were again at the head of the procession, which continued to progress steadily in a southwesterly direction. The days were becoming increasingly warm, and the nights, while yet cool, had lost some of the bitter sting they had held on the High Plains. The grass became less plentiful and the first clumps of sagebrush passed beneath their horses' hooves.

Windy's eyes were locked on the horizon, and he spoke without looking at Kincaid. "If my rememberin' tools are working right, I say when we top that next rise up yonder, you're gonna be in for a sight you'd never expect to see in a million years."

Impulsively, Kincaid looked toward the distant rolling swell. "What the hell could there be to see, Windy? Seems to me like we're on the fringes of a desert and going deeper into it all the time."

"We are. Have you ever been to Mormon country?"

"Never have. Why?"

"You'll see. Damnedest, hardest-workin' bunch of people you've ever seen."

"What makes them different?"

"Nothin' except the fact that they think they're different. Kind of God's chosen ones, if you know what I mean."

Kincaid surveyed the increasingly barren landscape. "If they are the chosen ones, why the hell would God put 'em in a place like this?"

"Don't know. A feller named Brigham Young, their leader, is supposed to have seen the valley up ahead and said, "This is the place.""

"Well, judging from what I've seen so far, if I thought I had a special connection with God, I'd expect a little better shake than this."

"That's part of the deal. They expect they're supposed to suffer hardships. Appears a little strange to me too, but they don't seem to complain much about what they've got. Seem pretty damned pleased with it, to tell you the truth."

They were still nearly a half-mile from the crest of the rise, and Kincaid glanced rearward toward the supply wagon bearing its precious cargo.

Noticing the concerned look on Kincaid's face, Windy asked, "How's Dark Star doing?"

"Not good. Worse, if anything. I checked on her last night and again this morning, and she seems to be getting weaker all the time. She's still losing quite a bit of blood."

"Well, if she can hang on for a little while longer, we might be able to get some help for her. Those Mormon people have had to fend for themselves for quite a while now, and should know what they're doing. They've got quite a few wives and maybe one of them will know how to help her out."

"What do you mean by that?"

Windy eyed Kincaid quizzically. "You really don't know anything about the Mormons, do you?"

"Didn't know there was a hell of a lot more to know about them than about anybody else."

"There is."

"For instance?"

"Wait and see. They're just regular people, damned good people, but they've got some beliefs you might find a little strange."

"Like what?"

"Like I said, wait and see. As a bachelor, you might find their way of doing things a little more than strange."

"What the hell are you being so secretive about?"

"Nothin'," Windy said with a grin. "I just think you'll 'preciate bein' a single man a little more when we leave."

"Goddammit, Windy! I don't like it when you grin like that."

"Can't grin no other way, Matt. Mouth only works two ways. Up for glad, down for sad."

"It goes a little farther than that, Windy. That 'up' part is tied to a mischievous twinkle in your eyes. It usually means you know a hell of a lot more than you're telling."

"A closed mouth catches no flies, Matt."

Fifteen minutes later, Kincaid reined in on the crest and couldn't believe what he saw below them. There, in the midst of that parched land, was a precise checkerboard of verdant, neatly tended fields. Interspersed fields of newly tilled soil contrasted in their brownness with those producing crops, and aqueducts filled with sparkling water fed from a central canal like the outspread fingers of a hand. Neatly tended roads connected the fields to various farmhouses, and brawny draft horses could be seen clearing new land soon to be put under the plow. Tiny dots that were men and women bent at their labor were to be seen everywhere, and it seemed as though they were busily producing a mirage that shimmered below in the strong heat of the boiling sun.

"Ain't that some kind of sight, Matt?" Windy asked contentedly, as if the pastoral scene filled him with some kind of inner joy.

"I've never seen anything like it. Here, in a semiarid land, they've created a mecca, like an offering to God or something."

"It is. An offering to their God, anyway. They call it irrigation, like you've seen back East maybe, and they grow mostly wheat, which they say is the eternal seed of God. They're hardworking people, they don't give anybody any trouble, but they don't take any trouble, either. 'Cept maybe from a wife or two."

"What?"

"You'll see," Windy replied, grinning and urging his horse forward again.

"Where are they, Wokana?" Harbert asked, eyes ablaze, as he waved an impatient hand toward the fifteen braves sitting their ponies and watching him with expressionless eyes. "Is this what we've been waiting for? Fifteen lousy fucking Indians?"

161

"Many say they will come, Mr. Boss, but they do not want trouble from Wah-shah-tung."

"Washington! Hell, they don't know anything about this, and if we do what I aim to, they'll never know until it's too late."

"Too late for who, Mr. Boss?" Wokana asked with a steady stare. "You or us?"

"Who gives a shit! Without me you're nothing, just a bunch of goddamned Indians waiting for a handout!" Harbert snapped, turning abruptly and walking away.

McCauley and his partners had been watching from a short distance away, and when Harbert approached, the miner said, "Is that the big bunch of reinforcements we've been waiting for, Mike? Hell, you've lost more featherheads just getting this far than you've got replacements."

"Maybe old Harbert wants to follow these bastards all the way to Texas, Bill," Reno said, chewing a stick methodically while he watched the agent. "That's fine for him, but it ain't for me. Way I count it, we're close to twenty days behind schedule for startin' to work that mine. Seems to me like we're just pissin' in the wind by listenin' to our friend and partner there. This ain't gettin' us nothin' but saddle sores."

There was a hint of desperation on Harbert's face, the look of a man who had played his entire poke on a last hand of cards and come up empty. "Now look here, fellows. Things happened that I didn't count on. The train, the dynamite, so few Indians showing up for the big kill, that sort of thing. Just give me a little more time and—"

"A little more time, Mike?" McCauley asked. "Twenty days seems to be a pretty generous amount of patience to me."

"I know it, but we can't stop now."

"No we can't. Not if we all want to ride back sittin' up right and proper in a saddle." McCauley furrowed his bushy brows and looked closely at Harbert. "But I reckon if me and old Reno there put our minds to it, we could figure out a way to get you to tell us what bank you left that letter in. Reno kind of likes that sort of thing, don't you, lad?"

"Be a pleasure, Bill. Every bit of it a pleasure."

"Look, hold on now," Harbert said, backing a few steps away and showing genuine fear for the first time. "They've still got a ways to go, through desert country. We'll take 'em the first chance we get, I promise you that."

McCauley watched the agent with no hint of emotion. 'First chance we get, huh, Mike? We've been ghostin' 'em for fourteen days now and ain't done nothin' worthwhile yet. What do you call a chance?"

"They're gonna be passing through broken country, suffering from the sun and lack of water. We'll take 'em somewhere in there. They've gotta be tired, and they'll let their guard down sooner or later."

"Only way to make a man let his guard down is to beat it down, Mike. You've got three days after they leave them farmers. If we don't have our Paiute by then, you're a dead man."

"You'll have 'em, Bill. You'll have 'em. You've got my word on that."

McCauley hawked up a wad of phlegm and spat over his shoulder before wiping his lips with the back of a hand. "I think you're bein' out-thunk, Mike. But I'll give you three more days."

"Thanks, Bill," Harbert said with sincerity. "You won't regret that decision."

"Mike, the only thing I regret is ever havin' laid eyes on you. You don't play the game right, and you're gonna regret it more'n me. We're fourteen days out from that bank right now. Ain't nobody gonna catch us 'tween here and the Mexican border after you're dead."

The two men stared at each other in an extended silence before Harbert hunched his shoulders in a shrug and walked away.

When they reached the valley floor, Kincaid slowed his horse and waited for Red Hand to catch up, then stepped down and led his mount as he walked beside the Indian.

"Red Hand, we're going to try and find some help for Dark Star. The folks that live here are called Mormons. According to Windy, they're fair, honest and decent people. Nobody could work this hard"—Kincaid waved his hand in a sweeping gesture to indicate the manicured fields and thriving crops before them—"without having some special value for life. I think they will do the best they can to help another human being."

The Indian remained silent, his eyes locked on the crystal-clear water coursing through a manmade ditch off to the right. Finally he glanced toward Kincaid, and there was a mixture of grudging respect and disbelief in his eyes.

"They have made the water to come here?"

"Yes they have. It's called irrigation. What they do is called farming."

"Farming?"

'Yes, they are called farmers."

"You said another word before."

"Mormons?" Kincaid asked, running a hand across his neck and trying to think of a simple explanation. "Let's see, how can I put this. All right, among the Indian tribes there are Paiute, Bannock, Shoshone, Crow and others, correct?"

"That is correct."

"Well, among white people there are Americans, Germans, Italians, Irish and so on. Now, I know all Indians believe in a supreme being, a God, but they don't all worship him in the same way. The only thing that makes Mormons different from other white people is their religious beliefs. The way they worship God."

Kincaid turned his horse onto a wide road that led through a field of towering wheat, the stalks of which bent under the heavy yield of golden grain. Red Hand stared at the lush greenery. It was obvious he was impressed, even though he had no concept of what farming was all about.

"They must have good medicine, these Mormons."

"I believe they think you make your own medicine in life, Red Hand. Just like you did when you led your people off the Sand Ridge. I'd like to ask a favor of you, and I'd appreciate it if you'd pass what I'm going to say along to your tribe."

"I will."

"Fine. These people have worked hard for what they have, and I'd say they're pretty damned proud of their accomplishments. And when people are proud of something, they're also damned protective of it. Kind of like the way you are about Dark Star. Do you understand what I'm saying?"

"Some."

"That's enough. I would like you to tell your people not to take anything, to touch anything, even so much as drink from the ditches, unless we are invited to. We have come to them for help, they didn't come to us. So we're their guests. Guests take only what they are given and do not take or ask for anything more. Is that clear?"

A look of defensive pride crossed Red Hand's face as they

entered the fields and felt the coolness of the farm country wafting on a gentle breeze.

"My people wander the land, taking only what they need," he said, staring straight ahead now, "and they believe that all growing things are to be shared by every man. They do not understand that some things are forbidden and other things are not. But they will do only what I do. If I drink, they drink. If I eat, they eat. If I take the white man's food, they will take the white man's food. I have no need to tell my people anything; they will live by my example."

"That's good enough for me," Kincaid replied, swinging into the saddle once more. "Now I will go to find help for Dark Star. She has woman problems and I know nothing of such things."

Kincaid cantered to the head of the column and caught up with Windy again.

"Know what, Matt?" the scout said as Kincaid fell into pace beside him.

"What?"

"The government is tryin' to make farmers out of these reconstructed Indians, seems like they should hire a few Mormons to show 'em how."

"The Indians, especially the Paiute, have no concept of property or possession, Windy. Only a concept of pride. Trying to make a farmer out of an Indian is like trying to milk a statue of a cow."

Windy grinned and looked across at Kincaid. "That's not bad, Matt. Not bad at all. Even old Howzer couldn't have said it better."

Kincaid started to reply, but held his words as he saw a tall, broad-shouldered man, thick of waist and arms, quit his field and walk toward the road. He stooped to pick up a rifle that was propped against a tree as he came toward them. A full beard touched the second button of his woolen undershirt; he wore a black felt hat, and wide suspenders held up gray pants tucked into high black boots. There was a sternness about him, the look of a man who had been given nothing in life and who had worked to earn everything in his possession. And there he stood, one man alone, facing two platoons of mounted infantry and an entire tribe of Paiute. There was no fear in his eyes, only the look of a man who knew right was on his side and

165

who lived upon the strength of higher convictions.

Kincaid reined in his horse and the entire procession halted.

"Good day, sir. I am Lieutenant Matthew Kincaid, commanding officer of an escort force from Easy Company, Wyoming Territory."

"Good day to you, Lieutenant. Welcome to Deseret. My name is Prescott Smith. How may I be of service to you and yours?"

"We are only passing through, Mr. Smith, on our way to the Skull Valley Reservation. We would very much appreciate water for our people and mounts."

"And that you shall have." He glanced once toward the nearby ditch and then back to Kincaid. "I would prefer that you not drink from the canal, because the soil along the banks is not sturdy enough to accommodate a great deal of traffic. May I invite you to drink from the well at my home and refresh your mounts at the watering troughs?"

"Thank you, sir. Also, I have an extremely ill person in my charge." Kincaid hesitated, watching for any change in the man's expression as he spoke again. "She is a young Indian girl suffering from women's problems. I'm afraid she'll die if I can't get help to her right away."

The word "Indian" seemed to have no effect on the Mormon, and his eyes left Kincaid's face to sweep down the column.

"Where is the lass?"

"Back there, in the lead wagon."

"Follow me, Lieutenant," Prescott Smith said, turning away to walk down the road. "The womenfolk will be happy to do whatever can be done within God's will."

The procession moved forward again, following the somewhat stern figure in the lead, whose head now snapped around toward a field they were passing, which was halfway down the lane to where a large, square frame house, painted white, sat nestled within a grove of trees.

"Boys!"

The children, some of them young men actually, looked up from their hoes and the eldest asked, "Yes, Father?"

"Get to the house. We have visitors."

"Yes, Father." The ten youngsters, ranging in age from ten to eighteen, laid down their tools and scampered toward the house with the irrepressible exuberance that only young people can demonstrate.

"Those are my sons, Lieutenant," Prescott Smith said over his shoulder, without looking back. "As it's Saturday, there is no school and the girls are working with their mothers at the loom."

Kincaid, somewhat puzzled, glanced at Windy.

"Mothers?"

"That's what the man said," Windy replied, tossing his chaw away and clearing his mouth. "Don't expect no coffee, tobacco or liquor, Matt. These people have got a way of thinkin' that might surprise you."

As if upon cue, six women stepped from the large building onto the courtyard when Prescott Smith passed by the well, and two more emerged from the barn. Their clothing was unpretentious and there was a look about them of swarthy health, which indicated they were not entirely confined to domestic chores. The women wore full-length aprons sheltering sturdy bodies. Smith stopped before them and turned back to Kincaid.

"Lieutenant, I would like you to meet my wives."

"I . . . I'd be pleased to . . . sir," Matt responded as his eyes swept over the women, all of whom appeared to be more patient than beautiful. The eldest was possibly forty, and the youngest, the two who had walked from the barn to stand beside the others, were no more than twenty.

"Rebecca, Jessica, Grace, Ruth, Sara, Clara, Jennifer and Louise," Smith said, indicating each with a bob of his hand. "Ladies, I present to you Lieutenant Mathew Kincaid."

The wives offered an abbreviated curtsy, while Smith's attention went to the first woman he had introduced.

"Rebecca, the lieutenant has a young lass with him who is in need of medical attention. Would you see to her needs, please?"

"Indeed, Prescott," she replied before looking up at Kincaid with compassionate eyes. "Where is she, Lieutenant?"

Kincaid waved a hand for the wagon to be brought forward, and seeing Red Hand step out to walk beside the conveyance, he glanced down at the woman while removing his hat.

"Thank you for the help, ma'am. Her name is Dark Star, and the man walking beside the wagon is her husband-to-be."

"What seems to be the nature of her problem, sir?"

"Well, ma'am, I don't really know how to put it," Kincaid replied, searching for the proper words. "She was molested by a man about twenty days ago and has been bleeding ever since."

167

Clutching her skirts about her thighs, the woman nodded quickly and stepped forward to reach into the wagon bed and place a hand gently on Dark Star's fevered forehead. After a moment's hesitation, she glanced toward the other wives.

"Jessica? We'll need a hot sitzbath. Please prepare one. Grace, please fetch the arnica. Ruth, if you would be so kind, please bring some hedge-nettle tea to my room. Sara, we'll need some turpentine and clean cloths. Clara and Jennifer? I would appreciate your help in preparing for the comfort of this lady. She's feverish and should be bathed in cool water from the well after her bath."

Without a word, the women turned to their assigned tasks and Rebecca looked up at the towering Smith. "Prescott? Would you be so kind as to have the young lady carried to my room? The sooner we begin, the better off she will be."

"Certainly," Smith replied, taking a step toward the wagon as if to carry Dark Star from the wagon himself. Then he stopped and looked at Red Hand, who had been watching the proceedings with confusion equal to his curiosity. "Shall I help you transport your lady to her room, son, or would you rather do it yourself?"

Confused by the word "transport," Red Hand looked at Windy.

"What he means, Red Hand, is that they want to help Dark Star. To do that, they have to get her into one of the rooms. Do you want to carry her by yourself, or do you want help?"

Red Hand hesitated as if making a final decision, then reached into the wagon and lifted the young woman up and over the side with little apparent effort.

"Just follow me, young man," Rebecca said, crossing the yard with hurried steps.

Prescott Smith nodded his satisfaction, then turned to the children, who had gathered a respectful distance away. There were sixteen of them, and many were miniature copies of the women who had been sent to assist Dark Star.

"Boys, I want you to fill the troughs and help with watering Lieutenant Kincaid's stock. And you girls, fetch fresh water from the well and serve it to these people, and if they're hungry, bring them food."

Kincaid had watched the entire proceedings with amazement. He stepped down from his mount and handed the reins to a boy of ten, who stepped forward shyly and led the animal away.

"I can't thank you enough, Mr. Smith, for your kindness and hospitality."

"Don't give it a second thought, Lieutenant. We are all travelers down the road of life, and an extended hand of welcome should be offered to each of us as he passes by. Unfortunately there are those who would bite that hand, therefore we must be wary. But the Lord has been good to us and we like to share when we can."

Windy's horse had been led away as well, and now he stepped forward. "Excuse me, Mr. Smith, but I'd like to talk to the lieutenant just for a moment. Matt, as soon as my horse is watered, I think I'll do a little backtracking. Harbert's police have likely seen us come here, and they might let their guard down a little till we leave. Maybe I can get close enough to find out what we're up against the rest of the way. When do you plan to pull out?"

"In the morning, Windy."

"That gives me enough time. See you when I get back."

Kincaid would have mentioned the need for caution, but knowing it wouldn't be heeded, he turned again to the Mormon. "Mr. Smith, is there a place nearby where we could make camp? I'd like to let Dark Star rest for the night and press on in the morning. Also, I would like to leave a detachment of troops here to protect you and your family. I hope I haven't brought trouble to your doorstep, but there is a certain element following us that I'm sure would delight in taking the women captive."

The big man smiled wearily. "Trouble is not a stranger at our doorstep, Lieutenant. We, as Mormon people, have not always been accepted with open arms ourselves. There are several acres of ground lying fallow adjacent to this section, and there is an artesian spring there. You are welcome to use that. One of my sons will show you the way when your mounts have been cared for. If you wish to leave some troops here for the ladies' protection, please do so."

"Thank you. I think it would be in the best interests of all of us."

"Then so be it. Did I hear you mention leaving in the morning?"

"Yes. I estimate we're about four days out from Skull Valley, and I'd like to get these people to their new home as quickly as possible."

Prescott Smith stood a moment to think and calculate. "Yes, I'd say you should be able to cover that distance in four days. Please say hello to Brother Young for me when you get there."

"Hiram Young? He's the agent at Skull Valley. Do you know him?"

"Yes. He is an elder in the Church, and he helped us set up a primary school for the children who live around here. He's a good person, doing the Lord's work in the best way he knows—by helping his fellow man, be they red or white."

Kincaid smiled with relief. "That's good to hear. Red Hand and his people are due for a break of some kind."

A boy of perhaps fifteen approached and stood several feet away, waiting for his father to acknowledge his presence.

"Yes, Martin? What is it?"

"We have finished watering the horses, sir. Is there anything else we can do to help?"

"Yes there is, son. Take that wagon to the barn and load it half full of straw. Use some of the winter quilts and make a proper bed in the back for the sick lady."

"Yes, father."

Prescott Smith turned his attention again to Kincaid. "Would it be inconvenient for you to drop the quilts by on your return trip to Wyoming Territory?"

"Not at all, Mr. Smith. And thank you."

Red Hand descended the steps from the house at that moment, and walked toward them. He looked like a man awakening from a particularly pleasant dream, one that he could not believe or ever recapture.

"How is the young lady, son?" Prescott Smith asked with kind concern in his voice as Red Hand approached.

"They are taking good care of her. Your wife Rebecca says she thinks Dark Star will be all right."

"Good. Excellent."

Red Hand's fathomless black eyes held on the Mormon, but there was a renewed brightness to them, a look of hope and promise. And Kincaid heard the Paiute say two words he had never heard him say before.

"Thank you."

170

"You're welcome, son," the Mormon replied. "Thank the Lord you got her to us in time."

Red Hand nodded and walked toward his people, and Kincaid watched him briefly before turning again to Prescott Smith. "He is their chief. A good man who has justifiable cause for his distrust of whites."

"There are many like him out here, Lieutenant. One day, perhaps we can all live together in peace and share in the bounty of this great land. Now if you'll excuse me, I'll gather my sons and return to the fields. There is plenty of light left and much to do before this day is done."

"Certainly, Mr. Smith. And thank you again for your assistance."

The Mormon smiled and offered his hand. "We do the best we can with what God's given us. And that includes an open heart. I'll see you when you return."

"You will, sir," Kincaid replied, returning the powerful grip and then releasing the Mormon's callused hand. "I'll give Mr. Young your best when I see him."

"Please do that," Prescott Smith said, moving away.

After the farmer had gone, Kincaid turned to find Lieutenant Dalby.

"Lieutenant? Come here, please."

"Yessir?"

"I want two squads left here tonight to protect this farmhouse. A four-hour relief is to be in effect."

"Right, sir," Dalby said, but his eyes were on the back of the receding Mormon. "Were those all really his wives, sir?"

"Apparently so."

"And were all those children his?"

Kincaid felt a hint of annoyance. "Marriages generally result in children, Lieutenant."

"But isn't that illegal, sir? Polygamy, I mean. He's breaking the law, isn't he?"

Now Kincaid was thoroughly irate. "Whatever he's breaking, Lieutenant, he can damned well keep on breaking it as far as I'm concerned. Restrict your concerns to military matters and leave the questions of civilian law to the proper authorities, a select group of idiots that you might deserve, but as yet do not have membership in."

"What, sir?"

171

"Post the goddamned guard, Lieutenant!"

"Yessir. Right away, sir."

Kincaid watched Dalby hustle toward the soldiers assembled nearby, and shook his head in obvious dismay.

"Where the hell do they come from?" he mumbled to himself, as he walked toward the well to draw a bucket of water.

fourteen ───────────────

The midday sun seemed to hang in the sky, hammering on barren soil mainly devoid of plant life, with the exception of flourishing sagebrush. The landscape was broken and uneven, with numerous draws and ravines, while pinyon and juniper provided what little shade was to be found on the high ground.

Kincaid had just returned from checking on Dark Star, who rested as comfortably as possible in the jolting wagon. A healthy color had returned to her skin. Though weak, she could smile again and engage in short conversations. But when he rejoined the head of the column, his concern went to Windy. The scout had not returned from his night's foray, and trusting in Windy's inherent resourcefulness, Kincaid had moved the column out at dawn. Nearly twenty-four hours had passed now, though, and he couldn't shake the feeling of abandonment from his mind.

Even in his mental discomfort, Kincaid tried to force unsettling concerns from his mind and concentrate on selecting the least arduous course for those behind him to follow. A hot breeze drifted from the shimmering body of water to the northwest, known as Salt Lake, and Kincaid had just taken a sip of water from his canteen when he heard Sergeant Olsen call out from behind him.

"Lieutenant Kincaid! Look over there, sir. Looks like Windy's comin', and he's got somebody with him."

Kincaid twisted in the saddle and his head swiveled in the direction indicated by Olsen. Relief swept through him as he recognized the big roan with the round-shouldered man on its back cradling a rifle in his arms. He couldn't make out who the other man was, riding just ahead and to the left of the scout, so he turned forward and negotiated a dry wash while waiting for Windy to catch up with them. Minutes later, Windy inter-

173

cepted them at a quartering angle and reined in beside Kincaid

"Afternoon, Matt. Kind of hot, ain't it?"

"Kind of hot! Where the hell have you been, you old bastard? I'm not much for worrying, but I'll have to admit you've been on my mind more than a little these past few hours."

"Worry's a lot like religion, Matt. It kinda creeps up on you when you think somethin's wrong. I'd like you to meet a feller," Windy said, bobbing the rifle barrel toward the man now off to his right. "That there is Wilbert Jenkins. Leastwise that's what he told me his name was."

"What's his line of work?"

"Chasin' Paiute, mostly. He's one of Harbert's partners. Caught him tryin' to sneak away last night."

Kincaid's eyes hardened and Jenkins tried to match the stare before glancing away.

"What the hell are you and Harbert up to, Jenkins?"

"I ain't got nothin' to do with it, Lieutenant," Jenkins replied, his tone surly and defensive. "It was all Harbert's idea. Him and Bill McCauley."

"Bill McCauley? Who's he?"

Jenkins fell silent and Windy spat and said, "Old Jenkins here don't talk too good unless he's got a gunbarrel under his ear. He was chatterin' like a chipmunk last night, though, and I think he had enough scare in him to tell the truth. Harbert's got some partners, Jenkins here and three others. Seems they want these Paiute to work a mine they high-graded from some poor old bastard back East."

Kincaid hadn't taken his eyes off the man. "That right, Jenkins?"

The miner gave no response and continued to stare straight ahead.

"Anyway," Windy added, "Harbert killed the agent that was sent out to replace him. He was behind that ambush in the South Pass, and now he plans to take us tomorrow morning."

"Where?"

"At a place called Chitworth Ravine. I know the place, and we've gotta cross it to get to Skull Valley. They'll have the advantage of surprise and should've been able to wipe us out if we hadn't found out about it."

"How many men has he got?"

"About seventy Indians, Bannock and Shoshone mixed, along with the three whites."

Kincaid studied what the scout had said. "That's a sizable force, Windy. But how do we know that Jenkins there is telling the truth?"

"'Cause he was tryin' to get away last night. Said he didn't want any part of what was goin' on and that he'd had it with Harbert, McCauley and the whole damned lashup." Windy reached over and shoved the barrel of the Sharps beneath Jenkins' right ear. "Ain't that right, Jenkins?"

Jenkins lurched away from hot metal and looked at Kincaid pleadingly. "Yes. That's right. I ain't got nothin' to do with it, Lieutenant. That's why I was tryin' to get away. You've gotta believe that."

"I don't have to believe anything you say, Jenkins," Kincaid said coldly. "But I do believe you're guilty as sin, and you'll be right by my side when the ambush occurs tomorrow. It won't happen the way Harbert's got it planned, but if anything goes wrong, you'll be the first dead man to hit the ground."

Kincaid turned in the saddle and called back, "Sergeant Olsen! Bring the wagon with the Gatling forward!"

"Yessir!"

"Windy, you said you're familiar with this Chitworth Ravine?"

"Been there a time or two."

"Is there anyplace where we could hide the Gatling, camouflaged with sagebrush and the like?"

"I'll find one, Matt, if there's one to be found. Let me have a little look-see, and maybe we can use ourselves as decoys to bring on the attack in just the right place."

"That's what I was thinking. Does Harbert know you've captured Jenkins?"

"Not that I know of. Jenkins was headin' north like a cat with snuff up its ass when I caught up to him."

"Good. We'll assume he doesn't know." Kincaid paused to give the captive time to absorb what he was going to say. "If he does, I think we'll see it on Jenkins' face just before I put a bullet through his brain."

"Where the hell is Jenkins?" McCauley asked, joining the group gathered beneath a pinyon tree. "Anybody seen him?"

"I talked to him just before dark last night, Bill," Logan offered. "He seemed a little upset about something and mentioned being tired of the whole damned thing."

175

"Do you think he snuck off, Bill?" Harbert asked.

Reno was leaning against the tree trunk, and he watched the agent closely. "If he has any sense he did. This is the most fucked-up operation I've ever seen."

"Just hold on, Reno, all right? It'll be over tomorrow morning."

"Yeah, sure," was Reno's derisive reply.

"Well, to hell with him," McCauley said. "If he's gone, that's just fine. Make it a four-way split instead of five. Let's get on with it. What's your plan, Mike?"

Wokana and the Shoshone chief, a young Indian with a curling sneer and an arrogant bearing, stood slightly off to one side while Harbert knelt down in the center to draw a map with a stick in the sand.

"Here's Chitworth Ravine," he said, scratching a long, curving mark, "and those wagons will have to cross right about here and come out here. This particular section of the ravine is formed in a long 'S' shape. It's fairly steep on either side and we'll hit them just when they get to the bottom, here. Wokana and I will be waiting around the west bend, here, about a hundred and fifty yards from the crossing, with the Bannock. Crow Foot will have his Shoshone, along with you three, out of sight beyond the ridge on the far side. The ravine's about a hundred yards wide, so both forces will have about the same distance to travel."

He paused to look up at the men surrounding him. "Do all of you understand that?"

Crow Foot allowed a sullen nod, which was matched by Reno's, and the others indicated that they did.

Harbert looked back down to use his stick again. "All right Crow Foot's people will cut across behind them, here, and we'll take them from the front, here. There is no way they can escape. Remember, we will take no survivers among the army. They will be our primary target and try not to hit the Paiute, if possible." He glanced at the two Indians again and smiled. "You fellers can have your fun with them later."

"What time you figure they'll show up at the ravine?" McCauley asked.

"From where they are now, they couldn't possibly get there until sometime tomorrow morning. I make it around ten o'clock or so. We'll be in position long before then. Remember, every soldier must die. This is abandoned country around here, and their remains won't be found till long after we're gone."

Reno studied the map in silence for long moments. "How are we supposed to know when to come down from the other side? If this thing's gonna work, we'll have to hit them at exactly the same time." Then he added, "If it works at all."

"It'll work, Reno. I'll fire the first shot, and when you hear my gun go off, you bring your people down."

McCauley scratched his beard in thought. "Looks like it should work. How about the dynamite? What if they use that again?"

"I don't think they have any left, and even if they do, we'll be on 'em too fast for 'em to use it. We've got both a numbers and a weapons advantage on them. Most of our people are armed with repeating rifles, Remingtons and Spencers, while all they've got are single-shot Springfields. It should be like shootin' fish in a barrel once we trap them in that ravine."

"Fish in a barrel, huh, Harbert?" Reno snapped. "If this plan works as lousy as the other ones you've come up with, I hate to think who the fish are gonna be."

"Have you got a better plan, Reno?" Harbert asked, glancing sharply at the gunman "If you do, let's hear it."

Reno snapped the twig in his hands, tossed it aside and walked away with no reply.

Brilliant shafts of light stabbed across the vacant land, and there was instant heat as the sun surged into the sky to blaze its scorching trail across the heavens. Four men stood beside the empty supply wagon that had transported the Gatling, while a fifth stooped to trail a stick across the sand.

"The trail goes down to the bottom of the ravine right about here," Kincaid said, "and about twenty yards to the left is a washout, cave sort of thing. The front of it is well covered with brush, and the gun is hidden inside. Malone and Watson are with it now, having spent the night in there, as you know."

"Lieutenant Dalby, you will be positioned here, around this curve to the left. If they're waiting for us where I think they are, they'll be out of sight and won't be able to see you coming up the ravine. Once the attack starts, if it does, you can close on them and have a clear field of fire from the rear. The other platoon will escort as usual.

"Red Hand, your armed braves are to be on either side of the people in the center, leaving about ten yards of separation.

If we come under fire, your unarmed people are supposed to lie flat on the ground to avoid being hit, while your braves drop to one knee and return fire.

"Sergeant Olsen, your platoon will be riding slightly farther ahead than normal, and they will protect the front while the Gatling and Dalby cover the rear." He studied the map for several seconds before shrugging his shoulders. "I guess that's about it. Can you think of anything I left out, Windy?"

"Nope. Seems like you covered it pretty good."

Kincaid obliterated the marks in the sand before rising. "I'll ride in the lead with Sergeant Olsen, and when we get to the ravine, Windy will drop back to coordinate things to the rear. If we leave now, we should be at the crossing in about four hours, which would put us in position between ten and eleven. Do you have anything to add, Windy?"

"Nope. 'Cept it don't really matter what time we get there. If Harbert's got another ambush planned, he's probably already got things set up."

"All right, let's move out. Lieutenant, take your platoon and angle southwest now. Follow the ravine until you come to that bend I described, and expect to move in at exactly ten-thirty. Don't tip your hand until after you've heard the engagement begin."

"Yes, sir. You can count on me."

"I hope so. A lot of lives are riding on your use of proper judgment. And perhaps your military career as well. Keep those factors in mind."

"I will, Lieutenant," Dalby replied with a crisp salute, before turning and striding to the head of his platoon.

The long march ground on through the increasing heat of another blistering day. When Kincaid checked his watch again, it was exactly ten o'clock and he could see the ragged edges of the ravine approximately half a mile away in the distance.

"Our timing should be just about perfect, Windy. Is that slight depression over there the trail down?"

"Yup. I'd make it to be about fifty yards to the bottom."

"Fine. You fall back to the rear just when we break over."

Windy nodded while his keen eyes searched the landscape shimmering before them in the intense heat. "Dalby should be in position by now, and since we haven't heard any firing, I'd say our hunch was correct. With this southeasterly wind blowing, Harbert will attack from the west to keep us from hearing anything he doesn't want us to hear."

"We'll soon find out. Let's keep everything looking natural when we go down."

At ten-twenty, Kincaid's horse entered the cut bank and moved toward the bottom of the ravine, its legs braced against the incline. As if casually looking at the scenery, Matt's head slowly turned toward the left and his vision passed by a natural-looking pile of sagebrush.

"Ten minutes, Malone," he said just loudly enough to be heard as he looked to the front once more.

"Bloody good show, sir," came the muffled reply.

The Paiute were bunched together on the narrow trail, but they fanned out again when they reached the bottom. The wagon carrying Dark Star creaked down the hill, followed by the other two, with Windy being the last person to enter the sloping trail.

Dust rose in swirling eddies, and the only sound to be heard in the eerie calm was the moaning of a steady wind sweeping between the walls of the ravine.

Kincaid could feel his heartbeat quicken as he looked back to see Windy reach the bottom, and he wondered momentarily if they had been wrong about the suspected ambush. Then the first shot rang out and his head snapped toward the sound. The hoofbeats of running horses accompanied the shot, and Kincaid saw the first Bannock mounts burst into view from around the bend to the west.

"Sergeant Olsen! Bring your platoon forward and form a skirmish line!"

"Yessir!"

Kincaid saw his mounted infantrymen gallop by him on either side, and as if sensing another presence rather than expecting it, he looked toward the far ridge. Thirty more horses pounded down the trail at an angle that would put them to the rear of the column.

Olsen gave the command to fire, and Kincaid heard the crashing roar of rifles blazing in response to incoming rounds snapping overhead, fired by the charging Indians. Off to his left, the Paiute had instantly dropped flat to the ground and the armed braves were firing their weapons from kneeling positions.

The Shoshone wheeled their mounts in the center of the ravine and turned to bring the rear of the column under attack, while Windy leaped from his horse and began throwing brush away from the indentation in the ravine wall.

"Go to it, Malone!" he yelled to the grinning Irishman crouched behind the Gatling. "Let's see if the damned thing still works!"

Without hesitation, Malone began cranking the gun's rotating bundle of six barrels around as he swept the rapid-fire weapon over the Shoshone. Several startled Indians tumbled from their plunging mounts and others went down on dead or wounded horses. Kincaid saw two white men in the lead plunge to their deaths, while a third, wearing a flapping duster, spun his horse and broke for the other side of the ravine. Matt raised his Scoff and aimed, but before he could pull the trigger, he heard a blast from behind him and saw the rider spill from the saddle with a bullet through his spine. Recognizing the unmistakable sound of Windy's Sharps, Kincaid took aim on the milling Shoshone and dropped two in rapid succession.

Quitting the battle, the stunned Indians lashed their ponies and raced toward the eastern curve, and Kincaid glanced sharply in that direction. Dalby's platoon emerged from the shelter, riding in a firing line with weapons ablaze. The Shoshone, thoroughly confused now, broke ranks and scattered in all directions, with many more falling to weapons from Dalby's command and the incessant chatter of the Gatling gun. Kincaid took aim on the lead rider, squeezed the trigger, and an Indian named Crow Foot flopped over the rear of his horse.

Kincaid's attention went to the battle raging toward the front of the column, and he saw a pitched, hand-to-hand conflict, with numerous riderless horses rearing and plunging in the middle of the frey. One man stood out from the rest, and Kincaid immediately recognized the screaming, cursing figure of Dennis Michael Harbert. He took aim on the agent, but a soldier blocked his view and Kincaid spurred his mount forward.

When he caught sight of Harbert again, the bearlike man was lashing with his coiled whip at Bannock on either side, and trying to force his way rearward in an attempted escape from the crushing mass surrounding him. With the agent nearing open ground, his horse reared and Kincaid pulled his mount in, took careful aim, and pulled the trigger. The bullet slammed into Harbert's back just above the hips and his arms flew out to the sides, the whip dropping from his grasp, and he pitched over backward to lie dead upon the ground.

The narrowness of the ravine held in the crashing reverberation of exploding shells, and a pall of smoke hung above the fierce battle. Kincaid's eyes swept over the scene in search of Wokana, whom he saw bludgeoning a soldier to death with the butt of his rifle. Again he maneuvered for position to fire, and then his eye caught something else.

Red Hand had leaped up from his kneeling position and swung onto the back of a riderless horse. He spun the mount around, and Matt could see that he was unarmed except for a Paiute digging stick, which he raised above his head as he angled toward Wokana. There was cold, deadly determination on his face as he bore down on his old enemy.

When Wokana finally turned and noticed Red Hand, the Bannock smiled in cruel triumph and raised his rifle. Red Hand's arm lashed forward before Wokana could fire, and the smile on the Bannock's face quickly vanished, to be replaced by the shocked look of a mortally wounded man. The digging implement was imbedded in his chest and protruded out through his back, the fire-hardened point now red with blood. The rifle fell from Wokana's grasp and he clutched the stick in both hands and tried to pull it free, but to no avail. He slumped forward against his pony's neck, twisted and slid to the ground.

Red Hand's expression didn't change as he watched his dead foe lying motionless in the sand, and he stared at him for several moments before turning the horse away.

The battle had raged for nearly ten minutes, and there were men's bodies lying everywhere, interspersed with dead horses. The firing had become sporadic, with what few surviving Indians there were fleeing to the opposite side of the ravine and out of range.

"Shall we go aftem them, sir?" Dalby asked, his face red with excitement as he turned his horse in beside Kincaid's.

"No, Lieutenant. It wouldn't accomplish much even if you did catch them. I think all the leaders of this thing are dead, and those who got away won't be causing us any more trouble. See to it that an aid station is set up for the wounded and get me a casualty count as quickly as you can."

"Right away, sir," Dalby replied, turning away.

"Lieutenant?"

"Yes, sir?"

"You did a hell of a fine job. I'd like to congratulate you."

Dalby grinned. "Thank you, sir. I'd say I've survived my baptism by fire. I'm not sure, but I think I got two of them myself."

Kincaid returned the smile. "Is your gun empty?"

"No, but it's hot, Lieutenant. And the sun didn't have anything to do with that."

"Fine. Get that report to me just as soon as possible."

"I'm on my way, sir."

Kincaid turned his mount and rode toward the wagon where Dark Star was lying, and he saw Red Hand, still mounted, heading in that direction as well. Both men stopped beside the wagon at the same time, and Red Hand looked down at her.

"It is over now, little one. Wokana is dead."

Dark Star opened her eyes tiredly. "It is good, Red Hand." Then she noticed that he was mounted, and her eyes widened slightly in admiration. "I didn't know you could ride a horse."

Red Hand watched her as he reached forward to stroke the mount's neck. "I never said I couldn't ride one, Dark Star. I only said I didn't want to ride one."

Kincaid smiled and walked his horse toward the cave to supervise the packing up of the Gatling gun. Even amid the carnage, he felt a sense of satisfaction. They had traveled nearly four hundred miles and fought the mountains, the cold, the heat, the desert, and finally the Bannock. And most importantly, they had won.

Kincaid felt especially proud of Easy Company as he stepped from the saddle and walked up to stand beside Malone.

"She's a bleedin' beauty, Lieutenant," the Irishman said with a grin, as he patted the barrel affectionately.

"I'm sure you didn't mean that literally, Private, but I'm afraid that's the case," Kincaid replied with a weary sigh as his gaze swept over the dead Shoshone. "Let's load the damned thing up, deliver Red Hand's people and then head home. There's plenty to be done back at Outpost Nine."

"More latrines, sir?"

"Not right away, Malone," Kincaid said with a smile. "Let's have a beer first when we get back, then we'll see."

SPECIAL PREVIEW

Here are the opening scenes
from

EASY COMPANY IN COLTER'S HELL

the next novel in Jove's exciting
High Plains adventure series

EASY COMPANY

coming in October!

one _____

_____

The dispatch rider, Private Clayton Pomeroy, rode for his life. He was a nervous gent to start with, and the band of Indians swarming after him didn't help any.

He glanced back, his face contorted by fear.

"Band" and "swarm" were dead-on, he decided.

Dead wrong, actually. He was given to exaggeration. There were only four Indians, not enough to *swarm*. But the danger appeared real enough.

He'd ridden out of regimental HQ early that morning, bound for Outpost Number Nine and Easy Company. He'd been told the mount he'd drawn could run forever.

He split the air now with curses as he realized that forever wasn't far away and that the durned horse could run so far because he ran so *slow*.

The early morning on the gently rolling High Plains of Wyoming had been pleasant enough. Spooky perhaps, with the early light filling the draws with purple shadows and creating worrisome shapes elsewhere, but pleasant and uneventful. But then, along about noon, with the high sun flattening the plains and turning them a brilliant yellow, the Indians had ridden out of a draw and gotten on his tail.

After the first whoops and yells they'd fallen silent. That was kind of spooky too.

Pomeroy asked his mount for more speed, but didn't get it.

He thought of emptying his Scoff at the hostiles. But he also didn't figure that would do much good. They were probably too far back, and he'd miss.

He lay over his mount's neck, deciding to let the hostiles tell him when they'd come into range. If the first slug didn't get him, then he'd know. And he'd cut loose with his Scoff and—

Damn! They'd be using rifles, the brand-new repeaters the

government kept giving those bastards. They'd still be out of range.

The plains flowed under his mount's hooves, the sandy soil, the buffalo grass with its two-foot roots, bunch grass, grama grass. Perfect for a goddamn cemetery.

He figured he was about halfway to Outpost Nine. But halfway didn't count. He sure as hell hoped the message for Captain Warner Conway was important. It could be Pomeroy's epitaph.

He dipped down into a draw and his mount labored up the far side. It wouldn't be long. Maybe he should just hit the ground and make a stand. Pomeroy's Last Stand. It didn't have the same ring as another, more famous Last Stand, but he'd be just as dead.

His horse stretched out as the ground ran level for a distance. Pomeroy glanced around to see how close the hostiles were now. . . .

And almost had a heart attack!

There was one practically running up the ass end of his horse, and he was grinning.

Jesus! Merciless, cold-hearted bastards. They were toying with him. He grabbed for his Scoff.

The Indian closed fast, reached out and grabbed Pomeroy's hand. "Please. We mean no harm. Please stop."

Pomeroy stared at him, wild-eyed. His horse kept running.

"If you do not stop, then we will have to kill you," shouted the Indian.

Since his dash for safety hadn't gone as planned, Pomeroy threw on the brakes and his weary horse stumbled to a halt.

The Indian grinned again. And his three companions grinned too. Pomeroy was chilled to the marrow. "It is a nice day for a hard ride," said the Indian, "but this is far enough."

Pomeroy finally noted the absence of warpaint. Could these be what were called friendlies?

"We think you must be riding for the Americans at what they call Outpost Nine. Is that right?"

"Yeah, goddammit, Outpost Nine. An' you 'bout scared me half to death. Whyn't you *say* somethin'?"

"We did, and you rode faster."

Pomeroy didn't care for the implications. "Jeez, you fellers is real lucky I didn't shoot and kill you."

"We are Cheyenne," said the Indian, as if that were sufficient rebuttal (and it probably was), "from the village of Chief Walks Bent Over."

"You're from the reservation?"

"Yes."

"How come you're off it?"

The Indian responded crossly, "We were still on it when we saw you."

What? He'd been riding through a Cheyenne reservation? They could get themselves another dispatch rider next time. "So whaddaya want?"

"I am Brave Elk. And this is a gift from Walks Bent Over to the American, Kincaid, at the outpost." He handed Pomeroy a worn notebook.

"What is it?" asked Pomeroy.

"We have kept it this past year. It is from the Greasy Grass."

Pomeroy, young and new to the frontier, wondered what the hell the greasy grass was. "You're sure he'll want it?"

"We think he will. It is our gift for being a friend. Goodbye." They turned to leave.

"Hey," cried Pomeroy, "you don't know if there are any more of you fellers up front of me somewhere, do you?"

"The path to the American post is thick with danger," said Brave Elk portentously. "Ride with care." Brave Elk, like many Indians, had a nice sense of humor.

Pomeroy's eyes bulged. "You-all don't feel like ridin' along a ways, do you?"

"If we wished to ride farther, we would deliver the gift ourselves. But we must return to the land that the White Father has given the Cheyenne. He has been so good to give us land that we have always lived on . . . we do not wish to make him mad."

"Good thinkin', Brave Moose—"

"Elk."

"Same thing."

Brave Elk smiled thinly, held up a hand palm outward, and said in Cheyenne, "May the Great Spirit spit on you." Then he and his friends rode off.

Pomeroy's mount had been contentedly nibbling at the grass. The dispatch rider had a hard time getting him moving again.

187

A few hours later he spied Outpost Number Nine in the distance. It was his first visit, and he hadn't known what to expect. What surprised him was that it looked like a fort. Not some casual, token outpost—a shack in the wilderness—but a real fort.

And he was quite right. Outpost Number Nine, which squatted atop the highest rise within a mile's radius and which commanded an unimpeded field of fire, with no draws or gullies, for about a quarter-mile out from its walls, was indeed built like a fort.

There were high walls or ramparts, behind which guards strolled, peering out over a chest-high parapet. The walls, as he drew closer, revealed themselves as composed of sod and timber, and they appeared to form a large, square fortification, unbroken save for the eastward-facing main gate and a gate to the paddock, which he saw and identified at the southern end of the Post.

What Pomeroy didn't realize was that a "fort," in army terminology, was not a physical description but a designation. No fortification below regimental level was supposed to be called a fort. A number were, of course, but inaccurately.

Pomeroy rode through the main gate and immediately saw that all the post's housing was built right into the walls. That was what the guards walked on. While soldiers were sleeping, there were guards walking right over their heads . . . and likely *peeing* right over their heads too. Pomeroy smiled. He hoped the roofs were thick, which they were, mercifully, though not quite thick enough to withstand the winter meltdown and the spring rains.

Directly to Pomeroy's front, on the far western side of the parade, was the orderly room, Easy Company headquarters. Pomeroy rode toward it, skirting the flagpole in the center of the parade. The everpresent plains wind was making the flag at the top of the pole stand tall, but at ground level the air was calm. And right warm, thought the dispatch rider.

Pomeroy dismounted and marched into the orderly room.

First Sergeant Ben Cohen looked up from behind his desk.

"Message for Captain Conway from Regiment, Sarge," said Private Pomeroy, handing over the dispatch bag. "Also got a gift here for someone named Kincaid . . . from another someone named Walks Crooked and the Brave feller."

Upon hearing his name, the tall, raw-boned person of First Lieutenant Matt Kincaid, company adjutant, appeared from an adjoining office. "Brave Elk? From Walks Bent Over?"

"That's them, sir. They s'prised me on the way here. I almost kilt them 'fore I found out they didn't mean no harm."

"Is that so?" Matt said laconically. "I'm Kincaid What have you got for me?"

"Just this, sir." Pomeroy handed over the worn notebook. "He said they'd had it a year. I'd be careful though, sir— handling it, I mean. Injun said it came from some greasy grass."

Matt vanished into his office with the notebook, and sergeant Cohen took the dispatch into the CO's office to give to Captain Conway.

Cohen reappeared and went back behind his desk just as Matt was coming back out of his office. "There's no name on this book, Sergeant, but it reads like it might have belonged to Kellogg."

"Mark Kellogg? The journalist who was with Custer?"
Matt nodded.

"But they didn't do anything to him, sir, besides kill him. Didn't take his clothes like they did the rest, didn't mutilate him."

"Yes. But no one found anything that Kellogg had written, either, which was kind of unusual, seeing he was there to write." Matt weighed the book in his hand. "Maybe I'd better send it on for some kind of verification."

"If it's the real thing," said Cohen, "you'll never see it again, sir."

"No doubt. But what if it's not the real thing, just the notes of some poor, dead soldier, if indeed it came from where Brave Elk had said it did?"

"'Scuse me, sir," Pomeroy broke in, "but what's the greasy grass?"

"That's what the Indians call the Little Big Horn, soldier." Matt flashed him a quick smile, forgiving him for his ignorance. Then he asked Cohen, "What did the captain get?"

"Dunno, sir. He's readin' it now."

Captain Warner Conway had broken the seal on the envelope,

removed a set of orders, read them...and then read them again

Now he leaned back in his chair, a faraway look in his eyes ...

It had been 1872 five years earlier. Warner Conway, a captain then as now, had taken his leave back East. And as was customary when they spent his leave in the East, he and his black-haired wife Flora, passed the time on the spacious Maryland estate of Flora's family. Most of the time, at any rate. But there were parties about the state to attend, as well as functions in the nation's capital, and there were the Washington sights to see. Tourist attractions. Warner and Flora had been out West for so long that with every passing year they felt more and more like tourists

One such tourist attraction was the exhibit of paintings that hung in the Capitol Building, and on one afternoon, Warner and Flora Conway were part of a small crowd that stood before a large painting.

The painting was by Thomas Moran one of several Moran canvases on display. It showed a deep, yellow-sided canyon with an apparently prodigious waterfall in the distance. The scene was awesome And the painting was entitled *Grand Canyon of the Yellowstone*

"Warner," murmured Flora. "Do such places really exist?"

"Congress thinks they do. When they got a look at these paintings and some photographs and eyewitness reports, they—"

"Lookit them falls." said another tourist "How high d'you suppose they are?"

Warner Conway looked at the tourist, a stout man a good deal shorter than himself, and answered, "They measured them out at three hundred and eight feet." He turned to his wife. "Flora, remember when we went to Niagara Falls? Well, these are supposed to be twice as high."

"No kiddin'?" said the tourist. "That a fact?"

Warner wouldn't have guessed the man's name was Flora. He and his wife exchanged smiles and decided to humor the fellow. "Yes it is," said Conway. "And beyond those falls is the plateau. Enormous, almost eight thousand feet high, and filled with boiling geysers and sulphur springs and the Lord only knows what else "

"Awww," said the man, "come on."

"It's a fact," declared Warner Conway. "Back in 1807 there was a man called Colter. He'd been with the Lewis and Clark expedition, but the year before, he'd left them to go on his own, trapping and exploring. That way, I suppose he figured that if he found something great, it would be his."

"That makes sense," said the man.

"Well, he stumbled into this place, likely the first white man ever to see it. But when he came out and described what he'd seen, no one would believe him. They figured he was just spinning yarns, as Mountain Men are apt to do, the grander the better. But he told the stories so well that they became legend and this place came to be known as Colter's Hell. Then Old Gabe went on in and came back out—"

"Who's Old Gabe?"

"Jim Bridger. He came out telling of boiling springs and steaming fountains and this cliff of black grass, and they didn't believe him, either. They called his stories 'Jim Bridger's Lies.' Of the two names, I kind of prefer Colter's Hell. Anyway, that plateau's just as virgin as what's in that painting there, and it's going to remain so."

"How come?" inquired the stranger.

"Because Congress just made it a National Park."

"What the hell's a National Park? Pardon the French, ma'am."

"I'm not exactly sure," replied Warner Conway slowly. "Just a place where everything gets left alone, to live and die— the land, the trees, the animals, everything."

The man thought it over. "I dunno," he finally said. "That don't sound American to me. I mean, look at that place. A feller could make a bundle sellin' tickets to look at that, and *that's* American."

Warner Conway shook his head slowly. He had to agree that that was the American way, up until then.

"Well, somebody'll do it, you wait and see," said the man. "By the way, long as we're talkin' so much, my name's Hiram Peckinpah. You're infantry, aintcha?"

"Sort of," said Warner—the trim on his uniform was certainly light blue. He introduced himself and Flora to the pushy but pleasant fellow, and then explained the difference between regular infantry and mounted infantry.

"So you ride horses, so what? You're just like regular infantry, only lazier."

Conway was preparing a retort when Peckinpah grinned disarmingly. "I sell food, myself. An' hardware. An' hotels. An' guns. Just about everything. I'm an entry-pre-noor. I'd give yuh my card, 'ceptin' it wouldn't do me no good, you being in the army. But, talkin' about food, I'm hungry. How about joinin' me fer dinner?"

The Conways declined.

"My treat. Mind yuh, that don't happen often."

"Thank you, no, Mr. Peckinpah—"

"Hiram."

"Hiram. But we'd rather look around some more, and then there are some places we have to visit."

After Peckinpah had hurried off, Flora said, "Funny little man."

"Funny?" Warner Conway was thinking about "the American way." "I suppose so."

"Oh, Warner. Do you think we'll ever get to go to someplace like this?"

"Maybe, someday. But I just remembered, we have to go to the Adamses for dinner. We'd better hurry."

"The Adamses? Who are they?"

"Classmate of mine. Sam. He met you a few times." He watched for a reaction, but there was none. "It's a party for a lot of my classmates. There are some I'd like to see."

"But not Sam," she said, reading his expression.

"No. Sam was always . . . envious." And again he eyed her very closely.

"Envious? Of what?" She was oblivious to his meaningful stare.

Warner Conway smiled, remembering. It was well that he could remember the fiercely competitive Sam Adams.

Conway straightened in his chair and barked, "Sergeant Cohen! Matt!"

The two men entered the office, the rangy Kincaid and the shorter, bearlike Sergeant Cohen. "What's up, sir?" asked Cohen.

"We're going to Colter's Hell."

Matt grinned, but Cohen frowned. "We? All of us?"

"You've been wanting to get off post, haven't you, Sergeant?" Conway smiled. "I figure fifty, sixty men. We've got

192

about a week to decide. Come on, Ben, don't look so unhappy."

"Jes' thinkin' about the work, sir, to say nothing of the saddlesores. It's gonna be some move."

In 1864, the year Montana was declared a United States Territory and Bannack City became its first capital, a small mining camp sprang up in the west central part of the territory and was named Last Chance Gulch.

The next year, when Virginia City replaced Bannack City as the capital, it was still Last Chance Gulch.

But by 1875, when Last Chance Gulch became the territorial capital, that small mining camp had grown to accommodate more than three thousand souls and had been renamed Helena.

And it was in Helena, in the Spring of 1877, that U.S. Marshal William Quaid gave his young deputy marshal, Cal Murphy, an assignment. Young Murphy, twenty-three going on fifty, had recently returned from a successful six-month manhunt.

"Do you remember the Raffertys, Cal?"

"Natcherly. I remember last year, after they rid south from here, heard they was biddin' t' turn into right serious outlaws. Got them some pards, even worse than they was, an' played hell down t' Radersburgh an' Bozeman an' Virginia City an' the mining country." He shook his head in sorrow.

"And we were thinking we were going to have to stop them."

"You mean *I* was gonna have to stop them. They was once my buddies." Both Murphy and the Raffertys were Irish and local boys, but while Cal was small, wiry, hard, fair and straight, Tom, Jim and Jack Rafferty were all squat, muscular, mean and crooked. "But they ain't my buddies no more, not since they went wrong," he concluded.

Marshal Quaid eyed a wall map.

"But we figured they was finished," Cal went on. "Disappeared last summer after they got down kinda close to what you might call Sioux country. Leastways, Custer woulda called it that." He grinned, showing tobacco-stained teeth. "We figgered the hostiles musta done 'em in."

"Well, they didn't," said Marshal Quaid. "Last fall, soon after you took off after the Pittman gang, they showed up again. Same stuff, down around Yellowstone City, 'Ginny City. I figure"—he regarded the map again—"that they got a hideout of some sort, south of Yellowstone City, somewhere in the mountains there."

"You don't mean Colter's Hell, do you?"

"No. Ain't no point in them going that far. All that's up there is boilin' water and geysers."

Murphy had never been to Colter's Hell, but he'd heard differently. He didn't say so, though. Wouldn't make any difference. He'd go where the trail led.

Nonetheless, he too expected to locate the Raffertys somewhat closer. "They still operatin' in the 'Ginny City area?"

"Three, four weeks ago I would have said yes, but now they've dropped out of sight again, same as last year."

"Mebbe the Indians did get 'em this time."

Marshal Quaid shook his head slowly. "It was a better bet last year. Them hostiles was nailin' everyone then. But this year's a whole different story. The Sioux Nation's just about had its back broke, Chief Joseph's on the run. Hey, if you run into that old bastard, give 'im a howdy for me."

"Will do."

Marshal Quaid's eyes narrowed as he peered into some imagined distance. "No sirree, I don't plan to wait another six months to find out the hostiles didn't get them."

"Get who?"

"The Raffertys. Who else?"

"Had me confused there for a second."

"Well, get unconfused real fast, Cal. Find those Raffertys, them or their scalps. They've done run out of rope."

Murphy had headed for Virginia City, and from there had trailed southeast, scaring up leads where none were apparent. One pestered cowpuncher had managed to remember some "fellers," and a flustered saloon gal had babbled something about a mean, heavyset gent with the initials "T.R." tattooed on his butt—courtesy of his brothers, Cal recalled—and still another gent, a hollow-eyed drifter, had tossed down a shot of rotgut and said something about Yellowstone.

By early summer, Murphy had made Yellowstone City, but

the trail didn't stop there. It headed south, climbing into the mountains.

Murphy had moved real gingerly then, following the Yellowstone upstream. He figured they were somewhere close by.

But they weren't. Folks in both Emigrant and Emigrant Gulch—flanking the Yellowstone west of Emigrant Peak—had seen some men answering the descriptions, but they weren't around anymore.

"Where'd they go?"

"Upriver. We figgered they was hunters or trappers or mebbe even gummint folk. That's a gummint park up there now, y'know."

The Raffertys, government folk? That was either a big laugh or he'd made a big mistake somewhere along the line. But he had no choice, so he climbed on.

The traveling wasn't hard. There was a trail alongside the Yellowstone, just about wide enough in most spots for two wagons to squeeze by. And judging from the wear and tear on the trail, a number of wagons had done just that.

More folk were visiting the park than he'd figured on. He'd heard it was going to be popular, but not that soon.

He climbed steadily, but moved more and more slowly as the air got thinner and his horse had more trouble breathing.

Finally, as summer was beginning to crest, he reached the park. He didn't know where the boundaries were, but he saw something steaming off to the side and he figured he was there.

He continued following the river upstream as it curled east and then began to curl back around to the south. He found himself riding into a slight trench, a shallow ravine. Slopes of yellow rock began to lift away from the river's banks.

Then, at the lower end of the twenty-four-mile-long Grand Canyon, the trail left the river and climbed to run along the edge of the fourteen-hundred-foot-deep ravine, the Grand Canyon of the Yellowstone. Cal Murphy followed the trail, his wonder increasing with each careful step his horse took.

At length, something more than ten miles later, he dismounted and stood about where the painter Thomas Moran must have stood when he painted his picture. He gazed at the distant Lower Falls, their turbulent thunder audible even at that distance, and surmised, *I'll say it's going to be popular*.

But he wasn't there to sightsee. He had work to do. He grained his horse, mounted and rode on.

As the day grew late he reached the plateau proper, which the Indians called the "Summit of the World," and angled west, following a set of wagon tracks over grassy meadows and in among fir and aspen.

The place abounded with game. If he'd kept a list, he would have written bear, moose, elk, buffalo, bighorn sheep, deer, antelope, wolves, coyotes, rabbits, mice....

A trumpeter swan soared overhead. Murphy thought it was a big goose....

There didn't seem to be any species lacking—even live stock. Cattle with a Rocking K brand.

What the hell? Had he wandered back outside of the park? If not, what were these cattle doing here?

Murphy lost the track he was following, and soon after that; as it rapidly became a pitch-black, moonless night, he got lost himself.

He rode slowly through the trees. He didn't think a wild animal was apt to jump him at night, unless his horse stepped on a bear's foot or something, but maybe the animals way up here were different. And further contributing to his unrest were the odd rumblings and hisses and gurgles and murmurs—not the soothing nocturnal sounds to which he was accustomed He rode with his right hand resting on the butt of his Colt.

At length he came out on what seemed to be an open patch of meadow. His eyes had become sufficiently accustomed to the dark to tell him that much.

He picketed his horse where it could graze, built a small fire and spread out his bedroll. It was about a half-hour between the time he came out upon the meadow and the time when, squatting in front of his fire, he figured the coffee and beans were hot.

Along about then his horse began to make noises and yank at its picket rope.

Murphy drew his Colt, kicked out the fire and waited It might be a cougar after the horse. Then again, it might be hostiles.

His eyes slowly became reaccustomed to the dark.

And then, suddenly, less than a hundred yards away, there was a huge roar and a white cloud shot up into the air, a dim, ghostly fountain, climbing and climbing....

It went on for better than four minutes.

Murphy wasn't in the path of the runoff, fortunately, but

he got sprinkled some, and damn!—that water wasn't cold, not by a long shot.

It was back into the trees for him, pronto, him and his horse. What in the world had he stumbled onto? Colter's Hell didn't begin to describe it.